THE BALKAN ROUTE

The Balkan Route

By

Cal Smyth

Fahrenheit Press

To Belgrade

Chapter 1

The silhouetted fishing boats reminded Inspector Marko Despotović of corpses that had floated down from Vukovar during the Yugoslav War.

Marko turned from the view of the Danube, lit up by the rising sun, picked up his Serpico-style sunglasses and slid them into his shirt opening. He smiled at his wife, who was sitting up in bed, at work on her laptop. She looked up and asked:

'Thought you'd finished your early shifts?'

'One more day of holiday to cover.'

Branka rose out of bed and adjusted her silk slip, said:

'I'll make you breakfast.'

His wife had already ironed his shirt, was writing up an article and was ready to make him breakfast. Marko put an arm around Branka's waist, pulled her warm body to him, said:

'Kiss me first.'

'Feeling romantic this morning.'

'I'm a romantic guy.'

As they kissed, Marko pressed his groin into Branka, who raised her eyebrows:

'Uh huh, really romantic eh big boy?'

Branka smacked him on the arm, just like she had the first time they'd gone on a date. But she'd kissed him that time too. They'd met when Branka was studying journalism and Marko had just joined the police.

Attractive rather than beautiful, it was her sense of purpose he'd noticed most. As an investigative journalist for *Danas*, her one-woman crusade to expose corruption in Belgrade was widely admired but also the subject of various death threats. But after the shit Marko had witnessed in Kosovo and the danger of breaking up the Zemun clan, he wasn't spooked by a few threats.

They'd been together since they were twenty, both now forty years old. He still found her attractive. They were both older and she had lines around her eyes. But when she smiled, her face lit up and the sex was full of love.

It wasn't as if he was Dragan Bjelogrlić, though he had been compared to the handsome actor.

He still had thick black hair and did enough exercise to keep fit – had to be to have a chance of winning a game against his tennis-playing son. He'd found one white hair on his chest a week earlier, but had plucked it in the hope more wouldn't appear. Marko kissed Branka on the head and headed to the front door, saying:

'Don't worry about breakfast, I'll grab some *burek* on the way.'

He paused by his son's door and silently spied in. At fifteen years old, Goran was too old to be checked on, but Marko couldn't help it. Goran was spread out on the bed, his long limbs dangling off it.

In the hallway, Marko reached up for his police standard Zastava revolver and holstered it.

Marko had built the high shelf when his son was little so that the gun was out of sight. These days, Goran could reach it with ease, but Marko trusted his son. Marko had never killed anyone, but he'd fired the gun in a few car chases.

Marko left the flat and went down to his car. Imagining he was in Al Pacino's Mustang, Marko drove his Ford Focus out of New Belgrade, zig-zagging the grid system one-handed.

The car was hardly Serpico cool, but better than the Yugo he'd had for ten years.

Cruising over the Sava, Marko passed Kalemegdan. The

medieval fortress still stood over the intersecting rivers despite being a battlefield in wars against the Romans, the Turks and the Germans.

Turning down into Stari Grad, Marko parked diagonally over the kerb on Simina Street. The street had once housed Belgrade's aristocracy, but Tito had supposedly made everyone equal and several of the buildings had been left to ruin since the fifties.

Marko opened the ornate metal gate covered in wisteria and heard his name called. He looked up and saw Milica on the stone balcony, wearing nothing but a towel as she leaned over and said:

'So the Inspector calls.'

'Just doing my duty.'

Marko smiled as he entered the building. Downstairs was derelict, but the second floor had a basic bathroom, kitchen and bedroom. Milica had added her own touches – a bookshelf, make-up table and *Pulp Fiction* poster personalising the bedroom.

Milica was his neighbour-cum-friend's daughter. Twenty-four years old, she had dropped out of university because of her heroin habit. Charged with possession after a car chase that ended with her in hospital, Marko managed to get her off as a neighbourly favour.

He'd known her as a neighbourhood kid, saw less of her as a teenager and hadn't thought about her since then. In the hospital, she was pale with needle marks on one arm and a cut from the car crash on another. Yet she still had a defiant beauty, wanting to get out of the life, but refusing to name names. Marko had tried:

'If I'm going to get you out of this, I need to know who the dealer is.'

'And I thought Dragan Bjelogrlić had just come to visit me in hospital.'

That line sealed the deal. Being compared to the actor had hit his vanity. He got her into rehab for a year and set her up in the flat. The place had been seized by the police in a drugs bust and he had the keys. With Milica's dad a recovering alcoholic and her mum living in Novi Sad, they were happy she was on her way to recovery. She'd even gone back to her literature course at university. Whenever she went to the toilet, Marko always did a secret search to check she was still straight.

Marko told himself he was doing it for his friend, but he was also excited every time he was near Milica. The first time he showed Milica the flat, she had shown her gratitude by giving him a kiss, which he had reciprocated before backing off. He resisted his impulses but popped in to see her whenever he could before work and had stopped telling his wife about the visits.

Still in only a towel, Milica sashayed into the kitchen to make coffee. With the Turkish coffee in a pot on the hob, Milica lit a Lucky Strike and stood in a provocative pose. Marko waved the smoke away and Milica pouted:

'I need to have one vice.'

'How's uni?'

'Got to write a paper on Ivo Andrić.'

'Yea?'

'You've never read him have you?'

'No.'

The pot of coffee came to the boil. Milica poured a cup and asked:

'Are you going to let me read your coffee?'

Marko checked his watch, said:

'Can't. Shift starts soon.'

He still had time, but out of warped loyalty to his wife, he wouldn't have breakfast with either woman. Milica took a drag of her cigarette, looked at Marko through the smoke and asked:

'Are you scared of what I'll see?'

'You know I don't believe that shit.'

'Maybe you should, might help with solving a case one day.'

Marko got up and Milica kissed him on the mouth, so he could taste her cigarette. He didn't like smoking, but with her, everything was alluring. Milica pushed him away, said:

'Go on, go to work.'

For the second time that morning, Marko said goodbye to a woman. As he started to cross to his car, a tram rattled past. Marko stepped out of harm's way. The only passenger was a gaunt old woman all in black, Marko not sure he'd really seen her or if she was just an apparition. His mum would say it was some kind of omen. But then she would also say he needed to eat.

He still had time to grab some *burek* before work, so he drove around the corner to *Pekera Trpković* on Gospodar Jovanova, where a black-windowed Audi was silently idling. Parking a few metres behind, Marko watched as the Audi drove off.

The car belonged to Dragan Mladić, a drugs dealer and hardcore Partizan fanatic who never seemed to be caught. Marko knew Dragan had supplied Milica even if she wouldn't admit it. On that late summer morning, Marko bore no bitterness. It didn't matter that a criminal had a better car than a police inspector. Without criminals, there wouldn't be police – so it was all copacetic.

Nemanja, the perpetually sweating proprietor, greeted Marko as he took a tray of *burek* out of the wood-burning stove:

'Good morning Inspector, mushroom for a change?'

'I'll stick with the cheese. And cut the 'Inspector', mister will do.'

Marko took a stool at the counter. Nemanja wiped his big hands on his white apron, sliced a slab of *burek* and placed it on the counter. Marko took his wallet out, but Nemanja waved it off.

'Come on Inspector, you know you don't pay in here.'

Two months earlier, Nemanja had been hauled in for tax evasion. He hadn't asked Marko to intervene, but it would be a shame if the place closed down, so Marko had a word with the tax inspector. Nemanja paid up his taxes but didn't get closed down.

Marko finished his *burek*, wiped the oil off his chin and gulped down some yogurt. He thanked Nemanja and got back in his car. He donned his sunglasses, put the Ford in gear and bumped over the tram lines. Some of the old buildings still bore bullet holes from the Second World War, but the stone gargoyles were lit up by the morning sun, preserving the ugly beauty.

Marko loved his city.

Pulling into the police headquarters on Bulevar Despota Stefana, Marko remembered when the street was called 29 Novembra – a Yugoslav national holiday. A BMW parked beside him, Inspector Jovanović inside. Jovanović was the same age as Marko, but dressed like a younger man and acted as if he was the older colleague. He claimed the car had been obtained at a police auction, the BMW seized in a drugs bust and never reclaimed. Jovanović also claimed his dress sense helped him integrate with the criminal underworld and get informants.

Marko knew it was a thin line. If a case could be solved with minor coercion, then fine. But they'd spent so many years fighting corruption, you couldn't succumb. Some police still did, he knew that.

Jovanović jumped out of his BMW, looking like he'd come from Miami in his white Armani jacket, and slapped Marko on the shoulder:

'Thanks for the holiday cover Despot.'

'No worries Jova. So you survived the Montenegro mafia.'

'Not a mafia guy in sight. Just rich Russians with their model girlfriends.'

The two inspectors strolled into headquarters together and walked up to the department for the fight against organized crime on the second floor. The place had been designed for giants, but Marko took the steps in his stride. Above the stairwell was a discoloured patch where portraits of Tito and then Milošević had once hung. The Chief of Police waved them both over to his office.

Ivan Dragić was a striking figure with his shock of white

hair, moustache and broken Roman nose – appearing in a haze of smoke.

Ivan had been prominent in the post-Milošević clean-up, making his name as lead inspector in the break-up of the Zemun mafia clan. In cynical moments, Marko wondered who had benefited the most. Belgrade was a safer city, that was true. But with the main criminal clans split up, it was hard to tell who was with which remaining gangs.

Ivan slapped Jovanović on the back and slapped a file into Marko's hands. He smiled at Jovanović:

'How's our country house?'

Jovanović sniffed and rubbed his nose:

'Caught a bloody summer cold. But apart from that, all in good order Chief, all in good order.'

'Good, good. Come on in and tell me about it.'

Ivan and three inspectors had a share in the Montenegro house. They'd asked Marko if he wanted in, but he'd opted out. Ivan turned to Marko and gestured at the file:

'Burglary in Banovo Brdo. Usual suspects. Sure you'll sort it. Take Nebojša with you. Let him see how it's done.'

Putting the file under his arm, Marko called for Nebojša, the guy just out of police academy – a young gun blazing with ambition and righteous indignation at any crime. Every day, Nebojša came into work clean-shaven and with his ironed shirt tucked in, hoping he would one day be given a real case.

First stop was the old woman who had been burgled in Banovo Brdo. The flat was full of tradition – table covered in embroidered cloth, Orthodox icons adorning the walls. Sweat trickled down Marko's head, but he knew there was no point asking to open a window. The old woman would cite *promaja* as a reason not to – the deadly draught meaning no breeze was allowed even in extreme heat.

With the woman seated, Marko started. According to the description she'd given the street police, the thief was gaunt and had a moustache.

While Nebojša watched from the side, Marko showed a set

of photos to the old woman – two of the ten men with a moustache. The old woman dithered between two photos:

'Both of these look a bit like him.'

'Both heroin addicts who burgle old people's homes. To be honest, we're not sure if this guy still has a moustache as the photo is old. But the other one is recent because we had him in for stealing from another vulnerable woman like yourself.'

'Yes, I think it's him.'

Marko got the woman to sign a witness statement, then asked to use the bathroom, where he pocketed a bottle of prescribed sleeping pills with her name on them.

Leaving the old woman's flat, Nebojša knew he was the junior partner, but couldn't help questioning Marko's method:

'You didn't give her much choice about which guy.'

Marko shrugged:

'The Chief wants an arrest and so does the old woman.'

'But what if the guy's innocent?'

'He's not. He's been arrested seven times for burglary and is a known smack addict. Getting him off the street for a while will help everyone, including himself.'

The rest of the morning was spent tracking down the thief. They found him with a load of junkies in a nearby flat, the guy half out of it. Marko slipped the old woman's pills into the junkie's pocket and let Nebojša find them – his younger colleague having to admit they'd got the right guy. Marko smiled to himself, remembering how he used to trick his son with 'magic'.

In the police interview room, Marko patted the junkie down for harder drugs than the old woman's pills but couldn't find anything. The junkie declared:

'I'm clean, man.'

'Get your clothes off.'

'You want to see my dick?'

'I want to see where you've put the smack.'

The junkie shrugged and took off his clothes. He spread out his arms:

'See.'

'Turn around.'

The junkie sighed and turned around. His arse was covered in some kind of oil. Marko shook his head:

'Why's your arse all oily?'

'So you can fuck me easily.'

Marko exhaled as he snapped on rubber gloves and said:

'I know where it is, so you want me to put my hand up there or you going to do it yourself?'

The junkie turned to face Marko:

'I'll do it myself.'

The junkie squatted and squeezed a shit onto the floor, a sealed bag of heroin dropping out with it. Marko screwed up his nose as he picked up the bag. At a guess, the amount was five grams, or 'ten dolls' as it was called on the street – 'a doll' being half a gram. The junkie had obviously sold what he'd stolen from the old woman and bought the smack. In case the junkie was feeling talkative, Marko asked:

'Who did you buy it off?'

'Found it.'

'You found ten dolls and thought you'd like them up your arse?'

'They were nice dolls.'

Marko could see that the junkie preferred being put in a cell and possibly bum-raped to naming whoever the main dealer was. Turning to Nebojša, Marko dismissed the junkie:

'Lock him up.'

By mid-afternoon, Marko was writing up a report, thirty minutes from finishing his shift. He couldn't wait to have a shower and wash the day's heat off his body. A family meal, perhaps a quick tennis match with Goran. Even if he got thrashed, it was always a joy to see his son in action. Marko's pleasant thoughts were interrupted by Ivan calling urgently from his doorway:

'Despotović, you've got a murder. Dorćol depot, now. I'll meet you there.'

Heading to his car, Marko knew some shit had gone down.

If it was so urgent that Ivan was coming along, some big shot had been killed.

Chapter 2

As Marko parked up in the Dorćol depot, he was hit with the smell of sewage. The street police had already cordoned off a haulage container, the officer on guard shooing away a stray dog that was nosing around. Flies were buzzing at the haulage container's doorway. Animals and insects had detected death. In the oppressive heat, Marko's shirt was sticking to his skin. He flashed his ID, slipped on plastic over his shoes and stepped inside the container.

It was cool inside, but this brought no respite. Forensics were busy swabbing what had once been a man, but was now just a torso and head in a puddle of blood.

Marko backed out of the container and strode around the corner. Out of sight by the riverside, he puked up his morning *burek*. With spittle dripping from his lips, he felt the hair on his arms rise.

His stint in Kosovo was the only other time in Marko's life when he had seen something so horrific. He'd done his best to forget it, but an unwanted image of ears being sliced off a man's head came to his mind.

Marko shivered off his memory and headed back to the crime scene, where Ivan was waiting for him:

'You know whose body that is in there? Milan Panić.'

Marko hadn't recognised the face, but he knew the name. Milan Panić was a well-known businessman, a man who had been chopped up. Belgrade had its share of killings but Marko had never come across a dismembered body. It was

Serbia, not Mexico.

While Ivan moved off to take a call, Marko re-entered the haulage container, his resolve hardened and his mind focused. Apart from Milan's dismembered body and a wooden chair splintered to bits, the container was empty. Had the businessman been murdered for what had been in storage? And why had the limbs been taken?

One of the forensics team stood up, a young guy called Stefan who had studied in America.

A bit pedantic and very full of himself, he gave Marko his initial thoughts without being asked:

'We'll need more detailed analysis but at this point the trauma would seem to indicate the dismemberment occurred while the victim was alive.'

Marko thought out loud:

'So he was meant to die in pain.'

'I can't verify that, but I can tell you it was done with a sharp instrument.'

'No shit. They teach you that in America?'

Stefan ignored Marko's sarcasm:

'Judging by the cuts, a lot of force was used.'

'What about the chair?'

Stefan didn't get it:

'What about the chair?'

'Two of the chair legs have been chopped off, as if it was all a bit frantic.'

'But the killer knew what he was doing. It's not easy to cut off someone's limbs so cleanly, especially while he's alive. Probably needed two people. One to hold him while the other did the cutting.'

Marko took that on board, finally gaining some useful information. He asked:

'And no trace of the missing limbs?'

'The blood patterns suggest they were picked up.'

Wishing he smoked, Marko left forensics to it and stepped out of the container. Cigarette in hand, Ivan came over, business-like:

'Initial thoughts?'

'Need to find out what was in storage and who Milan's enemies were. Possible revenge killing. Whoever did it was strong, knew how to cut off a person's limbs and did it while he was alive.'

The two of them were focused on solving the murder, their sentences clipped. Ivan added:

'He was found by his wife. She called it in and in a state of shock drove home.'

'We not bringing her in?'

'Interview her at her place. Be sensitive but find out what you need to.'

Ivan gave Marko the address. Internally, Marko shook his head at how even in a murder case, the wealthy got special treatment. With no time to dwell on it, he got in his Ford and sped to Dedinje.

Belgrade's rich elite lived in this leafy suburb. Tito had had a house there, complete with a private cinema. Then in the eighties and nineties, the nouveaux riches moved in – politicians like Milošević and criminals like Arkan, until the former was arrested and the latter killed.

Of course, many considered Arkan a national hero rather than a war criminal. Marko wasn't making a judgement either way, but he knew Arkan's wife still lived in Dedinje. A Turbo-folk pop star, Ceca was a Serbian idol in her own right – her palatial mansion in the neighbourhood of top politicians, 'businessmen' and ambassadors.

Some of the traditional stone buildings were beautiful, but were at odds with the White House-style mansions and modernist Dubai type designs – much of the construction illegal. Marko guessed Milan Panić had lived in 'style'.

Sure enough, the address led him to a building which looked a bit like a wedding cake. Marko knew Milan had made money from Panić Ajvar, but had it been this lucrative? A relish of red peppers and garlic, *ajvar* was the Serbian version of caviar. Everybody loved it, but most people ate homemade.

Marko got himself buzzed in at the electronic gate and

crunched his way to the mansion's entrance, the white stones to either side of the ornamental garden raked in a swirling shape. A security guard who looked like he'd been one of Arkan's Tigers stood in the doorway.

The guard inspected Marko's ID, let him in and led him through a white corridor towards a glass extension at the back of the house. He gestured for Marko to stop:

'Wait here. She's meditating in her spiritual retreat.'

'Looks like a conservatory to me.'

The guard didn't smile, but stood opposite Marko, who told himself to forget the funny comments. At least it was cool inside the air-conditioned mansion. The glass doors opened and Marko looked up.

Vesna Panić glided out of her 'spiritual retreat' in a white dress, her shoulders erect and chest out. She'd clearly had a boob job and maybe a face lift – Marko guessing she was ten years older than the forty something she looked. She was obviously modelled on her famous neighbour Ceca. It wasn't attractive to Marko, but he had to admit she had a presence as she looked him in the eyes and said:

'I'm so sorry, it was such a shock that the only way I had to cope was by meditating.'

Marko nodded in understanding, though he wasn't sure if he did understand. But people reacted in different ways to seeing a dismembered body. He'd been sick. She had meditated.

He put on his police voice:

'I know this is upsetting, but I have to ask some questions.'

'I understand Inspector.'

Vesna guided Marko to a vast lounge, all in white – walls, rugs and two chaise-longues opposite each other. If this was 'style', thought Marko, he was happy with his compact family flat in New Belgrade. The room was so bright, Marko wanted to put on his sunglasses.

Squinting, he sat across from Vesna and asked:

'Can you tell me how you found your husband?'

Vesna took a deep breath, closed her eyes, then opened

them:

'Milan had an early morning collection so he left the house at three. I knew he had a busy schedule so I wasn't expecting him until lunch. When he didn't turn up at the restaurant, I called his office and no-one had seen him.'

Vesna paused, then stared through Marko as her voice took on a husky tone:

'As I sat there, I had a vision of the haulage container and I felt a pull down to the Dorćol depot. The nearer I got, the more my skin tingled. I didn't want to look inside, but my feet took me and I...'

Vesna faltered, bit her lip, tried to stare into the distance but was unable to hold back tears:

'I... I saw his body.'

Marko gave Vesna time to wipe her eyes. He was sceptical about the whole vision thing, but hadn't he also had a vision from his time in Kosovo? Marko concentrated on practical police work:

'The container was empty. Do you know what was inside?'

'*Ajvar.*'

'So where's the *ajvar* now?'

'According to the office, it was collected and is on its way to Germany.'

Marko couldn't believe that a man would be murdered over jars of *ajvar*:

'Your husband didn't keep anything else there?'

'No. My husband had no secrets from me.'

Marko knew from experience that a husband could keep secrets from his wife, but Vesna spoke with such certainty he was inclined to believe her. He asked his next question:

'Did he have any enemies?'

Vesna laughed, her sadness broken for a moment:

'Inspector, my husband was a politician and then a businessman. Of course he had enemies. But he survived the nineties and his enemies are all in prison or dead.'

She had a point. But if the killer wasn't an enemy and the murder wasn't about what was in the container, Marko had no leads. In vague hope, he asked:

'Did you notice anything unusual about the container?'

Vesna glared at him in a burst of anger:

'Apart from my husband's dismembered body?'

'I'm sorry, I'm just trying to find any clues that might lead to the killer.'

'No, nothing that I remember. I'm afraid as soon as I saw the body I blanked out. I don't recall calling the police or driving back here.'

Marko thanked her and was let out of the house by the security guard. He sat in his car and thought things through. Milan Panić's wife was certainly a case – a mixture of fake tits, spiritual visions and sudden bursts of anger. But none of that helped him solve the murder.

To start his research, Marko called his wife. He knew that before becoming a businessman, Milan had been Minister of Economy in the post-Milošević government. But Branka would know more. They used each other sometimes, making sure there was no conflict of interest, both understanding the other's work. As soon as she answered, he asked:

'What do you know about Milan Panić?'

'I wrote a couple of articles on Milan. He brought in privatisation laws then bought up several state-owned companies before anyone knew it was possible. Milan was cleared of fraud while others went to prison.'

Marko thought about it. Milan would have enemies. But as Milan's wife had implied, the killers weren't working for an aggrieved politician or businessman. That would have been two guys in balaclavas shooting Milan in the head outside his house. That was so nineties and Milan would be long dead.

Branka was still on the phone.

'Something happened to him?'

She wasn't a crime reporter and news would soon be out so Marko wasn't worried about revealing the murder.

'Yea, he's dead. Guess I'll be late home.'

Marko would have to check with Milan's office and get a list of present-day associates. It was going to be a long day and night. Branka wished him good luck and he was just about to drive off when Vesna strode out of her mansion. Marko wound down his window and Vesna leaned in, her eyes gleaming as she held out a badge:

'Inspector, there was something. I completely forgot that I put it in my pocket. I found this by the container entrance.'

Marko looked at the Partizan badge in her hand. Vesna explained:

'Milan supported Red Star.'

Marko snapped into action, rooting around for a plastic packet. Holding Vesna by the wrist, he tipped the badge into the packet. She'd already got her fingerprints all over it. Forensics didn't need his too. Vesna realised her mistake:

'I'm so sorry, I wasn't thinking.'

Marko was thinking fast. He would send the badge to forensics, but at least now he had something to go on. If the killers were Partizan supporters, he knew who to ask.

Marko drove to Stari Grad and pulled up outside Café Insomnia on Strahinjića Bana, or Silicon Street as it was known. Dragan Mladić's Audi was there as Marko knew it would be. Partizan were playing Tottenham away in the mid-week Europa League qualifier, so Dragan and his crew would be watching the match on TV.

The café-bar was packed, members of Dragan's gang standing with a silicon stunner on their arm or sitting with one on their lap. Dragan was at the bar, one arm around a blonde, a bottle of 'deer' beer in his other hand. Marko was a big guy, but Dragan was a shoulder wider.

Marko made his way through the melee and displayed his ID. Dragan gave it a dismissive glance:

'And what?'

'Looking into a murder and heard that the killers might be Partizan supporters.'

Dragan finished his beer and gave the bottle to the top-heavy blonde to get him another.

Dragan smacked her backside as she passed, then turned to look at Marko – Dragan's rugged good looks offset by a scar above his right eyebrow, aging him a few years over his thirty-six.

He knew Marko was an inspector but didn't think he had the clout to be useful or a threat. He repeated his words:

'And what?'

Marko held Dragan's gaze:

'And I wondered if you knew a guy or two who might have done it.'

Dragan burst into laughter:

'So I'm just going to name some Partizan fans who I think killed some guy?'

Marko laughed back, at himself as much as anything:

'Yea, it was a long shot.'

Dragan smiled and patted the stool next to him, said:

'Why don't you watch the match with us, take your mind off the case.'

Dragan called over to the blonde:

'Biljana, bring two beers. And where are those *ćevapčići*?'

The young stunner shrugged:

'Vlada and Dušan were supposed to bring the sausages.'

'So where the fuck are they?'

'How do I know?'

Dragan got out his iPhone and made a call:

'Nenad, where're my *ćevapčići*? The match is starting in ten minutes… well bring it for half time then. And when you hear from those two cousins, tell them I want a word.'

Dragan ended the call, took one beer from the blonde and gave one to Marko. Needing a drink, Marko didn't decline. He'd never met a fellow Serb who didn't want to take their time.

It was amazing any murder cases ever got solved. He wanted to leave, but told himself to be patient. Clinking bottles, Dragan said:

'To life.'

'To life.'

They both took a swig. Dragan lit up a Davidoff, offered the packet to Marko, who refused:

'Smoking kills.'

'So do guns.'

'What will you do when the government bans smoking in all public places?'

'Say fuck you.'

Nodding at the TV, Marko said:

'Surprised you didn't go over to London for the game.'

'Didn't have a visa.'

'Hasn't stopped you in the past.'

Dragan smiled. Maybe this inspector wasn't such an idiot as had been made out. Marko put his bottle down:

'Cheers for the beer.'

Trying to act calm, Marko ambled back out to his car. But his mind was racing with what he'd overheard Dragan say on the phone.

Two of Dragan's guys hadn't turned up, two guys who were supposed to bring *ćevapčići* from Nenad's, the butchers on Bulevar. The clues indicated that the killers were Partizan fans and used to cutting off limbs.

Marko was on fire as he gunned up Bulevar Kralja Aleksandra. For decades, the longest street in Belgrade had been called Bulevar Revolucije. In the nineties, the pavements had been lined with dealers selling black-market cigarettes and coffee off their car bonnets. The clean-up had seen the street renamed and only proper shops remained. One of those was Nenad's butchers.

Marko parked over the kerb as Nenad came out carrying a tray to his van, wearing his red-and-white striped apron, more hair on his arms than his head. As Marko accosted him, Nenad got his words in first:

'Sorry got a delivery to make. Be closed for an hour.'

'I know, you're on your way to Dragan. He sent me to ask where Vlada and Dušan are.'

It was a ruse using Dragan's name, but Marko doubted he'd get any information showing his police ID. Nenad slammed his van doors shut and waved his hairy arms in the air:

'Wish I knew. Neither turned up for work today.'

Marko felt it in his bones that he was on the right track and went into police mode:

'You got their full names and address?'

Nenad paused by the driver's door, looked Marko up and down. He didn't look like one of Dragan's men. Seeing he'd been sussed, Marko bluffed:

'Yea, yea, I'm police, but I've got a deal with Dragan. Said I'd check Vlada and Dušan haven't done anything stupid.'

Nenad didn't have time to think about it. He had to get the *ćevapčići* to Dragan, so he said:

'Vladimir and Dušan Ivanović. They're cousins. Live together in Zemun, on Cara Dušana.'

Nenad drove off and Marko ran to his car, mobile to his ear as he called Ivan to relay the names and address:

'I'm on my way, but I'll need backup.'

'Where are you now?'

'Bulevar.'

'Okay, I'll have men ready and I'll call Jovanović. He's in Zemun now, just finishing his fish soup. I'll get him there. You sure it's these two guys?'

'We'll need more concrete evidence, but they're two Partizan supporting butchers who've gone AWOL.'

'Good work Despotović, fucking good work.'

Marko got off the phone, got in his car and set off to Zemun.

Chapter 3

Holed up in their ground-floor flat, Vlada and Dušan were slouched on the sofa-cum-bed, eyes dilated as they watched the build-up to the Tottenham versus Partizan match on TV. They'd spent the day smoking dope to come down from the mescaline. They wanted to watch the match in the bar, but Dragan had told them to stay put until he called.

Dušan's mobile rang. He answered it in slow-motion and listened as he got instructions from Dragan:

'Listen, a police inspector will come to your door in a minute. Let him in, he's going to collect the limbs.'

'We just let him in?'

'Yea, don't worry, he's on our side.'

'You sure boss?'

'Course I'm sure, I pay him.'

'Okay, gravediggers!'

Vlada woke from his slumber and joined his cousin in chanting the nickname for Partizan fans:

'Gravediggers! Gravediggers!'

Dušan smiled at his cousin and had a mescaline flashback, seeing Vlada hacking madly into the businessman. Vlada in the red-and-white striped apron that hardly tied around his waist – looking like a real life Obelix. Vlada had always been a big lad. Working at Nenad's Butchers, he put on more weight and the joke was that he ate half the sausages he sold. Dušan looked like either he didn't eat much or had worms, neither of which was true. He liked *ćevapčići* as much as his cousin, but he also liked cocaine and LSD, which is what he spent all his wages on. And his habit kept him thin. They'd worn the same apron for ten years at Nenad's, Dušan resigned that they had to wear Red Star colours rather than Partizan black and white. It was the first time Dušan had noticed how bright and aligned the stripes were. And they seemed to be moving like rivers in opposite directions at different speeds – the red river pulsating along while the white one flowed slowly.

Was he being shown that Red Star was the team to support, not Partizan? Dušan knew that mescaline could alter a person's way of thinking, but making him think he could support Red Star was too fucking much.

Outside Café Insomnia, Dragan shook his head as he ended the call. Those two cousins were off their fucking heads, which was just as well as it meant they carried out jobs for him without question and were easy fall guys. It was a shame they would no longer be useful. Dragan shrugged and went back in to Café Insomnia for the start of the match.

Marko drove fast over the Sava, veered right to drive alongside the Danube – the quickest way to get to Cara Dušana in Zemun being along the riverside. At a tram intersection, a tram's metal rod had come unattached from the electric cable above the street. Several Yugos were blocked in, the drivers shouting at the tram driver, who in turn shouted back at them. Marko swerved onto the tramline, weaved between the tram and Yugos.

Dušan was taking a piss when there was a knock at the door. He called out to Vlada but only got a grunt. Forgetting his mobile on the bathroom shelf, Dušan zipped up and went to the front door. He squinted through the peephole, saw the ID and opened up. Inspector Jovanović smiled:

'Dragan sent me. You got the limbs?'

'Yea man, in the ice-box in the bath.'

Dušan gestured to a doorway and nipped back to the TV. He had no idea why Dragan wanted the limbs and didn't care. There was a match to watch.

Jovanović entered the bathroom and pulled a face of disgust. The kitchen didn't have a sink, so the bath was piled high with dirty dishes. Next to the toilet were scraps of newspaper instead of toilet paper. Jovanović checked the limbs were inside the ice-box, then took the box.

He looked in at Vlada and Dušan on the sofa. Apart from the kitchen and bathroom, it was the only other room. Did the cousins fuck each other? Jovanović asked:

'The match started yet?'

The cousins' eyes were glued to the screen. Only Dušan answered:

'Just kicked off.'

Jovanović took out his Zastava CZ99 and shot Dušan in the head. Vlada opened his mouth, his eyes wide. Jovanović shot him in the face. Taking a civilian handgun out of his jacket pocket, he placed it in Vlada's hand.

Marko screeched into the street the same time as Ivan and police backup arrived. They saw Jovanović's BMW parked up and heard the shots. Instantly alert, the group simultaneously whipped out their guns. A call came out:

'Guys, just me, all done here.'

Marko and the others lowered their guns as Jovanović exited the building, holding up the ice-box.

The next hour was spent containing the scene. Jovanović explained how he'd had to shoot in self-defence and found the ice-box of limbs in the bath – he was congratulated by his colleagues and the Chief of Police.

Marko stood to the side, feeling uneasy. It seemed like they'd got the right guys. Milan's limbs were there as evidence. But there was something not quite right about Jovanović turning up and killing both men before they could be questioned. And Marko knew full well that evidence could be planted. But he couldn't see what Jovanović would gain from it, so maybe he was just being sour that Jovanović was getting all the glory. As if reading his mind, the Chief came over:

'I know you did the leg work on this. I'll see it gets noted.'

'Pity we didn't get to talk to them, find out their motive.'

'Who gives a fuck why they did it. Probably just off their heads. Place stinks of cannabis and I bet if we did an autopsy, we'd find their blood full of amphetamines or some shit.'

Ivan patted Marko on the shoulder:

'You did good work Despotović. This could have been a major murder fuck-up and we've sorted it in less than four hours. That must be some fucking record for solving a murder case.'

'I'll expect a pay rise then.'

Ivan laughed:

'Go get some rest.'

Marko did as he was instructed and drove the short distance home to Block 45 in New Belgrade. He should have felt happy. It was the best detective work he'd done in years. Maybe it was natural to feel deflated once the adrenaline had drained out.

Pulling up outside his block, Marko didn't notice the black-windowed Audi until he got out of his car.

Once more on the alert, Marko's first thought was that Dragan was after him for using his name. But with the Audi's back window down, Marko could see the man sitting inside wasn't Dragan. The guy was in a suit too tight for his waist as he leaned over:

'Marko Despotović?'

'Uh huh.'

The man reached out a podgy hand, Marko recognising him as he said his name:

'Željko Radović, Minister of the Interior. Can we have a quick chat?'

Back in the nineties, a ride in a politician's car could have meant the end of your life. This was a new Belgrade, but

Marko still stood his ground:

'You know, it's been a long day.'

'I know, I've been informed of your part in solving Milan Panić's murder.'

'Word gets around quickly.'

'Yes it does. Why don't you come in? Or we could talk in your flat if you prefer?'

Marko sighed. The man wasn't going to go away. He got in the car, sitting next to the coiffured Minister, a muscled chauffeur in the driver's seat. The Minister asked:

'So, would you say the case was satisfactorily solved?'

'I think it's good to solve a murder.'

'Bit convenient though, the killers killed, limbs found. Don't you think?'

Marko didn't respond. The Minister didn't need him to:

'I'm going to be honest with you. The government's aim is to make Belgrade free of corruption. This is for the city itself and also for Serbia as a whole so it can join the EU.'

Marko was ready to sleep. Politics had always bored him. The Interior Minister continued:

'I'm convinced this case is corrupt. Not you, I hasten to add. I believe you acted in good faith. But I'd like you to keep the investigation open, to find out how your colleague and the Chief of Police had it so quickly solved.'

Marko had heard enough:

'First, I'm no snitch. Second, it was me who led them to the killers.'

'Yes, because they played you for a fool. Has a murder ever been solved so quickly?'

Marko's jaw throbbed in fury. What the hell was the Interior Minister implying? And yet, his words echoed Ivan's, planting doubt in Marko's mind – had he been used by the Chief of Police? He said:

'I need to get to my family.'

'It's your family I'm thinking of.'

'Sorry?'

'I need you to look into this. If you don't, you might find it hard to support your family without a job. And your son's budding tennis career might not get very far.'

Marko exhaled. The Interior Minister was no fighter, but the chauffeur obviously doubled up as a bodyguard. Marko tried to find an excuse:

'Look, I'm not the right person for this. If there is corruption, and I say *if*, I'm not going to be trusted with that information.'

'On the contrary, you're exactly the right person. Nobody thinks you're a danger, just someone to use. And in fact you're better at your job than people think. Do you remember why you became an inspector? Think about it.'

Marko got out of the Audi without a word. He watched the car ease away from the kerb. In between two tower blocks, a group of boys kicked a ball about on a concrete area with goals painted onto the walls. Grizzled men drank from brown beer bottles while they grilled red peppers on makeshift barbecues – the aroma drifting into Marko's nostrils and stinging his eyes. All around, people carried on with their lives.

Marko's life had just got a lot more complicated.

Chapter 4

Marko crossed over the street to his building. His son had spent years hitting a tennis ball against the side wall, much to the annoyance of people in the ground floor flats. What Marko needed now was a game to take his mind off the day's events.

Marko checked the time. It was almost nine, so Goran would be home from the tennis academy. They could go to the local courts, have a quick father and son match.

Marko knew that the Interior Minister's son went to the same tennis academy over by the Partizan stadium, so he hadn't been surprised that the Minister knew about Goran. They'd never met before because both sons were old enough to go alone and their parents had busy working schedules. What troubled Marko was what the Minister had said about Goran's tennis career.

As for the murder case and possible corruption, Marko needed time to process it all. If the Minister was right, it undermined all he'd done that day as a police inspector. But he wasn't going to be bullied by a politician. He would think about it later. First he needed to see his family and to eat.

Before Marko could enter the block of flats, Gojko called out from his first-floor balcony:

'Good evening neighbour.'

Marko looked up and replied:

'Hey neighbour.'

It was a long-standing joke between them to greet each other in this way. Gojko was Milica's dad. He was three years older than Marko. When they'd been kids on the block, Gojko had taken Marko under his wing, getting him on the basketball court when he was younger than the others. But Gojko's real love was books. He'd just started university when he was conscripted during the Yugoslav War. He survived, but the horrors he'd witnessed stayed with him. When he came back, he almost drank himself to death. His wife left him and his daughter took after him in her love of literature and addiction. Milica blamed her dad and hadn't talked to him for two years. Gojko asked:

'You seen Milica this week?'

'Popped in this morning. She seems to be doing okay. Studying hard.'

'What's she reading?'

'Ivo Andrić I think she said.'

'Of course, the great Yugoslav writer. Born in Bosnia, brought up by Croatian parents, lived and died in Belgrade. Each nation claims him as their own, but does it matter?'

Marko shrugged, not having an answer. Even if he'd been in the right state of mind, neither literature or nationality debates were his forte. Gojko put up a hand:

'Stop in on your way up. I've got an Ivo Andrić.'

Before Marko could say that he needed to get to his family after a long day, Gojko left the balcony.

Marko went into the building and took the steps to Gojko's flat. The door was open so he stepped inside. The main room was lined floor to ceiling with bookshelves, the books in alphabetical order – the system in place matching Gojko's sobriety. Gojko hadn't touched a drop of alcohol for three years, not since Milica had started taking heroin.

On the floor were several boxes of books. Gojko had turned his passion into a job. He went around obtaining collections from the homes of old professors who died and selling the books on the street.

Standing on a chair, Gojko removed a thin paperback from the top left corner of his bookshelves and chucked it down to Marko, who caught it and read the title:

'*The Damned Yard.*'

'A novella. *The Bridge on the Drina* is his famous novel, but this is also an important work. Explores the arbitrary nature of power and how imagination is a means of escape from containment.'

'Sounds fun.'

'It's for Milica, not you.'

Gojko got down from his chair. Marko stood with the book in his hand, unsure how he was going to give Gojko's gift. Gojko put up a hand:

'I know she won't accept anything from me. Just say it's from you.'

'Okay, will do.'

'I appreciate it. You want a drink?'

Gojko raised a glass of cherry juice:

'No alcohol.'

'It's been a long day. I need to see Branka and Goran.'

Marko raised the novella in salute and got the lift up to the fourteenth floor. Entering the flat, he was greeted by the smell of *gibanica* – his wife's speciality. Marko un-holstered his Zastava and shelved it with the Ivo Andrić book for Milica. Branka called out from the kitchen:

'Just in time.'

'Okay, just let me shower.'

As Marko washed away the day's heat and gore, he thought about the Interior Minister's question. Did he remember why he became an inspector? In his first year, Marko had shown his mettle by arresting two bank robbers.

The two guys were from the now defunct New Belgrade clan. Seeming to think they were immune from being captured, the two robbers hadn't bothered disguising their faces. So when Marko had read their description, he was sure he'd seen them around. As a good neighbour he got information as to which block they were in. With a colleague, he staked out the block, waited until one of the robbers went to buy cigarettes, then followed.

It hadn't taken much to arrest them, the flat full of cash and guns. Marko had gained respect from that case, but he'd lived off it for too long.

Marko changed into clean clothes, cleared his head and went into the kitchen. He gave his wife a kiss on the head and his son a high five, Goran desperately swallowing a mouthful so that he could speak. Marko grabbed a 'deer' beer from the fridge, sat at the table and filled his plate with *gibanica* – adding *ajvar* next to the layers of filo, egg and white cheese.

All he'd eaten that day was some *burek* at five in the morning. And he'd puked that up. There hadn't been time to think about food and he hadn't had any appetite anyway after what he'd seen. But now he was starving.

As Marko ate, Goran spoke in excitement:

'Dad, I'm seeded in the Pančevo Open. And not just that, there's going to be some scout from Pilić Academy watching – that's the one in Germany, the same one Đoković went to. Radovan's dad arranged it.'

A piece of *gibanica* stuck in Marko's throat. Normally, he would have been overjoyed for Goran. But Radovan was the Minister's son and his suspicions were instantly raised. Branka frowned, not used to Marko's non-response:

'It's such great news. It's a real opportunity. Maybe we've got the next Novak Đoković at our table.'

Marko swallowed his food, regained his composure and smiled:

'Sorry, some cheese got stuck. Yes, it's brilliant. So why don't we head out for a match after food, show me some of your aces.'

'Sorry dad, but I said I'd meet Jelena, celebrate the news.'

'Yea, I guess the news is more important than playing your dad.'

Goran's face fell and Marko instantly regretted what he'd said, realising how childish he sounded. Their bond as father and son had always been strong and it was wrong of Marko to question it. Before Marko articulated an apology, Branka reprimanded him:

'Come on, he's excited.'

'I know, I'm sorry son. It's been a long day.'

Goran nodded and checked his mobile which bleeped with a text. Branka said:

'It was on the news about a businessman being murdered. Were you involved with that?'

'Yea, but I don't want to talk about it. Sorry.'

Goran looked up from his phone and switched on the TV by remote as he said:

'Radovan said his mum is on TV talking about you.'

Before Marko could protest, the Interior Minister appeared on TV, standing outside the flat in Zemun. Flanked by the Chief of Police and Inspector Jovanović, the Minister was giving an interview:

'As I stated earlier, outstanding police work has solved this horrific case. Chief of Police Ivan Dragić has been instrumental in breaking up criminal clans. And Inspector Jovanović should be commended for his bravery in apprehending the murderers of businessman Milan Panić. Credit is also due to Inspector Despotović, whose detective work I understand led to the murderers. However, we must be ever-vigilant in ridding this city of crime. It is a sad day for the family of Milan Panić and such murders must not occur again.'

Goran turned from the TV, genuine respect on his face as he tried to make up to Marko:

'Wow Dad, you solved it?'

Marko shrugged and feigned modesty:

'Just doing my job. But if you want to call me Sherlock Holmes, you can.'

On the surface, Marko was showing his usual humorous persona. But underneath, he was trying to work out the Interior Minister's words. Did they have a hidden meaning?

'Come on Dad, what happened?'

'Really, it was awful, I can't go over it.'

'Okay, but why did they kill him?'

'Who knows? Off their heads on drugs I guess.'

Goran checked the time and jumped up:

'Got to meet Jelena.'

Marko high fived his son and said:

'Just remember, you need any advice about women... I know nothing.'

As their son left the flat, Branka did the sign of the Orthodox cross:

'Thank God our son's never been involved with drugs and crime.'

'God or good parenting?'

Or even good luck, thought Marko. He wasn't anti-religion, but he didn't believe either.

Branka wasn't devout, but she went occasionally to keep up the tradition. His wife smiled:

'My two boys. My husband solved a murder case and my son got seeded for a tennis tournament.'

'Don't forget your own achievement.'

'What's that?'

'Making the best *gibanica* in Serbia of course.'

Branka threw a tea towel at him and he was pretty sure he was going to get lucky. Branka sat opposite him:

'This is a real opportunity for Goran.'

'I know.'

'Imagine if he won and got chosen for that tennis Academy.'

'It's not so easy, not everyone can be Đoković.'

Marko had played basketball at school and his team had won national championships, but making it as a professional was a different ball game, one that very few achieved. He loved seeing his son on the tennis court, but he was also aware of how difficult it was to have a sporting career. Branka didn't understand:

'You're usually so supportive of him.'

'I'm just being realistic. Do you know what age Đoković

went to Germany? When he was twelve. He went professional at sixteen.'

'So this is Goran's last chance. Don't you want him to have it?'

'Of course I do. But even if he got offered a place, do you know how expensive it would be?'

'We'd find a way.'

'Anyway, if the Interior Minister's arranged for a scout to be there, it's probably just part of a backhander for his son to be watched.'

'What happened to innocent until proven guilty? Looks to me like he's doing a good job making Belgrade a less crime-ridden city.'

'You think some politician does more than the police?'

'It's not a competition. Come on, I know what you guys do. But he's also having an effect.'

Marko looked across at his wife. They shared almost everything, but telling her about the Interior Minister's request-cum-threat wasn't going to work. Branka's journalistic instincts would kick in. She would ask a million questions, turn it into an investigative article. Marko was against corruption as much as she was, but he was less evangelical. Whereas Branka had a utopian aim, Marko solved crimes as they came along, knowing corruption would never disappear. He was more cynical than his wife. He was also a loyal police inspector. He could have his doubts, but until proven guilty, his colleagues were innocent. Marko rose from the table, said:

'I told Gojko I would drop a book off to Milica.'

'Now?'

Marko could see Branka wasn't happy, but he needed to go for a drive and clear his head before he said anything he regretted.

Chapter 5

As the bodies of the two butchers were carted away and the press dispersed, the Interior Minister and the Chief of Police stepped to the side so that they could confer in private. Lighting up a Marlboro, Ivan got in there first:

'Murder solved in record time. You have to hand it to my men.'

In public, the Interior Minister had spoken positively, but in private he voiced his concern:

'It is how quickly the murder was solved that makes me wonder.'

'What exactly does it make you wonder?'

Ivan looked straight at the Interior Minister. He wasn't cowed by the politician, who was ten years younger and only in the post for a year. The Minister held his ground:

'It makes me wonder how it was solved so quickly. The inspectors on this case, Despotović and Jovanović, did they have inside information?'

Ivan bristled:

'First, the case was solved through sheer good police work. Second, if we had needed inside information then I would have had no hesitation in sanctioning its use. In this city more than any other, it's how cases get solved.'

'I'm well aware of how things work in this city, that's precisely why I've been implementing the anti-corruption drive.'

'You? Who do you think broke up the Zemun clan?'

'I apologise. The work you did was phenomenal. But we can't rest on our laurels. If Serbia is going to stand a chance of joining the EU, we have to be seen to be free of corruption.'

Ivan blew out smoke:

'Do you know what the murder rate is in Portugal? 1.2 per 100,000. Exactly the same as Serbia. In fact last year, there were actually 11 more murders in Portugal. Yet Portugal is in the EU and Serbia isn't.'

'Which is exactly the point – we're not in it.'

'Who wants to be? I'm no politician, but last I heard, the EU was fucked. If you ask me, we're better off looking after our own country by ourselves.'

'That's what the government is trying to do. I'm no economy minister, but at present Serbian products aren't sold to EU countries. Which countries are making money from *ajvar*? Bulgaria, Turkey, Macedonia. And think of the future generations. Wouldn't you like your children and grandchildren to travel freely around the world?'

'We can go to Europe without a problem these days.'

'What about the UK?'

'What about it?'

When Željko was at university, he'd dreamed about going to Oxford or Cambridge. Of course, it was possible to get a visa, but wouldn't it be better to travel to the UK without hassle?

Ivan had lost interest. He knew how to talk the talk, that was one of the reasons he'd reached his position, but he was bored of talking with the Interior Minister. Keeping everything controlled in Serbia was the best option if you asked him. But he couldn't be bothered to prolong the argument:

'Policing in Belgrade is in good shape. The Zemun clan has had their hold broken and murders are down. In this particular case, it was all done according to the book as far as I'm aware. But if you have evidence to arrest either of my inspectors on charges of corruption, let me know.'

The Interior Minister nodded in resignation. He didn't want to antagonise the Chief of Police too much:

'I recognise the good work your men do. I just want to ensure we keep up that good work.'

Ivan flicked his cigarette away and rejoined his men. The Interior Minister slid in to his Audi.

The chauffeur drove away from the scene, the Minister mulling over the conversation with Ivan. He wasn't sure who had got the better of it, but he was sure he was in the right. He accepted that the Zemun clan had been broken up, but that didn't mean corruption had been eradicated. Did anyone really believe that Milan Panić was murdered by two butchers, who were then conveniently shot dead by the police?

The problem was that the population of Belgrade had become immune to crime and corruption. When Željko Radović had become Minister of the Interior, he'd made a vow – a vow that had turned into a rousing speech:

'For too many years, murder and corruption have become commonplace in this city. How many deaths will it take to bring about change? Journalist Slavko Ćuruvija shot dead outside his home in 1999. Case still unsolved. Former Prime Minister Ivan Stambolić kidnapped from a park in 2000. Found murdered three years later. Prime Minister Zoran Đinđić assassinated in broad daylight in 2003. Four years until his killers were found guilty. It is time to end all this death in Belgrade. It is time to restore justice to this city.'

He'd got a standing ovation that day in Parliament. And TV cameras had captured it. He had a recording at home.

The Audi pulled up outside Željko's apartment on the corner of Francuska Street, opposite the National Theatre. He had an hour before dinner at the German Ambassador's diplomatic residence. Enough time to see his wife and son, remember what all the hard work was for.

The apartment was on the third floor, sparely furnished with antique chairs on the parquet flooring and a balcony overlooking Trg Republike. He'd texted his wife and son, saying he was on TV and would pop in. He wasn't expecting a welcoming committee, but was ready to be greeted with respect.

Instead he found his son fixated on his Xbox game, blowing apart enemies on the huge, flat-screen TV. Željko attempted to interrupt:

'No hello?'

'I'm in the middle of a game.'

'Did you see me on TV?'

Radovan didn't take his eyes off the screen as he killed more enemies:

'No, I was playing this. But I sent the message to Goran like you asked.'

At least something done for his father, thought Željko. Although ultimately it was for his son's benefit.

If the tennis scout was going to watch his son, police corruption had to be looked at. That was the deal he'd made with the German Interior Minister, who no doubt had his own agenda.

Željko left his son to it and crossed the parquet flooring into the kitchen, where his wife was at her laptop, a glass of red wine to the side. Željko smiled:

'Anything for me?'

Keeping her eyes on her laptop screen, Slavica pointed to the kitchen unit:

'Bottle's over there.'

Slavica wasn't beautiful, but her toughness turned him on. They'd met as student union representatives. It had certainly not been love at first sight, but as two ambitious young people, they'd recognised a kindred spirit.

They'd worked together for a year without any sexual chemistry, until after a successful campaign, she had told him to fuck her. Her order had aroused him and he'd obeyed.

While Željko had made himself a career in politics, Slavica had risen to dean of faculty – taking a brief maternity break before getting back in the saddle. He poured himself a glass of wine and tried to get her attention:

'Well that was an eventful day. Milan Panić murdered then the killers shot by the police.'

Slavica looked up:

'Oh yes, I saw the breaking news online.'

'How did I come across?'

'Like the Minister of the Interior should.'

'You don't think I made a big enough impression?'

'Not every speech can be as good as your acceptance speech darling.'

Željko sighed. Was his acceptance speech the highlight of his bloody career? His wife had turned her attention back to her laptop:

'I was just checking the history of a student who was accused of taking drugs. It seems she was arrested for possession of heroin, but after a year in rehabilitation, went back to her studies.

'Straight A's since she has returned so I can't see the need to set up disciplinary action.'

'Maybe someone does her essays for her.'

Slavica snorted:

'She wouldn't be the only person to do that. I seem to recall someone getting quite a bit of help with his PhD.'

'Just a little.'

'A little? It takes three years to do a PhD. We got yours done in under two.'

'It was necessary for my career.'

'Of course, but don't pretend to be innocent.'

Željko wasn't often lost for words, but was still trying to form a reply when Radovan entered the kitchen. On his way to grab a Coke from the fridge, Radovan asked:

'When's that tennis scout coming?'

Željko couldn't hold his tongue anymore:

'The work I do for this country, this city and this family deserves more respect. I dedicate my time to eradicating crime so that my wife and son can have boundless opportunities in the future. A little gratitude wouldn't go amiss.'

Željko's wife and son looked at him mid-poise, Radovan with the fridge door open and Slavica with her hands hovering over the keyboard. Radovan shut the fridge and said:

'So are you meeting the scout later or not?'

Željko sighed:

'Yes.'

His son left the kitchen and his wife said:

'Not bad, but not as good as your acceptance speech.'

Željko downed his wine in impotent fury. He was about to march out of the kitchen when Slavica said:

'I refer back to your acceptance speech because that is your benchmark. If you wish to maintain your career, that is the height you should aspire to. Now, go and sort out a deal with the German Interior Minister and get that tennis scout to see our son in action.'

Chapter 6

Marko drove over the Sava, following the same route he'd taken at six that morning. Ada Bridge was lit up at night. Marko didn't know how much it had cost, but in his opinion the investment had been worth it. Belgrade had suffered enough economic woes and deserved to preserve its beauty. By the time he rounded Kalemegdan, he felt calmer and even a little guilty.

He should have been happier for his son and shouldn't have taken his frustration out on his wife. But he still needed time to think.

Milan Panić had been murdered. That was clear. Marko had gone from one clue to another that led to the two cousins. Had it been luck? Was it good detective work? Or, as the Interior Minister suggested, had it all been set up?

If the Interior Minister was right, Marko had been played for an idiot by his colleague and the Chief. But what did Jovanović and Ivan gain from it? And how did the Interior Minister know the case was corrupt? What evidence did he have?

With the Interior Minister making a veiled threat, Marko had no inclination to question the case or his colleagues. And yet, it niggled.

Realising he'd been sitting in the car outside Milica's for ten minutes, he got out. The lights were out in her flat. He called her mobile and got no answer. He had nowhere else he needed to be and had a spare key so let himself in.

He'd give her an hour. On the way out of his own home, Marko had grabbed the Ivo Andrić book Gojko had given for his daughter. If Milica didn't turn up, Marko would leave the book for her. It was irrational, he knew, but he was annoyed she wasn't there. What did he expect, that she waited there like Sleeping Beauty?

Not knowing what to do with himself, Marko sat on Milica's bed and started reading the novella. The prologue about a dead monk didn't excite Marko, so he skipped to the first chapter, set in the 'damned yard' of the title.

The prison yard was full of criminals and murders who told stories to pass the time, but the governor was more brutal than the inmates, claiming that no-one was innocent and using whatever method possible to extract a confession. So who was worse, the criminals or the authorities? That's what Marko guessed the writer was asking.

Marko was too tired to read on. He put the book by the bed and lay down to rest. His overworked mind wouldn't let him sleep. Where was Milica? She was probably out with friends, maybe even a boyfriend. He felt a surge of jealousy.

He tried to be rational. He had a wife. Wasn't Milica allowed a personal life? But what if she brought a guy back to the flat while he was there?

Marko looked at the *Pulp Fiction* poster on the wall, Uma Thurman in a smouldering pose.

Milica had only been nine when the film came out, so Marko guessed it was retro heroin chic.

Maybe she'd got back onto drugs. Marko knew she didn't inject but she could be taking morphine for all he knew. He leapt up off the bed and started searching the flat. He opened kitchen drawers and bathroom cabinets. He checked under the bed and in the wardrobe. He didn't find any evidence of drugs, but an addict could be good at hiding. In the back of his mind, he knew he was transferring his anger, but he couldn't stop. He heard the front door as he was rooting through her underwear. He shut the drawer and called out:

'It's me.'

Milica came into the bedroom, but didn't seem excited to see him as she slumped onto the bed. Marko said:

'Thought I'd surprise you.'

'Or to check if I was hiding drugs?'

He bluffed:

'Of course not, I trust you.'

'If I wanted to hide it, you wouldn't find it anyway.'

'What's that supposed to mean?'

'It means what it means.'

'I didn't come here to argue with you. I've had a bloody hard day.'

'Well I had a hard day too.'

Marko doubted she'd had a harder day than he had, but he asked:

'So what was so hard?'

'I was accused of being on drugs.'

'Were you?'

'Of course I wasn't.'

'Who accused you?'

'Another student. And then I had to explain myself to the professor.'

'Why did they accuse you?'

'Because I fell asleep in class.'

'Was it that boring?'

'I was tired. And it's your fault!'

'Mine?'

'Yes, because I waited for you at six this morning and I couldn't sleep before that in excitement.'

'So did you explain you were tired to the professor?'

'Yes, I even showed him my arms in case he didn't believe me.'

Milica held out her left arm and slapped it. Marko shrugged:

'So what's the problem?'

'The problem is what people think about me. They all think

I'm a fucking junkie.'

They lapsed into silence. Marko sat and put an arm around her:

'Hey, come on, who cares what people think? I've been waiting for you.'

'I wait for you every fucking day. Tonight I went to the cinema, if that's okay.'

'So what did you watch?'

'Are you checking I really went to the cinema?'

'I like films, just wondering what you saw.'

'There was a Srđan Dragojević retrospective at the Kinoteka so I saw *Wounds*. I thought if I couldn't see Dragan Blagojević in real life, I could watch him on screen.'

Marko picked up the Ivo Andrić book and offered it to Milica:

'I, er, got this for you.'

'Really?'

Milica took the book and looked at it in wonder as if he'd just given her a diamond ring. He said:

'It's just a book.'

Milica looked up at him:

'It's more than that. It shows you listen to me, that you care about me, that you maybe even lov…, no I won't say it.'

Marko squirmed at Milica's emotional response, feeling guilty he was receiving praise for a gift that had been from her dad. He'd just done what Gojko had told him to.

Milica grabbed Marko by the shirt and pulled him on top of her. He didn't have time to resist and they kissed hard. As they both took a breath, Marko tried to regain his senses, but Milica reached down, unzipped him and grabbed his hard cock. Unable to stop, Marko pulled down Milica's knickers and went inside her.

They collapsed on the bed in a sweaty tangle of limbs and clothes. Milica said:

'I need a cigarette and coffee.'

'Me too.'

'Really?'

'Okay, no cigarette, but I'll have a coffee.'

'You'll have to let me read it.'

'Fine.'

Marko didn't have a brain left to protest. If Milica wanted to read his coffee, he'd go along with it. Getting off the bed, Milica picked up the Ivo Andrić novella that had fallen to the floor.

She opened the book to the first page:

'You haven't written anything.'

She found a pen and handed it to him along with the book:

'Come on, you have to write an inscription.'

'Like what?'

'Like, To Milica, my beautiful princess, with all my love Marko.'

Marko hesitated. If he wrote something like that, would it come back to haunt him? Would Milica show it to his wife? Milica seemed to read his mind:

'Don't worry, nobody will ever see it. I would never hurt you.'

Marko wrote 'To Milica, from Marko.' Milica took the book and pen from him:

'Not even any 'love'?'

Milica drew a big heart around the inscription:

'At least that's a sign of our love, even if I put it there.'

Milica went into the kitchen and put Turkish coffee on to boil. Marko followed and felt remorse. He had just been unfaithful to his wife who he loved and fucked his friend's daughter.

Could he have fucked up any more? Milica looked over her shoulder at him:

'Are you okay?'

'Told you, had a hard day.'

'You certainly were hard big boy. Sit down and tell me.'

Marko did as he was told. He had to tell someone. Milica placed two cups of Turkish coffee on the table and sat down to listen. Marko took a sip of the bitter coffee and said:

'Heard of Milan Panić?'

'The 'businessman'?'

'Yea, well he was murdered this morning.'

'Probably did some shady deals.'

'Probably. The business certainly did alright. I was up at his mansion in Dedinje to interview his wife.'

'A rich widow. Was she nice-looking?'

'Not my type.'

'What type was she?'

'A not so rich man's version of Ceca. Probably had the same surgeon do her tits.'

'I see you got a good look at her.'

'Couldn't help noticing.'

'Ceca's a bit passé by the way. Jelena Karleuša is the queen of Balkan pop these days. Even accused Beyonce and Kim Kardashian of copying her style.'

'Guess I'm out of touch. Anyway, the widow certainly had a presence. Claimed she had a vision of where her dead husband was.'

'Did you believe her?'

She was bloody convincing.'

Marko grimaced as he downed the rest of his coffee. Milica reached across and turned the cup upside down on its saucer. Marko continued:

'Anyway, I went from one lead to another and tracked down the murderers. Only they were killed before I got there.'

'By who?'

'By my colleague – in 'self defence'.'

'You think the police are involved?'

'I don't know. But I was on my way home when I got stopped by the Interior Minister.'

'Like you do.'

'Exactly. He told me the case is corrupt and he wanted me to keep investigating.'

'Shit. Do you think he's right?'

'I don't know.'

'Sounds fucked up. I'd leave it be.'

'Would if I could, but I don't think the Minister's going to let me.'

'What can he do?'

'Don't know that either. But if he's right, I've been played for an idiot.'

'As you said to me, who cares what people think?'

Milica turned Marko's cup back over and examined the patterns of brown sludge. She frowned:

'There are different paths that converge, but one leads to darkness.'

Marko bit his lip to not laugh at the vague statement. Concentrated on the cup, Milica said:

'The paths lead from death and there's going to be another – a death of someone close to you.'

Marko listened but was sceptical. Milica already knew about the murder and had simply made up the other. But she looked up at him, deadly serious:

'Marko, you shouldn't pursue this. It will only lead to another death. Someone close to you, someone you love.'

'Okay.'

'Promise me.'

'Okay.'

Marko kissed Milica on the lips and got up to leave. It had been a good idea to see her. Not just the sex, but talking over the case and even having his coffee read. It was wrong to have sex with her, but he felt relieved and reinvigorated.

The next day, he would have to write the case up. At the same time, he would just check things over.

Chapter 7

Back in his chauffeured Audi, Željko was driven to Dedinje. The Prime Minister still drove around in an old Yugo, proving his everyman credentials. But Željko wasn't taking any chances. His whole mantra was about ridding the city of crime, so there would be plenty of people who wished him harm.

The car and driver came with the job, expenses covered. His driver was former Special Forces who had Zemun connections. Whenever Željko needed to procure women, domestic *rakija* or information on people, his driver provided it.

The meal was taking place in the German Ambassador's diplomatic residence. The German Interior Minister would be there, having flown in for a few days. And as a special guest, the tennis scout had been invited.

Željko would have preferred the meal to be in a restaurant, but the Germans had insisted.

Željko hoped the food was good. He was starving.

The informal meeting was as important as an official one, the meal sanctioned by the Prime Minister. Two interior ministers with information for each other. And a tennis scout as personal bait.

Driving into Belgrade's wealthiest area, the Audi passed Milan Panić's mansion. The Economy Minister turned businessman had been murdered for his sins. According to his German counterpart, Milan Panić's *ajvar* business was a cover up for drugs. This in itself didn't surprise Željko, but the lack of police interest in this connection was worrying.

That was why getting Inspector Despotović to do some digging was a good move. He might need more persuading, but his family's welfare would get him on side.

The chauffeur pulled into the drive of the diplomat's beautifully maintained residence and Željko felt a surge of patriotic wrath. In Stari Grad, you could find buildings that bore bullet marks from the Germans in the Second World War. And central Belgrade still had the remains of NATO bombing from 1999. Yet the German Ambassador had a house on the most expensive street in the city.

Željko exhaled as he approached the entrance, fixing a smile on his face. Long-term planning was what made a career, not short-term aggression.

He was welcomed by the German Ambassador, an ageing man of little importance. With his glasses, grey beard and corduroy trousers, he looked like a literary professor. He was simply useful in hosting the meal.

The German Interior Minster, Marcus Hoffman, was a confident man. Out of office, he wore waistcoat and jeans, a typically German version of casual attire. The tennis scout, Karl Babel was tall and broad shouldered in his v-necked sweater. Of course none of the three Germans spoke Serbian, so Željko had to speak their language – having studied both German and English. Željko asked:

'How do you like Belgrade?'

The tennis scout nodded in appreciation:

'The women here are something else.'

Babel had played professionally and had a lot of contacts on the circuit. Working as a scout at Pilić Academy for several years, he was used to being invited to various countries and had made a habit of fucking women wherever he went.

Željko smiled in pride. The whole world knew Serbian women were the best. On cue, a cute waitress came in and served food, the Germans smirking as she bent over the table.

As they ate, Hoffman nodded his approval:

'This is good.'

Željko smiled but thought the German Interior Minister knew nothing about Serbian cuisine.

The *ajvar* was shop-bought rather than domestic and the wine was expensive but not full- bodied. At least he'd brought some domestic *rakija*.

Every time the waitress left the room, the tennis scout commented on the beauty of Serbian women. It was getting tiresome. Željko was starting to wonder if it was really worth making a deal with the Germans. As the Chief of Police had said, why didn't they just concentrate on their own country?

With the meal over, the two interior ministers sat to the side, a *rakija* in their hands. It was the best thing about the meal, thought Željko. Hoffman said:

'I see that the businessman's murder has been solved.'

'The police work was exceptional.'

'Pity such murders have to occur in the first place.'

'We have exactly the same murder rate as Portugal, an EU country I believe.'

'And if Serbia is to join, the corruption needs to be sorted.'

'It's under investigation.'

'The businessman's murder was not an accident. He was connected to the Balkan drug route. It's extremely strange that the Serbian police haven't made this connection.'

'If Serbian police are involved in corruption, no-one wants it resolved more than me. I want Serbia free of crime for its own good, not just to appease the EU.'

Željko wasn't just going to sit there and kowtow to his German counterpart. It was humiliating enough as it was. Hoffman hadn't finished:

'That drug route has to become non-operative within Serbia. EU membership is dependent on it.'

'You know, since Kosovo's independence, the Albanians

took over most of the route.'

'The Albanians aren't trying to join the EU.'

Željko took a hit of *rakija*, felt the burn in his throat. Why was the German Minister so concerned about the drug route? What was Hoffman's agenda? He didn't care if Serbia joined the EU. Germany had been rebuilt after the Second World War because it had been granted reparations. What had Serbia received after NATO bombing? Nothing. He expressed his thoughts as politely as possible:

'Most Serbs have no interest in being part of the EU. The only reason I do is for Serbia's own benefit.'

'And your own personal gain. Your son's future remember could go one way or another.'

The German Minister raised his glass of *rakija* to the tennis scout who was trying to chat up the waitress. She left the room and the scout raised his glass:

'To Serbian women.'

Željko downed the last of his *rakija*, fired by resentment. He got the picture. The German Minister had used the same tactics he had with Inspector Despotović. An offer-cum-threat about his son's future. If the tennis scout was going to consider Radovan, Željko had to root out corruption and block the Balkan drug route. And the tennis scout had his own requirements.

Željko hoped his son had enough talent to warrant it.

Chapter 8

Marko accepted the back slapping as he entered police headquarters. The mood was jubilant and Marko went along with it. Jovanović had nailed the murderers but Marko had done the detective work and his colleagues appreciated it.

Viktor Antić, a drugs squad veteran who'd been part of Ivan's Zemun clean-up crew and had a share in their Montenegro house, called out:

'Finally got off your arse Despot.'

'Thought I'd show you amateurs how it's done.'

Viktor had also been part of the 'Balkan Warriors' operation that broke up the Serbian-South American coke cartel. A year earlier, the drug lord Darko Šarić had been arrested after five years on the run. It was Viktor's persistence that led to the arrest. With his beard and tufts of hair that resembled helmet horns, Marko always thought of him as Viktor the Viking.

Even the clean-shaven rookie Nebojša looked at Marko with new-found respect, no longer seeing a slightly past-it cop but a shrewd inspector.

Ivan called Marko into his smoke-filled office, where Jovanović was waiting, leaning on a cabinet in his t-shirt under Armani jacket and slip-on loafers, Jovanović coming across as a man who shot murderers on a daily basis.

Marko could hardly see his boss through the smoke, but he knew a window would never be opened. It was better to die from cigarette smoke than suffer the deadly draught. Ivan sat behind his desk, picked up his Marlboro from the ashtray and pointed at his two men:

'Great work from you two yesterday.'

Ivan took a drag of his cigarette. If Jovanović's look was a Belgrade version of Miami Vice, all Ivan needed was a cowboy hat and he'd be a Serbian Marlboro man. Marko knew Ivan was anti-American, but that didn't stop him smoking their cigarettes. Most Serbs remained angry at America and the West for the NATO bombing. Marko had been saddened rather than angry.

He loved his country, but he also loved American detective films and TV cop shows. Ivan exhaled:

'Now back to the daily grind. I need a report, a good one. For once, the media are showing us in a good light, even B92, so we need to keep up appearances. I've got the Interior Minister breathing down my neck, complaining you got the intel from a criminal source.'

Jovanović shook his head in disgust:

'Fucking politicians.'

Marko defended himself:

'I went to Dragan but not as if he'd tell me anything. It was just what I overheard.'

Ivan waved a dismissive hand:

'You know I don't care how you got the info. But I want a report to show everything was above board. You okay to write it up Despotović?'

'Sure Chief. Had enough excitement yesterday.'

'Good. Jovanović will fill you in with his end of events, so you can incorporate that. Here's the initial forensic file.'

Ivan slid over a document. Marko gave it a quick scan. The two butchers had been shot in the head by Jovanović and died instantly. One of the cousins was found with a handgun in his grasp. So it looked like a clear act of self-defence on Jovanović's part. What the forensics report didn't show was how Jovanović had come to be standing in front of the butchers unopposed.

Marko took out a notebook and asked:

'Ok, so how did you get into the flat?'

'The door was unlocked. The football was on loud so they didn't hear me. I know, I should have waited for backup, but once I was inside, I had to keep moving.'

'And they just sat watching TV?'

'Yea, until I was right in front of them.'

'But you shot them in self defence?'

Jovanović bridled:

'Where you going with this Despot?'

Marko raised his hands in peace:

'Hey, we're on the same side. I'm just thinking what the Interior Minister or the press are going to ask.'

From behind his desk, Ivan nodded:

'Despotović is right. Let's get it clear.'

Jovanović shrugged:

'I saw the bigger of the two cousins had a gun beside him. I told him to raise his hands and he went for the gun. I didn't have a choice.'

Marko spoke as he made notes:

'What about the other cousin?'

'He reached for the gun so I shot him too.'

Marko closed his notebook, smiled and gave a wide-armed gesture:

'Okay, that should do. I'll get my events down too.'

Marko started to head out of the office, then popped his head back in:

'You think I should check the scene, make sure the report is corroborated by logistics?'

Jovanović frowned:

'I told you how it went down.'

'Just don't want anything coming back to bite us. I'll bring the laptop, write it up while I'm out.'

Ivan stubbed out his cigarette and said:

'Do what you need to do. Just have the report on my desk by the end of the day.'

Leaving Ivan's office, Marko was pleased with how he'd engineered things. On the surface, he was the same laid-back guy everyone knew, doing what his boss asked.

Either Ivan and Jovanović were clean or they were good at bluffing. They'd shown no sign of being involved in anything but police work. Maybe the Interior Minister's insinuations were false. But then wasn't Marko also bluffing? Acting as if he was happy to write a report that supported all their good work when he would also be using the opportunity to see if he'd been set up by corrupt colleagues.

One way or another he was going to find out. Even if he'd been played for an idiot the day before, at least he'd got his taste for investigation back.

Chapter 9

On his way to Zemun, Marko drove through New Belgrade. Not in a rush, he decided to drop in on his mum. He'd seen her on Sunday, but she would complain if he didn't see her during the week.

She lived in Block 70, two blocks away from his own home. As a kid he had played basketball on the outdoor courts and kissed Branka by the riverside. New Belgrade had been given a bad reputation in the nineties, films like *Wounds* depicting it as an urban ghetto.

Marko had watched *Wounds* back when he was in police academy. He'd smiled at the satire – dictatorship turning disaffected youths into gangsters who were propelled to fame on TV.

But he didn't think it worked as a thriller. The trouble was he'd seen *LA Confidential* in the cinema a few months earlier and was still in awe of that film. It was unfair to compare the two films, but Marko preferred the American neo-noir tale of police corruption and Hollywood glamour. Did that make him unpatriotic?

The *blokovi* were pretty ugly, but Marko had enjoyed his childhood and hadn't become a criminal. He had no hesitation setting up family in a nearby block.

Constructed in the years after the Second World War, New Belgrade was built by over a hundred thousand workers from the newly liberated Yugoslavia, Marko's grandfather one of the manual labourers. With no notable technological tools, most of the work was done by hand.

The project was a success for Tito's communist government. Apparently under Tito, everyone had been happy. Though Marko suspected that was because if anybody said otherwise, they lost their job.

Marko's father had been a card-carrying communist during Tito's time. At the start under Milošević, he'd carried on believing in the system. But the wars, dictatorship and sanctions had eroded his beliefs. By the time of his death, he was no longer a bus driver, but selling petrol on the black market.

Marko's dad had been warned off a couple of times until he was killed in a drive-by shooting.

It made the news for one day and was soon forgotten. Marko was in Kosovo at the time, doing his time in the army. His mum always claimed she'd felt a premonition and had worn black ever since. Marko hadn't been surprised by his father's murder and was almost numb to it.

Every day someone was killed.

When Marko had joined the force, he'd talked to the inspector in charge of his dad's murder.

But Inspector Stojanović had told him no clues had ever been found. There were so many drive-by shootings at the time, it was impossible to find the killers.

Five years later, Inspector Stojanović was arrested on charges of corruption and shown to be in league with the Zemun clan. Back in 2001, when the whole police force had joined with the demonstrators in rallying against Milošević for a final time, Stojanović had been the one who let the clan break into headquarters and steal all the weapons.

The corruption clean-up and clan crackdown of 2003 was more important than a personal case, so Marko didn't get a chance to question the corrupt inspector. And after that, too many years had passed. Marko wanted to forget his dad's death not dig into it.

Marko didn't believe in communism or any other creed, but he liked the idea of people from all walks of life living side by side. As a bus driver, Marko's father had inhabited the same building as Branka's dad, who was a doctor. And now Marko as a police inspector lived in the same building as a book seller.

Opening the door, Marko's mum broke into a smile:

'My son! I was worried about you. I haven't seen you for so long.'

'I was here at the weekend.'

'Should a mother only see her son at weekends? You could have been killed in a car chase for all I know.'

Marko's mum had never approved of him joining the police. Her constant worry was that he would die before she did.

Marko kissed his mum, who ushered him inside. As always, she was all in black. She'd been in mourning for her husband for twenty years. She hadn't turned into a waddling old woman, but her lined face made her look ten years older than her sixty-five years.

His mum had never recovered from his dad's death. Granted compassionate leave from the army, Marko came home to comfort his mum before the funeral. He still remembered how she was contorted with sobs, an undrunk glass of *rakija* in her hand as he hugged her, the roles of son and mother reversed.

On the hallway wall was a faded, framed wedding photo of Marko's parents next to a school photograph of Marko. Branka had given his mum more recent photos of her son's marriage and grandson in school, but they had been put in a drawer. His mum still lived in the past. She put a hand on her son's arm:

'Last night I had a dream that you died in a car chase. Nobody told me. I just read about it in the newspaper. When I went to identify your body, they said I had to prove you were my son by showing your birth certificate. So I came home and searched for the certificate, but when I went back, they had already buried you.'

Marko's mum opened a drawer and handed him a pair of

extra large y-fronts:

'I bought these in the market, just in case.'

Marko looked at the underwear. He was big but not that large and hadn't worn y-fronts since he was a little boy and had no choice. When he was a boy, his mum always said he should wear clean underwear in case he got hit by a bus and had to be taken to hospital. Once he joined the police, she changed her mantra, saying he should have clean underwear in case he got hurt in a car chase.

Marko's mum beckoned him into the kitchen:

'Come on, sit and eat. Have some *gibanica*.'

Marko knew she had *gibanica* because Branka had dropped some around. She still mothered him even though it was she who was looked after. With no-one to cook for, she'd stopped bothering. As much as Marko loved his wife's *gibanica*, he'd already had breakfast and it was too early for lunch. He protested in vain:

'Nothing, thanks.'

Ignoring him, his mum took out a plate of *gibanica* from the fridge:

'Sit and eat.'

Marko sat at the table as he was told. He gestured at a pile of documents that covered the table:

'What's all this?'

His mum's mouth spasmed into a nervous twitch before she replied:

'You remember after your father died I sold his car. I never officially notified the police.

Maybe the car has since been used for some robbery and I can be blamed. I can't find the papers, but I have the name of the person who bought it.'

'It was twenty years ago.'

'You think they don't keep records?'

'Who?'

Marko's mum leaned in, spoke in a hushed voice:

'The police.'

'I am the police.'

'So you have to find out if the car has been involved in any robberies.'

'Mama, we're not living under Milošević anymore.'

Marko's mum had lived under Tito then Milošević, with all the state paranoia that had induced. Marko's generation had the chance to see through the dictatorship. State television had depicted Serbs as patriots fighting for their nation, but radio station B92 had given a more sceptical view. On the internet, the whole world seemed to view Serbs as barbaric monsters.

That was hard to take as the truth was not so black and white. Atrocities had been committed on all sides, as he'd witnessed. But it meant Marko learnt not to believe everything he was told.

His mum shook her head and smiled sadly:

'My son, how can you be so blind?'

Chapter 10

His mum's words played on his mind as he drove to the cousins' flat in Zemun. Was he blind to what went on?

The flat was inset from Cara Dušana. Marko ducked under the police tape into a small yard with a back wall that had half fallen down, the tower of Saborna Church visible through the gap. The front door wasn't visible from the main street, so however Jovanović had entered the flat, no-one had seen him.

The door had been left ajar by forensics. Marko checked the lock. It was a deadbolt so either the door had been locked or open but not on the latch. Jovanović had said the door was unlocked, not open. How else could Jovanović have gained entry unless he was invited in?

Marko stepped inside the dank flat, the sink-less kitchen leading to a bed-living room.

Through the bathroom doorway, Marko glimpsed a pile of dirty plates in the bath.

The dead bodies had been removed but the sofa-bed was stained with dry blood. Thankfully, the butchers' brains had been cleaned off. An ashtray had the remains of a stubbed out joint.

Marko took out his mobile and called forensics:

'Hey Stefan, is the autopsy on the two butchers done yet?'

'Just writing it up. We've tried to match the speed of your detective work.'

Marko recognised Stefan's respect, so reciprocated:

'Well you helped out by telling me the killers knew how to use sharp tools. Listen, I need that perceptive mind of yours again. How much dope had they smoked?'

'27.3 mg.'

'Which is how many joints?'

'Maybe three.'

'So they were pretty stoned.'

'They needed it to combat the effects of 3,4,5-trimethoxyphenethylamine in their bloodstream.'

'What the fuck's that?'

'Mescaline.'

Marko took that in. So the two cousins had been off their heads enough to commit murder.

But wouldn't they have been too stoned to offer a threat to Jovanović? And where had the drugs come from?

'You bag their mobiles?'

'Didn't find any.'

'Neither of them had a mobile?'

'I don't know if they had one. We just didn't find one on their person.'

'Okay, thanks.'

Marko ended the call. Stefan's pedantic answers had unwittingly helped him again. It was hard to believe that the cousins hadn't had a mobile so someone had removed them from the scene.

The sound of plates clattering spun Marko around. A gypsy kid sprinted out of the bathroom and through the front door. Marko dashed after the boy, who headed for the crumbling back wall. Marko grabbed the boy's foot as he clambered through the gap. The kid kicked out and his dirty old trainer came off in Marko's hand.

Marko hauled himself over the wall, dropping down onto the cobbles below. The kid was up ahead, making a limping run for it towards Saborna Church the corner. Marko sprinted after the boy, still holding the trainer.

Lying in the shade, a stray dog gave a half-hearted bark, too hot to take part in the chase.

The boy made to turn right past the church, but then veered left. Marko was used to being wrong-footed by his son on the tennis court so took it in his stride. The kid was nimble but hindered by wearing only one trainer. Marko swung out a long arm and collared the boy against the church wall.

The boy was maybe ten years old. He attempted to struggle out of Marko's grasp, his dirt-stained face contorted in rage:

'Get the fuck off me.'

'Don't you want your trainer?'

The boy glared at Marko, who smiled back. He'd dealt with his own son's tantrums when he was the same age, remembering chasing Goran around the kitchen table to make him take some medicine.

'Swap. Your trainer for whatever you took.'

'Didn't take anything.'

'Well you won't need your trainer in a detention centre anyway.'

'They can't use it now, they're dead.'

Marko put his hand out. The gypsy kid sighed, dug into his pocket and handed over an old school mobile. Marko gave the boy his trainer but didn't let go of his collar:

'Where did you find it?'

'In the bathroom.'

'You often sneak into the flat?'

'I don't sneak in. They used to let me smoke with them.'

'You smoke with them yesterday?'

The boy hesitated. Marko took out a five hundred *dinar* note, said:

'How about some new trainers?'

The boy eyed the money as he hopped into his trainer. Marko pressed:

'What did you see yesterday?'

'You should know, he was police.'

'Flashy guy in a white Armani suit?'

'If you know, why you asking?'

'How did he get in?'

'Through the door.'

'I know that clever boy. Did the cousins let him in?'

'Of course. He's not a ghost.'

Marko let go of the boy's collar. The kid whipped the cash away and scampered.

Marko mulled things over. A gypsy kid's word against a police inspector's would never hold up in court and it wasn't something Marko ever intended to do. Just as he didn't intend to let anyone know about the mobile.

First he needed to eat and maybe Jovanović knew a good place. He called his colleague:

'Hey Jova, all fine at the scene. Thought I'd grab something to eat while I'm in Zemun. What's that restaurant you go to?'

'Šaran. Get the fish soup.'

'Cheers. Catch you later.'

Marko drove two minutes to the riverside, where the restaurant was. A balding waiter took his order with a grunt. Marko asked:

'You know Jova?'

'Yes.'

'I'm his colleague. He said he was here yesterday, said maybe he left his sunglasses.'

'No, he didn't.'

The waiter left, leaving Marko in no doubt that Jovanović had him on side. If Jovanović needed confirmation he was at the restaurant when he got a call from Ivan, he would get it.

Marko looked at the array of bars, clubs and restaurants that floated on the Danube, the *splavovi* connected to shore by wooden walkways. He knew Jovanović had one of the *splavovi* as a houseboat. It had initially been a summer house but after his divorce, Jova had turned it into his main home. For holidays, he went to Montenegro.

Conveniently, Jova was back in Belgrade on the day of Milan Panić's murder. By coincidence, he was also just around the corner from the cousins' flat when he got a call from Ivan to go there.

While he waited for his soup, Marko checked the mobile from the cousins' flat. There were no incriminating messages. The cousins hadn't been that stupid. But in the call log, someone listed as 'D' had called just before Jovanović had turned up and killed the cousins. Marko called the number and got a voice message:

'Leave a message. Or don't. Your call.'

Marko clicked off the phone. No name had been given, but the voice belonged to Dragan Mladić.

The waiter brought out the soup, roughly putting the bowl on the table so that a bit spilled. A carp's head looked up at him, the fish caught in the Danube. The waiter was surly and the tablecloth soiled, but the fish soup was the tastiest in Zemun, if not the whole of Belgrade.

Marko finished his soup, left money on the table and got in his car. Next stop was Nenad's Butchers. He didn't think Nenad had anything to do with setting him up, but he wanted to double check.

Marko drove over the Sava and skirted the city centre. Driving past Trg Republike, he recalled the anti-Milošević demonstrations that had taken place there. Marko hadn't been in the force long and had been called in to restrain the demonstrators. He'd done as he was ordered, but hadn't taken part in any of the beatings.

A few years later, Marko had joined other police officers in downing weapons as a final demonstration brought about the end of Milošević's regime. Marko avoided politics, but it was a relief when Milošević went. At least there was no longer the fear of which side to be on. He hadn't joined the police to protect the regime, but because he was a big guy who liked physical activities and solving problems. That and because as a teenager, he'd loved watching Al Pacino in *Serpico*.

Marko headed up what he still thought of as Bulevar and parked. The butchers was packed, though half the people inside seemed to be there just to chat rather than buy any meat.

Nenad and his wife were busy behind the counter. Marko bustled through and waited for Nenad to finish serving a customer. Nenad waved a hairy arm in despair when he recognised Marko:

'You again. Haven't you police caused enough problems? Isn't killing my employees enough? We're working our arses off here.'

'Just wanted to say thanks for the tip off.'

'Tip off? If I knew you lot were going to kill them, I wouldn't have given you their address.'

Marko looked at the counter of meat. He'd promised Branka he would bring some sausages for her to cook:

'I'll get some *ćevapčići* while I'm here.'

'I should charge you double.'

'I should get a discount for the extra fame and custom I've brought. Could be a new slogan – "*ćevapčići* to die for".'

Nenad wrapped some sausage meat and handed them over the counter, taking Marko's money and turning to the next customer. The guy was a genuine butcher, nothing to do with Jovanović or Dragan, who Marko would visit next.

Dragan's Audi was parked outside Café Insomnia. Everyone knew he operated out of the café, so it wasn't a surprise for Marko to find him so easily. No-one ever fingered him. They valued their lives.

Dragan wasn't inside, but Marko took a stool anyway. The girl behind the bar was pretty but too petite to make it as a silicon stunner. Marko asked:

'Dragan in?'

'Haven't seen him.'

'His car's outside.'

'And?'

The girl might not have been a mafia moll, but she still obviously cared more about keeping her job than revealing anything to a police inspector.

'And I'll have a beer then.'

The girl shrugged, slid him a bottle of 'deer' beer. As Marko drank, he wondered if he should leave. Knowing Milica was around the corner made Marko want to pop around to her, fuck to forget and drop his private investigation.

After he'd left Milica the night before and gone home, he'd told Branka he hadn't been able to meet the Interior Minister. Said he would try the next day, not quite making up with her, but getting there. Maybe he should just go back to his routine, write up the report and turn a blind eye to whatever was going on.

Dragan strutted out of a backroom, tucking in his shirt and zipping up his jeans. Just in case anyone hadn't realised he'd been getting a blow job from Biljana, who followed him out. He gestured for a beer from the bargirl and raised his bottle to Marko:

'Congratulations on catching the killers.'

'Sorry you lost two of your gravediggers.'

Dragan shrugged:

'Those cousins were always fucked up. You here to commiserate or you just can't keep away? People will start spreading rumours about us.'

'Just wanted to see if it was okay for me to name you in my report as the person who tipped off who the killers were.'

'Don't know what you're talking about.'

'So you didn't deliberately give me the cousins' names?'

'I just wanted to know why the fuck they hadn't brought my *ćevapčići* and you happened to be here. You can put that in your report if you want.'

'Must have been great detective work by me then.'

'Must have been.'

'Either that or one of us is really stupid.'

Dragan dead-eyed Marko before replying:

'How's that?'

'It's not too clever to leave a mobile phone which shows you called the cousins right after I left here and before they were killed.'

'Was your colleague who killed them, not me.'

'Be interesting to see what messages they received before they killed Milan Panić.'

As Marko got up to leave, Dragan asked:

'How's Milica these days? Heard you've got her shacked up around the corner.'

'And?'

'Think she'll stay on the straight and narrow forever?'

'If she stays away from you.'

'You think you're her saviour? Think you're better than me?'

'No, I think we're both idiots.'

Dragan burst into laughter. Marko strode out into the sunlight, dropped his sunglasses into place and drove to Dedinje. What was he doing sparring with Dragan, putting a death sentence on Milica? He should back off, but there was no point stopping now.

Marko pulled up outside Vesna's wedding cake of a mansion. The same bodyguard was at the door:

'She's in the middle of a meditation session.'

'I'll wait.'

Marko was prepared and held up his laptop. He sat on one of the chaise-longues, while the security guy stood to the side. It was awkward without a chair back, but Marko typed up his report to show how the police work that led to the killers was all above board.

Wearing only a kimono, Vesna glided into the room and sat straight-backed on the chaise-longue opposite Marko. Her eyes were clear but she seemed to look through him, her voice distant:

'Inspector, how can I help?'

'Sorry to intrude again. As you've been informed, your husband's murderers were found and killed. If that brings any relief.'

'Milan can't be brought back… but justice must be served.'

Her words sent a shiver through Marko. For some reason he thought of Karadžić. Wanted for war crimes in The Hague, the guy had disguised himself as an 'expert in alternative medicine' and evaded capture for several years. Marko wasn't judging whether Karadžić was guilty of war crimes, but the transformation was intriguing. Marko gestured at his laptop:

'I just need to clarify a few things for the report. You told me that you found the Partizan badge outside the haulage container.'

'That's correct.'

'It's quite small. Did you just spot it?'

'The whole day was full of omens and visions. Just like I felt myself pulled to the container, my eyes were drawn to the ground. But it all happened in a trance. I can't recall picking it up.'

'We only found your fingerprints on it.'

'I'm not sure I understand. Why are you telling me this? Haven't you found my husband's killers?'

'It's just that the butchers were Red Star fans.'

For a second, Vesna was thrown:

'You're mistaken. Milan was a Red Star fan, not his killers.'

Marko looked at his laptop and smiled:

'You're right, my mistake.'

He'd lied to catch Vesna out and she'd obliged. Vesna closed her eyes. When she opened them, they were full of hate. She spoke:

'My husband was brutally murdered. The killers were found and killed. Now leave me to grieve in peace.'

Marko was escorted from the mansion by the security guy. Inside his Ford, he sat and contemplated what he'd learnt. Vesna had made him think it was Partizan fans who had killed her husband. From there, he'd gone to Dragan who had accidentally on purpose supplied the names of the cousins. He'd got the address from the butcher and then Jovanović had been waiting to kill them. Marko didn't know why or what the exact connections were, but he had been set up. The Interior Minister was right. The case stank and he'd been played for an idiot.

Needing to keep up appearances, Marko drove to the

nearest café with wifi and set up his laptop. Vesna was bound to make a complaint, so he had to email his report to Ivan as soon as possible. He'd just pressed 'send' when his mobile rang. Seeing it was Ivan, Marko braced himself as he answered:

'Chief.'

'What the fuck are you up to?'

Chapter 11

Marko bluffed:

'Been writing the report. I just emailed it to you. Did you get it?'

That gave Marko a few seconds reprieve while Ivan checked his email:

'Yes, it's here, but what are you doing hassling Vesna Panić?'

'Didn't mean to hassle her Chief. Was making sure I had everything covered.'

'By insinuating she had made a mistake over which football club her husband supported?'

'Was my mistake. I can go back and apologise if you'd like.'

'No, stay away from her. She's distraught enough. Her husband's been murdered. We found and eliminated his killers. We don't need to bother her any more.'

'Okay Chief. Let me know if the report's up to scratch. I don't think the Interior Minister should have any complaints.'

'He better not have.'

'You need me to come in or can I call it a day?'

'No, go on home. You'll hear from me if the report needs altering.'

Marko let his boss end the call. He wondered if he'd overdone the innocent idiot role. But Ivan really couldn't have any complaints about the report. There was not a hint of corruption.

Were Ivan and Vesna involved in some cover-up? Or was it simply a case of a police chief protecting a wealthy citizen?

Marko didn't want to think about it any more. He'd found out what he needed to. Vesna and Dragan had set him up to find the killers and Jovanović had finished off the job. Maybe Ivan was also in on it. Marko had been used. But he'd gained respect out of it and he'd regained his detective instincts. He would go home and get the *ćevapčići* to his wife. He would forget what he'd found out and think up something to tell the Interior Minister.

Marko packed up his laptop and left the café. He was just getting in his car when the Interior Minister's Audi pulled up beside him.

Jovanović sniffed as he tapped his fingers on the cabinet, unable to keep still. Ivan glanced over from his pc:

'I'm trying to read here.'

'You think Despotović can be trusted?'

'If you let me read in peace, we'll find out.'

Jovanović's mobile bleeped with a message. While he read it and typed a reply, Ivan concentrated on his pc:

'His report is perfect. All above board.'

'So why has Dragan sent me a text saying Despot's been asking questions?'

'Did he make any accusations?'

'Don't know, but Dragan wants to meet.'

'So meet. Despotović hasn't mentioned him in the report. It shows how his detective work led to the killers and how you acted in self-defence.'

Jovanović snorted:

'He wouldn't know detective work if it bit him on the arse.'

'Despotović isn't inept. He just enjoys pretending he is.'

Ivan ran a hand through his shock of white hair, shook out a Marlboro from the packet and said:

'Even if he does suspect something he's not showing it. I'll talk to Vesna, see exactly what he said to her. You meet

Dragan, see what he's got to say.'

'What if Despot's worked things out?'

'What if he has? What can he do? He's got a wife and son. He knows to keep quiet. Like he always has done.'

Jovanović hoped Ivan was right because he wasn't going to let Despot fuck things up. The guy was a loser, always running home to his wife and son. The best thing Jovanović had done was get a divorce. The bitch got the apartment, but he had his houseboat. He loved his bachelor lifestyle and he didn't intend to give anything up. A message bleeped on his phone. He tapped the cabinet and said:

'Okay. I'm meeting him in an hour.'

'Good. Let me know what you find out.'

Ivan watched Jovanović pocket his mobile and wipe his nose. He hoped Jovanović wasn't becoming a coke-head. His drug-fuelled impulses were necessary to get the dirty work done, but it also meant he was on the verge of fucking up. Ivan lit his cigarette and said:

'And keep off the product. Nobody believes that summer cold shit.'

Standing between the Interior Minister's Audi and his own Ford, Marko asked:

'Your car or mine?'

'I think mine is more comfortable.'

Marko got in and said:

'You following me?'

The Interior Minister gestured to his chauffeur:

'My driver knows Vesna Panić's bodyguard. We heard you paid her a visit. I was in the area so waited for you.'

'Belgrade's a small world.'

'It would certainly seem to be the case. So, do you have any information for me?'

'Didn't know I'd agreed to give you any.'

The Interior Minister might have been right about the case being corrupt, but that didn't mean Marko was going to tell him anything. The Interior Minister smiled:

'I understand your reluctance. And perhaps my previous comments about your son's tennis career were uncalled for. I recognise you are in a difficult position, so let me make you a more positive offer. As you are aware, a renowned tennis scout will be watching the Pančevo Open, where both our sons will be competing. I can make it happen that your son is scouted as well as mine.'

Marko wasn't buying it:

'You can't buy sporting ability. Either he's good enough or he isn't.'

'That may be so, but let's say your son has the ability. He won't get very far if he doesn't get the support. And what if he does not have the ability? It would be a shame if he doesn't have any kind of career.'

Marko exhaled. In a way he preferred Dragan's more e x p l i c i t threats than the Interior Minister's convoluted ones, which tired him out:

'Look, maybe the case is corrupt, but even if it is, there's nothing I can prove.'

'Maybe I can help you. Let me tell you what I have discovered. I have it from an international source that Milan Panić's *ajvar* business was a cover up for drug smuggling.'

'It wouldn't surprise me, but where's the evidence? And that just shows his criminal dealings, not police corruption.'

'I'm also informed that Ivan Dragić used to go to school with Vesna Panić.'

This did surprise Marko, but still didn't prove anything:

'And?'

'And doesn't this strike you as a coincidence?'

'Is it a fact or rumour?'

'Unproven at this stage.'

Marko looked at the Interior Minister and weighed things up. Maybe the Minister had 'an international source', whatever the fuck that meant, as well as government backing, plus a chauffeur who had connections.

On the other hand, as Chief of Police, Ivan also wielded a lot of power. Jovanović was a loose cannon who could shoot people without hesitation. And Dragan was a drugs dealer who no-one crossed for fear of their lives.

If it was a case of politicians versus police and mafia, Marko thought the latter might come out on top:

'What are you hoping to do here, bring down the whole police department?'

'No, I simply want to root out corruption. You can help me do that. Or you can find yourself arrested as a corrupt inspector yourself.'

'Last time, it was losing my job you threatened me with.'

'Whatever is necessary to make you see sense.'

Marko wanted to laugh at the absurdity of the situation. Instead, he asked:

'What do you want me to do? Should I catch a police inspector and drugs dealer in the act?'

'I presume you are talking about Inspector Jovanović and Dragan Mladić. You could start by finding out how Dragan has carte blanche. I'm informed that he emerged unscathed after the Zemun clan was broken up. Do I have to do the detective work for you?'

Chapter 12

Marko sat in his car, debating whether to drive home or not. He'd wanted to tell the Interior Minister to go fuck himself with his various threats. It wasn't so long ago that politicians had been in bed with the Serbian mafia – until Đinđić's assassination in 2003, at least.

Marko had grown up during the Yugoslav War, lived through sanctions and NATO bombing.

If he lost his job, he would survive. Even if he was arrested on trumped up corruption charges, he could turn to Ivan for help.

The threat-cum-offer about Goran's tennis career could also be dealt with. Marko encouraged his son's sporting ambitions, but he was more concerned with Goran getting a good education and job in case the tennis didn't come off. What was more worrying was that the Interior Minister could make sure his son didn't have a future of any kind.

Marko had turned a blind eye to corruption because life was better than it had been in the nineties. Being in the police didn't pay well, but it was a job. His son hadn't had to live through war or bombing or economic crisis.

During the inflation years, shifty-looking men buzzed like bees on street corners, seeming not to move their mouths as they chanted the mantra of '*devize, devize*' – the word for 'foreign currency'.

People would dash out as soon as work finished to try and change Yugoslav *dinars* into German Deutschmarks –

the hard currency in Europe at the time. On several occasions, the money people thought they had in the morning was worthless by the afternoon. In his first week in the police, Marko's whole salary amounted to enough for one coffee. The world had since changed. Now the hard currency was Euros.

If Goran faced a bleak future, then Marko had to take action. To keep the Interior Minister off his back, Marko had to give him something. Plus, the information the Minister had given niggled. Marko had worked out that drugs were involved, but if Ivan and Vesna were part of it, that took it to another level.

Marko wasn't going to carry out some sting operation, but he could check a few things. He wanted to avoid Ivan and Jovanović. Who could Marko trust in the department? Ivan had his cronies. Probably the only person he could trust was Nebojša. Marko called the rookie:

'You still in headquarters?'

'Yea, they've got me printing out your report.'

'How about a bit of proper investigative work?'

'Sure.'

'I need to know if Dragan Mladić has ever been arrested.'

'Is this for the same case?'

'I'll tell you after you give me the info. Call me when you've got it.'

Marko knew it would take Nebojša a while to go through the arrest records, so he started driving back to the city centre. It had never occurred to Marko to check if Dragan had been arrested because he'd never come up in an investigation. Even when Marko had suspected Dragan was Milica's dealer, he hadn't looked into it. People didn't name Dragan and he had police connections.

On an impulse, Marko turned down at the Autokomanda intersection. On the bend, a patrol officer was parked up in an old police Yugo. With a copy of *Blic* draped against the steering wheel, the officer didn't look like he'd be stopping anyone for traffic offences. A speeding BMW would be in

Niš by the time the officer got up on the highway.

Gojko was under the overpass, sitting on a fold-up chair and engrossed in a book, several boxes of books on the low wall beside him. People waiting for buses picked up a book, looked at it, put it back when the bus arrived.

Across the road were the converted hangars of the former motorised forces command which gave the neighbourhood its name. With the constant traffic and noise, Gojko couldn't have chosen a less peaceful location. Maybe it was penance. When Gojko had heard Milica was back at university, he'd deliberately moved from Studentski Trg. She was bound to pass him on her way to classes and he didn't want to embarrass her.

Marko parked up and strolled over to Gojko:

'Hey neighbour.'

Gojko looked up from his book:

'Neighbour, what you doing here?'

'Was passing so thought I'd see how my old friend was. What you reading?'

Gojko held up the book. Marko read the title: *The Trial* by Franz Kafka. Gojko said:

'Read it when I was twenty, but got a set of Kafka so thought I'd give it a re-read.'

'I saw the film.'

'Orson Welles. Not a word for word adaptation, but it does capture the bureaucratic nightmare and the dread of not knowing what fate awaits you. You know he filmed part of it in Zagreb, with Tito's permission of course. They admired each other. Probably saw themselves as two dictators of greatness.'

Gojko was more into books than film, but he still had more knowledge than Marko, who just knew what he liked:

'*Touch of Evil* is my favourite of his.'

'You always liked your American films.'

'If there were any good Serbian films I'd watch them.'

'Come on. What about *We Are Not Angels*?'

Marko smiled. They'd seen *We Are Not Angels* together as

teenagers. He asked:

'When was the last time you went to the cinema?'

Gojko shrugged:

'Twenty years ago.'

'Maybe we're both out of date.'

'Not maybe. For sure.'

When was the last time Marko had gone to the cinema? With his wife in 1998. They'd gone to see *Godzilla* and the cinema had started shaking. At first the audience thought it was some kind of special effect. But then people started to panic, thinking NATO had begun bombing the city.

Marko and Branka ran out of the cinema with everyone else. There were no bombs. It was just a minor earthquake and people laughed in relief at their double misconception. Branka didn't find it funny. After that she refused to go to a cinema again.

Marko wouldn't go on his own. Besides, once he joined the police and they had Goran, he didn't have the time. If a good film was on TV he watched it. And in the last few years, Goran had shown him how to download all his old favourites. Marko had re-watched *Touch of Evil*, *Serpico*, *LA Confidential*.

'Anyway *We Are Not Angels* was a comedy. What about a good thriller?'

'Marko, we've had years of war, bloodshed and clan violence. People need to laugh. Besides, there hasn't been a film industry to speak of since Tito's time.'

'Doesn't have to be about war. Just a good detective thriller. Could call it Balkan Noir.'

Gojko laughed:

'Balkan Noir? Serbs don't need to watch that. They live it every day.'

Marko smiled, but Gojko turned serious:

'I feel the same. I've had enough horror for a lifetime. We complain about how the West portrays Serbs as monsters, but we do it ourselves. Milošević took us into two wars and left the country in economic ruin. We should be happy he's dead, but we still talk about him ten years later. We glorify our criminals and killers, give them nicknames and legendry status.

'Arkan is a legend in his death just as he was when he was alive. Legija makes newspaper headlines from behind bars. We make jokes – should have sent Legija to Kosovo, he would have sorted out the Albanians. I don't want to hear about them anymore. I want to talk about Ivo Andrić and Danilo Kiš or modern writers like Dragan Velikić and Aleksandar Đuričic. I want Serbia to be known for its literature, not killing.'

Gojko paused for breath, his rant over. He started to gesture at the books he sold, but gave up and let his hand drop.

Marko understood his old friend. It would be good to forget, but Serbs lived through their history. He wanted to make a joke of it, but couldn't think of one. He was saved from having to respond by his phone ringing. Nebojša was calling him. He told Gojko he had to go and took the call as he went back to his car. Nebojša told him what he'd found out:

'Dragan had one arrest in 2003.'

'Who was the arresting officer?'

'Jovanović.'

'And who signed his release?'

'Just the initials I.D.'

Marko knew what the initials stood for: Ivan Dragić. He exhaled as it dawned on Nebojša:

'The Chief of Police?'

'Uh huh.'

Marko was working it out. At the time of the Zemun clan clean-up, Dragan arrested and then released by Jovanović and Ivan. A few years later, Dragan was one of the city's main drug dealers and went untouched. That couldn't be coincidence.

For years, Marko had deliberately remained ignorant. Now, knowing the little that he did could get him killed.

He wouldn't get away with claiming innocence forever. He needed to know a lot so that he could have a bargaining tool. This wasn't for the Interior Minister, this was for him and his family.

He wasn't going to check on Ivan. His home in Senjak would have security and he would be too canny to leave a trace. Jovanović was more reckless. Marko suspected Jova's 'summer cold' was the result of cocaine. If he was snorting, maybe he was also dealing and maybe Marko could find evidence of this. Nebojša interrupted Marko's thoughts:

'What's this about?'

'Look, forget what you just told me okay?'

'Come on Marko, let me in on this.'

'You sure?'

'I'm sure.'

'Then you're surer than I am. What car have you got?'

'A Yugo.'

'Meet me in the Hotel Intercontinental car park in thirty minutes.'

For the first time since being assigned to headquarters, Nebojša had been given an investigative task. Checking arrest records was hardly what he'd been fast-tracked for, but it was better than photocopying. What should have been a two-minute check had taken longer because the arrest records system was so outdated, with only the last few years being documented on computers.

He wasn't sure about Marko's methods, but the older inspector had been fair to him. It wasn't much of a stretch to see that Jovanović was in liaison with a known dealer. How else did a police inspector drive a BMW?

Nebojša didn't want to think that the Chief of Police was also involved. Ivan was a legend for breaking up the Zemun clan. Checking on your boss was hardly a good career move. On the other hand, rooting out corruption from the very top could make his name. Nebojša's ambition drove him on. It didn't matter who had to be checked.

Chapter 13

Marko pulled up alongside Nebojša's old Yugo in the car park of The Hotel Intercontinental.

It seemed an appropriate place to meet, being the scene of Arkan's assassination.

Arkan's murder had been more of a shock than Đinđić's. The Prime Minister had already survived assassination attempts. He knew his attempts at reform made him a target. Arkan had always been immune. Whether he was a war criminal or a national hero, Arkan had iconic status in Serbia. He was the most powerful criminal and militia leader in the Balkans. Who would have dared to kill him?

Fifteen years after his murder, there was still a swirl of rumours. Some said Arkan had been killed because he knew too much when Milošević went on trial for war crimes. Others said his death was set up by Western spies because he had too much information on them. The theory Marko favoured was more local: With Arkan going into politics, he'd taken his eye off emerging criminal clans and they saw an opportunity.

As New Belgrade mob boss Bata Trlaja had said, Belgrade was 'a pond too small for so many crocodiles.'

Bata was murdered a year later.

After Arkan's murder, the Zemun clan ran riot for three years in a crime and killing spree.

On the surface it was to avenge Arkan, but it also benefited the clan to eliminate any competition. It took Đinđić's murder to bring about the crackdown. Not easy when the clans had far more armoury and money than the police.

It was difficult to chase an Audi in a Yugo. Drive-by shootings happened daily, mafia cars known as 'Audis of Death'. The police even started to play a betting game: who will be killed today?

Marko got inside Nebojša's old Yugo, the two men hardly fitting inside. Marko's Ford had air conditioning, but the Yugo's obviously wasn't working. As sweat dripped down the side of his head, Marko opened the window without thinking. Nebojša looked over in horror. Before he could say '*promaja*', Marko closed the window. Nodding at the hotel's entrance, Marko asked:

'How old were you when Arkan was killed?'

'Ten, but I remember it well. It was on TV all day. Did you take part in the investigation?'

'No, I hadn't made inspector yet.'

'Maybe he's still alive.'

That was another theory – that Arkan had faked his own death. Marko dead-panned:

'Yea, he's on the moon with Elvis and Hitler.'

'Come on, everyone knows the Americans didn't actually go to the moon.'

Marko didn't know if Nebojša had understood his joke. In Belgrade, everyone had an opinion about everything. Marko was different in that he joked rather than judged. Maybe it was time he got serious:

'I'm looking into police corruption. I want to find evidence of Jovanović's connection to Dragan, in particular if he's involved in drug smuggling.'

'You know, I thought you were the kind of cop who coerced suspects into confessions.'

'I am that kind of cop. That junkie we arrested? I planted the evidence on him.'

'You put the heroin up his arse?'

'What? No, I put the old woman's medicine in his pocket. Threats, deals, bribery – if you want to make arrests, they're all necessary.'

'So why do you care about Jovanović and Dragan?'

'Because drug dealing and murder cross the line. And because the Interior Minister is breaking my balls.'

You're working for the Interior Minister?'

'I'm not working for the Minister, I'm being 'coerced' by him.'

Marko looked at Nebojša. The rookie was full of zeal and obviously ambitious. Marko asked:

'How did you make inspector so young?'

'I got fast tracked after I arrested a car thief.'

'Must have been some arrest.'

Nebojša wanted to say that he'd noted down the stolen car when it came on the message boards. That he'd researched on social media and found guys bragging about their new BMW that matched the description. And as a patrol officer he had single-handedly made the arrest in the street. It was all true. But as Marko was being so honest, Nebojša also had to admit a truth:

'The car belonged to the Interior Minister's wife.'

Marko raised an eyebrow. Nebojša wasn't so naïve that he didn't see a career opportunity.

Still, Marko wanted to make sure Nebojša understood the situation:

'Finding evidence of police corruption could get us killed. The Interior Minister won't protect us. You still in?'

'I'm in.'

'Okay, we'll go in your car because Jovanović knows mine.'

'Where we going?'

'To Jovanović's houseboat in Zemun quay.'

Nebojša drove alongside the Danube, past the main stretch of *splavovi*, the nightclubs not open yet but the restaurants packed. The path between the road and river bank was full of couples out for a summer stroll. Marko thought about the times he'd walked with his wife. Not so often now, but a lot when they were younger, always avoiding certain bars. You could be shot for being in the wrong place.

Belgrade in the late nineties had been a crazy place. The war was over, but in its place was inflation and economic crisis. With no jobs or opportunities, everyone partied like it was nineteen-ninety-nine. The *splavovi* were where you hung out if you wanted to be seen with criminals. Inter-clan warfare was rife. One night, a club would be packed with ravers. In the morning it would be burnt down.

From their balcony, Marko and Branka had seen the fires at night. Just as they had sat with a beer and watched NATO's bombs rain down on Belgrade, lighting up the sky like fireworks.

Branka pregnant at the time, their son as old as the century. Marko wondered where fifteen years had gone.

Nebojša interrupted Marko's thoughts:

'What about the Zemun clan – did you have a hand in breaking it up?'

'Yea, I was there in 2003 when we blew up their headquarters in Šilerova Street.'

Marko was a rookie inspector in 2003, so had simply followed orders. Ivan was the lead inspector. Marko had made a few arrests, but hadn't been involved in any major shoot-outs.

They passed Hotel Jugoslavija, a formerly glorious monument of a country that no longer existed, the west wing still in ruin fifteen years after being bombed by NATO. The former Yugoslavia stretched south and west to the Adriatic. What Marko missed the most was easy access to the sea.

Nebojša slowed as they approached Zemun quay, a less busy area. The *splavovi* were smaller and more dotted apart, individual houseboats rather than a set of restaurants and clubs. Marko pointed out of the windscreen:

'Jova's is the last one. Turn off here and park up.'

Nebojša did as he was told, parking off the main street.

The two of them watched for movement in Jovanović's houseboat. Nebojša asked:

'Think he's in?'

'Can't see his car.'

'If he's hiding drugs, it doesn't look like he's got much security.'

'You think he doesn't have someone watching?'

'What do you mean?'

'His houseboat might not have CCTV, but one of those people is paid to keep an eye on the place.'

Marko gestured at the quay. A young lad was fishing. An old man was cleaning his nets. An old woman was sitting on a step, scaling a fish. Marko said:

'As soon as I set foot on the walkway, one of them will call Jovanović. I'll make it look as if I'm visiting. If he's not there, I'll break in. If he arrives before I'm off, text me.'

Marko took out the cousins' mobile he'd taken from the gypsy kid, called Nebojša so he had the number. He put his own phone and his gun in the glove compartment. If he needed a quick escape, the Danube might be the only option. Marko got out of the Yugo, jogged down the bank towards the riverside.

The young lad, old man and woman all looked Marko's way without even pretending not to.

Maybe all three were paid to keep a look out. Marko ignored their stares, stepped onto the wooden walkway and strode over the slats towards Jovanović's houseboat.

There was no obvious security. The walls were made of wood and the windows were single glazed. It was easy to break into. But with the long walkway, if an alarm was sounded, Marko would have to get back to land before Jovanović arrived. He banged on the door and called out:

'Jova?'

No answer. If he was at home, Marko would pretend to

be paying him a visit.

Marko didn't bother knocking again and stepped around to the side of the hut, the walkway going all the way around, swaying slightly with his movement. Blinds covered all the windows so he couldn't see inside. He knocked on the glass and called Jovanović's name again.

Marko tried around the back, where there was another door, this one made of glass. He rattled the handle, but it didn't open. He looked around and found a metal bucket next to steps leading into the water. He swung the bucket full force into the door, smashing the glass. He reached in, unlatched the door and yanked it open.

Nobody inside and no other rooms to explore. The hut was en-suite, a mini kitchen unit in one corner and a sofa bed against a wall. Movement caught Marko's eye. A black cat sprung from its hiding place behind the sofa and nipped out of the door.

There was no sign of anything feminine. A bachelor pad. A framed photo showed Jovanović fishing, Jova's son by his side. Marko checked behind the frame, but didn't find anything. He wasn't expecting to find a heap of cocaine on the table, but if Jovanović was on the take, there would be coke hidden somewhere.

Marko's eyes alighted on a shelf above the fridge. There were three jars of *ajvar*. Not domestic but Panić brand. Marko grabbed a jar, unscrewed the lid and dipped in his fingers.

He pulled out a sealed packet. Marko had expected to find a small amount of cocaine. This was maybe fifty grams of heroin.

A police inspector's salary wasn't great, so Marko understood Jova's need for more money.

But this was part of something bigger and more sinister. Worst of all, it was a waste of *ajvar*.

Marko's mobile bleeped with a text. He checked and read the message from Nebojša: 'get out'.

Jovanović waltzed into Café Insomnia as if he owned the place. He nodded to Dragan at the back of the bar, said:

'I need a piss.'

Dragan took a hit of *rakija* and lit a Davidoff. He watched as Jovanović came out of the toilet, rubbing his nose. In his youth, Dragan had taken his share of coke, but once he'd made a deal to become a major dealer, he'd quit. He waited for Jovanović to take a seat:

'You ready now?'

'Ready for anything. Don't I get a drink?'

'The bar's behind you.'

Jovanović laughed. He leapt up, went to the bar and got a beer. After his line of coke, he needed a drink. He winked at the waitress. Most of the silicon stunners sitting around were attached to Dragan's crew. But a waitress could be impressed with a police inspector who played both sides and had a houseboat to take her to. He'd hardly sat back down when Dragan asked:

'Why didn't you take the mobile from the cousins' flat?'

'I took the one I saw. I didn't have time to look around for another. It's not a problem. Despot's already handed in the report. You're not mentioned and neither is the mobile. He can't go and get it checked now.'

'So why was he stirring up shit?'

'He doesn't know shit.'

'He's not as stupid as you think.'

'So people keep saying. Personally, I think he's as stupid as he seems. But if he causes any problems, we know what his weak points are. He won't want anything happening to his wife and son.'

'Or his mistress.'

'Who's his mistress?'

'Fuck, do I have to do the detective work for you?'

Feeling coked-up fury rise inside him, Jovanović knocked back some beer. He'd had enough of Dragan's superior attitude. Okay, they were in his place, but he wouldn't even be sitting there if it wasn't for the deal that had been made:

'Hey, let's not forget who got you set up.'

'Who? You?'

Dragan's eyes deadened. In the past, he would have smashed his glass into Jovanović's face.

But his violence was another thing he'd learnt to contain. Yes, he'd made a deal. But Jovanović wasn't the broker. And the guy was starting to become a liability, snorting more coke than money he made from selling smack. Out of the two police inspectors, Dragan was starting to think Marko Despotović was the smarter one. Dragan looked at Jovanović with disdain, said:

'You've got coke on your nose.'

Jovanović pinched his nostrils and tried to form a witty reply when his mobile rang. Thinking it showed he had more important business than Dragan, he took the call:

'What's up?'

'You've got an intruder.'

'What? Who?'

'Some guy.'

'I'm on my way.'

Jovanović clicked off his phone, finished his beer and said:

'Got to go. Send me the name of Despot's mistress.'

'Look it up. You arrested her two years ago.'

Jovanović didn't have time to think up a reply, jogging out of the café.

Dragan downed his *rakija* and stubbed out his cigarette. It was a shame to mention Milica. He'd liked her before she started buying off him. And he could say he admired her for getting off smack. He understood her going from a drug dealer to a police inspector. She'd never mentioned his name when she was arrested. It wouldn't have mattered as his police connections would have got him off. But he appreciated her discretion. She was under Despotović's protection now, so it would be between him and Jovanović as to how it went down.

Marko looked through the blinds at a side window and saw a flashing blue light nearing the quay. Jovanović had arrived. Confronting him wasn't going to achieve anything. Marko would probably end up with a bullet in his head and Jovanović would cover his tracks, make it seem that Marko was corrupt. Nebojša wouldn't be able to prove anything.

If Marko ran back down the walkway, there was no guarantee he'd get to the end of it before Jovanović. If Jova didn't run him down, he could just pull out a gun.

Pocketing the heroin, Marko dashed out the back door and took the steps down into the Danube. It was a nice summer evening for a swim, but lowering himself fully clothed into the water wasn't much fun.

Marko dived under the hut and swam directly under the walkway back to shore.

He was taking a risk, but didn't see any other option. With his head just above water, Marko heard Jovanović's car screech to a halt. The depth shallowed, so Marko crawled forward with his mouth closed, water filling his nostrils. The walkway above him shook as Jovanović leapt on. If Jovanović looked down between the cracks, Marko would be spotted. But Jova strode straight to his houseboat.

Marko gave Jovanović time to get inside, counting to ten, not sure if it was too little or too much. He crawled out from under the walkway, spluttering out water as he scrambled up the grass bank. He forced himself into a run, trying to get his breath back. He heard shouting behind him, but didn't turn to look. He needed to get to Nebojša before Jovanović reached him. There were several Yugos parked up, but none of them were Nebojša's.

If Marko had had enough breath, he would have sworn. Was there nobody in this city he could trust? Had Nebojša left him high and dry, or rather low and wet? Without thinking, Marko headed into the streets of Zemun.

Finding himself at the back of the cousins' flat, Marko recognised the location – the same place he'd chased the gypsy kid that morning. It came to his mind that the Zemun clan's former headquarters on Šilerova Street wasn't far away. Seeing the tower of Saborna Church, Marko aimed for the church as a safe haven to hide. He felt as if he was treading water, his sodden clothes weighing down his movement. He stumbled across one cobbled street, turned into another and saw the church on the corner. A car swerved to a stop beside him.

Nebojša shouted out of the window:

'Get in.'

Marko scrambled into the passenger seat and Nebojša drove off, the old Yugo bouncing over the cobbles. Nebojša was as breathless as Marko:

'I had to move. The kid with the fishing rod was checking the cars. Did you find anything?'

Marko dug into his pocket and held up the packet of heroin:

'Found it in a jar of *ajvar*. There were two other jars.'

Nebojša looked over wide-eyed:

'Fuck, what are we going to do?'

'Go home so I can get out of these wet clothes.'

'I mean about Jovanović.'

'We see how he reacts.'

Chapter 14

Jovanović flung the jar at the floor. The glass smashed and *ajvar* splattered the wooden tiles.

Someone had broken into his home and stolen fifty grams of heroin. Jovanović was pretty sure that 'someone' was Marko fucking Despotović.

He hadn't managed to see the intruder's face, but the guy who had waded out of the water and made a run for it was Marko's size.

Jovanović's initial impulse had been to give chase and shoot the fucker in the back, but the thief was heading for the streets of Zemun and might be out of sight within a few turns. Even if he did catch the bastard, it would be a bit difficult to claim self-defence when witnesses would see him. So he had gone back into his houseboat to check what had been taken.

If it was a thief out to make a killing, all the heroin would have been taken. But only one packet had gone. Jovanović was sure Marko had nabbed it. What was the fucker up to? Was he planning to use it as evidence?

Ivan and Dragan had both said Marko shouldn't be underestimated. Maybe they were right.

But nor should he be. He would make sure Marko kept his find quiet.

Jovanović was ready to drive over to Marko's place, break into his flat, see how he liked it.

In an attempt to contain his growing fury, he phoned Ivan:

'I don't know what the fuck Marko is up to, but the bastard just broke into my houseboat. The guy can't be trusted. He's lost it. We need to contain him. I swear, I'm going to…'

'Slowly, slowly.'

At the other end of the call, Ivan lit a Marlboro while he sat in his garden. Jovanović sounded wired, so Ivan had to remain calm. He asked:

'Are you sure it was Marko?'

'Not a hundred per cent but I'll bet my houseboat on it.'

'Did you see him?'

'From the back, but I know it was him.'

'Why would he want to break into your home?'

Jovanović paused for a second. He hadn't given himself time to think up an explanation. He would have to go with the truth, partly at least:

'He took some dolls I had for my niece.'

Ivan inhaled and blew out smoke. He looked at the swirls of smoke vanish in the air to make himself calm. His desire to kill Jovanović subsided. He said:

'Maybe he has his own nieces. How many dolls did he take?'

'A hundred.'

Ivan almost crushed his cigarette. They were acting like teenagers, pretending to talk about dolls instead of heroin in case anyone was listening in on their conversation. But these days you couldn't be too careful.

Jovanović didn't tell Ivan about the other two jars. He would have to quickly sell the rest of the heroin in one batch, which would mean less money, but better than ditching it in the Danube.

A few seconds of silence as both men weighed up their options. Ivan broke it:

'Don't do anything stupid. I'll put a plan in motion tonight and develop it in the morning. You stay out of sight and trail him, but that's all. Understand?'

Jovanović nodded, busy forming his own plan. Ivan

repeated himself:

'You understand?'

'Yes Chief, I understand.'

Ivan ended the call and stubbed out his cigarette. He would apply tactics before letting Jovanović do anything drastic. In the morning, he would kill two birds with one stone by setting Marko and the Interior Minister against each other. Before that, Marko needed to be paid a visit. Ivan made a call to Viktor Antić.

Jovanović stared at the *ajvar*-smeared floor. He was calmer now. Ivan was right to an extent.

Acting on impulse could have consequences. But so could acting too slowly. He would follow Ivan's plan, but he also had his own ideas about how to put Marko in his place. First, he needed his floor cleaned. He strode out of his houseboat and called the kid over.

Marko got Nebojša to drop him off at Block 45. He would pick up his car later.

'Are you sure we shouldn't go to the Chief or the Interior Minister with this?'

'We need to wait and see if either of them can be trusted first.'

'You really think the Chief would be in on this?'

'Don't know. But presenting a bag of smack doesn't prove anything. Jova can just deny it and Ivan will back him up.'

'What do we do with the heroin?'

'I'll put it somewhere safe.'

What was he going to do with it? For Marko, the heroin was proof of Jovanović's corruption, but how could it be used as evidence? How could he prove it belonged to Jovanović when it was in Marko's possession?

In his sodden clothes, Marko waved the rookie off and trod towards the block of flats. An elderly neighbour was watering her pepper plants at the side of the building.

Marko remembered he was supposed to bring *ćevapčići* for Branka to cook. He'd completely forgotten. To appease her, he needed flowers. Maybe a plant would do instead. He turned to the old woman:

'Hey neighbour, how much for one of the plants?'

The old woman looked Marko up and down. She'd known him since he was a young man:

'I think you need dry clothes not a pepper plant.'

'I know, but I forgot to bring food for Branka so I need to make it up to her.'

'It takes more than a few minutes for peppers to grow.'

'I know that too. It's instead of flowers.'

Marko's neighbour shook her head as she dug up a plant and handed it to Marko:

'Have it for free. Good luck.'

Inside the flat, Marko headed straight for the balcony. Hearing him come in, Branka called from the kitchen:

'Did you bring the *ćevapčići*?'

'Afraid I left it in the car.'

'Shall I go and get it?'

'Uh, the car's in the Intercontinental car park.'

'And what's it doing there?'

Marko potted the pepper plant on the balcony, held it up as Branka came out to him:

'I got you this.'

Branka took in Marko's wet clothes:

'What happened to you?'

'Fancied a swim after a hot day.'

Marko's wife raised an eyebrow:

'I wasn't born yesterday Marko.'

'It's a long story. There was a guy with drugs, a chase, I fell in the water. This is this.'

Branka let Marko get away with his half-truths. She knew he couldn't tell her everything about work. But he had said he was bringing food for her to cook:

'Thanks for the plant but it will be a while before those peppers are ready to eat.'

'I'll make it up to you. Why don't we go out for a meal? We'll go for a walk to get the car, then pick Goran up, have a family meal out.'

Branka squinted at Marko:

'Are you having an affair?'

'What?'

'You're behaving strangely.'

'Just want to show my wife and son how much I love them. Come on, give me a hug.'

In his drenched state, Marko trod towards Branka with his muddy hands out. She couldn't help smiling as she backed away:

'Go away you dirty river creature.'

Marko smiled at his wife and said:

'Could you chuck me some dry clothes?'

Marko went to the bathroom and showered. Drying himself, Marko thought he saw a couple more white hairs on his chest. He chucked on the dry clothes Branka had left to avoid thinking about it. There were more important things to focus on.

The heroin find was going to bring him trouble, he knew it. Marko didn't know if Jovanović had recognised him. Until he saw Jovanović's reaction, he wanted to keep an eye on his family.

With their arms linked, Marko and Branka strolled to the Intercontinental. It wasn't the same feeling as when they were teenagers, but Marko loved his wife. He vowed to himself he would be faithful from now on. He would make sure Milica was safe, but no more sex.

Marko's car stank of meat that had been left in the sun for too long. He picked up the wrapped *ćevapčići* and chucked it in the nearest bin.

As they drove over to the tennis academy, Marko carried on with his semi-truths:

'I spoke with the Interior Minister. The tennis scout will keep an eye on Goran.'

Branka kissed him:

That's great news.'

They picked up Goran and went to Potkovica Restaurant near Slavija. To match the meaning of the restaurant's name, the first letter was in the shape of a horse shoe – the place famous for its Serbian cuisine, including horse meat. Branka asked:

'Did you get a pay rise?'

Marko put an arm around Goran:

'Just want to feed my son with the best before the Pančevo Open.'

Marko gestured at the horseshoe:

'Plus, good luck coming here.'

Branka laughed:

'Since when did you believe in things like that?'

'I don't. I just said that for you. I know my son doesn't need luck.'

Goran smiled:

'I don't know dad, some of those guys are almost ready to go pro.'

'Let's get some horse's blood in you for courage then.'

Branka tutted:

'Come on Marko, he shouldn't be drinking yet.'

'Just one glass.'

Marko ordered a bottle of Horse's Blood wine and horse meat pate for starters, getting into the theme. At some point he was going to face the repercussions of breaking into Jovanović's houseboat, but until then, he wanted to forget any thoughts of police corruption and enjoy the time with his family.

Though Marko couldn't help glancing at the doorway. What did he expect, that Jovanović and Ivan would follow him? He was becoming paranoid. Marko remembered the ending of *The Sopranos*, Tony Soprano always wary either of the FBI or mafia hitmen coming after him. A lot of people found the ending unsatisfactory, but Marko thought it perfectly summed up the state Tony Soprano was left in. Marko drank some Horse's Blood, tucked into the horse meat pate and told himself to relax.

By the time they drove home, Marko had managed to forget about the last few days. He pulled up outside Block

45 a happy family man. Until he saw the two unmarked police cars.

As Marko stepped out of his Ford, Viktor Antić and two other guys from the drugs enforcement section walked over. Viktor gave an apologetic smile:

'Need to search you Marko.'

'What?'

'We got a call that a person matching your description was seen doing a coke deal. Car matched too. Better we check this out, keep it in-house.'

'Come on Viktor, you know I don't do drugs.'

Viktor shrugged:

'Sorry Despot, orders are orders.'

Marko didn't know if Viktor was in on the corruption or really was just following orders. But what he did know was that Jovanović or Ivan was sending a message. He shrugged:

'I've got nothing to hide.'

Branka and Goran stood there wide-eyed as Marko placed his hands on the car and let Viktor pat him down. Not finding anything, Viktor gestured at the Ford:

'Need to check the car.'

Marko handed over the keys. He looked over at his wife and son:

'You two go on up. This won't take a minute. Just a misunderstanding.'

Viktor said:

'One of the guys will have to go with them. We need to check the flat too.'

'I know you don't have a warrant for that.'

'And you know it will be better if we check and give the all clear.'

Or, thought Marko, they plant drugs while he's out of sight. He said:

'We'll all go up together.'

While Viktor's two men searched the car, Viktor regaled Marko with a tale of a recent case:

'Hear about the bust we just made? We'd been told by an

informant that a lorry of peppers was a shipment of heroin. So we stopped it at the Kosovo border, questioned the driver and searched the lorry. The driver seemed innocent and we couldn't find any smack...'

Marko didn't know why Viktor was telling him the story. Was he trying to distract him? He looked over at his car to make sure the other two guys weren't placing drugs in the car which could then be 'found'. Viktor continued:

'But the intel we had was supposed to be dead certain, so we carried on searching. Took apart the lorry, even got the design plan from the manufacturer so we didn't miss anything. Still nothing. Brought in the sniffer dogs. They didn't find anything. After all the work, we were determined to find something. So we cut the fucking lorry in half. Nothing.'

Viktor looked over at his two guys:

'Nothing?'

Viktor's men shook their heads. They all headed up to the flat, Viktor still going on with his story:

'And we're thinking, shit, we've just cut a lorry in half for nothing. We're going to owe the transportation company big time. We were just about to give up, when one of the dog handler's lets his dog loose. The dog heads away from the lorry to the crates of peppers we'd unloaded, starts sniffing and pawing the crates...'

Marko didn't let the two guys out of sight as they checked the flat, while Branka and Goran sat in the kitchen. Viktor finished his story:

'You know where the stuff was? In each corner of the wooden crates, a triangular block encased it. A hundred and fifty-five kilos in total. Can you believe that?'

Marko just nodded, still uncertain why Viktor had told him the story. Was he genuinely a good cop? Should Marko tell him about the *ajvar*? But how could he prove it? Viktor was friends with Ivan and Jovanović. Even if he wasn't dirty, he might not trust Marko. Maybe Viktor had told the story about peppers to show Marko he knew about the *ajvar*.

Viktor's men turned to him. Lost in thought, Marko hadn't paid attention for a minute. Had the guys just planted something? Viktor slapped Marko on the shoulder:

'See, all clear, nothing to worry about and no need to file anything. No hard feelings eh?'

Viktor put out his hand to shake and Marko shook it. He was ready to play the game, whatever it was. He saw the men out of the flat and breathed a sigh of relief. It had been a good job he'd hidden the packet of heroin under the pepper plant.

Marko found Branka and Goran waiting for him in the kitchen. Branka asked:

'What was that about?'

'I'm not sure.'

Marko was sure he'd been sent a message. He just wasn't sure who had sent it.

Chapter 15

Marko couldn't face Branka's questions because he didn't know the answers. He wanted to go to bed and forget everything, but knew he couldn't sleep. Not looking his wife in the eye, he said:

'I need a drink.'

Marko stepped out to the balcony to get a bottle of homemade *rakija* from the pantry. But picking up the bottle, he knew drink wouldn't help him sleep. Looking down at the pepper plant, Marko thought about the heroin he'd hidden.

The heroin confirmed that Jova was on the take. Viktor's search had to have been instigated by Marko's discovery, but didn't mean Viktor was corrupt. Jova could have convinced his friend that Marko should be searched. More worrying was the idea that the Chief of Police was pulling the strings.

Had the Zemun clan been cleaned up because Dragan was an informant? That in itself was a natural part of police work, but was Dragan now the city's main dealer because of a deal with the Chief of Police?

The arrest records had shown that Dragan was released by the Chief just before the Zemun clan crackdown. How could Marko find out more?

An idea came to him. Maybe the *rakija* could gain him entry to Belgrade central prison. An official visit would get noticed by his colleagues and the Chief. So he would have to make sure it was off the books. He wouldn't gain access to any major guy from the Zemun clan, but there was someone who might talk.

Despite his mum nagging him about his dad's murder for twenty years, Marko had never gone to question Milo Stojanović. He still didn't want to talk to the former inspector about his dad, but maybe Stojanović could reveal a deal between Dragan and the Chief. If anyone knew about the deal, surely it would be a corrupt police officer who was put away because of it.

Marko stepped back into the flat. Putting his head around the kitchen door, he said:

'I need to go out.'

Branka was incredulous as she pointed at the bottle of *rakija* in Marko's hand:

'Where are you taking that?'

'Maybe it can help me find out what's going on.'

'Marko…'

He didn't wait to get into a discussion. Exiting the building, he glanced around to check Viktor or Jova weren't about to trail him. He didn't think they would, the message had already been sent, but Marko was starting to feel paranoid.

As he drove out of New Belgrade, Marko kept glancing in the mirrors, but no-one seemed to be following him. He tried to be rational. Just because Jova was corrupt, it didn't mean the whole force was. Jova could have put in an anonymous call to anti-narcotics and Viktor would have been obliged to follow it up. It was all conjecture.

Driving through the city centre, Marko reached Belgrade central prison, an imposing four-storey concrete block opposite Obelic FC Stadium. As some politician had announced proudly when Šarić was put away – this was a Serbian prison.

Šarić's arrest had been a real success story for the Serbian police. Viktor was a big part of that, so could he really be corrupt?

Parking up, Marko crossed to a corner shop and bought

three packets of cigarettes – Davidoff, Marlboro and Drina. He didn't know what Stojanović smoked, so he'd give him a choice – Swiss, American or Serbian.

Marko badged his way through the main gate and found the warden on duty ensconced in a smoke-filled room with another guard, the two of them laughing at the TV.

Marko saw they were watching *The Farm*, a reality TV programme where minor celebrities had sex and got into fights. The programme had been exported from Sweden, but in Serbia the contestants included criminals.

Kristijan Golubović was one of the few survivors from the 1995 documentary *See You in the Obituary*. Nearly all the other criminals interviewed had since been killed. After making the documentary, the director became a monk and ever since had lived in a monastery in Greece.

A known heroin dealer, Kristijan had been given a reprieve from his outstanding prison sentence so that he could appear on the show. In court, Kristijan had claimed he had no income to support his family so needed the TV money. An appeals judge postponed the sentence. Did the judge really believe that? Had he been threatened? Or paid off by Pink TV? Who knew?

But with a justice system like that, how were police supposed to put away criminals?

Marko guessed it was ironic that prison guards were watching a criminal on TV who they should be guarding. Maybe *Wounds* was a more prophetic film than Marko had realised – gangsters becoming reality TV stars. The warden turned from the TV with a smile and said:

'Kristijan kills me. I'm going to miss it when he's here not on TV.'

Marko remembered what Gojko had said about Serbs glorifying gangsters, but he went with the banter:

'Maybe you could have a show here – The Lock Up.'

'Think I'd rather watch him fuck some bimbo than wank in his cell. What can we do for you?'

'Wanted to see if I could have a quick word with Milo

Stojanović.'

'Got a court order?'

'No, but I got this.'

Marko held up the bottle of *rakija*. The warden shrugged and got on the phone:

'Who should I say is calling?'

'Inspector Despotović.'

Marko waited in the interview room, thinking if it was so easy to bribe a warden why did anyone end up in prison? He laid out the three packets of cigarettes on the table and waited.

Stojanović entered the room warily. In his fifties, Milo's muscled arms were starting to waste and his face was lined. But it wasn't just his age, illness was eating him. Cancer, Marko guessed.

Wearing a vest, the tattoos on Stojanović'c shoulders and upper arms were on display – a montage of heavenly Serbs killing Turks. When he'd been in the police, the tattoos had always been covered up.

Marko didn't know if Stojanović would remember him, but the former inspector squinted at Marko and said:

'*Inspector* Despotović. I remember when you were a rookie.'

'Fifteen years since then.'

'Twelve of them in this place. First time you've come to visit. You must have something you want to ask me.'

'Just thought we could have a smoke, chat about the old times.'

'What do I get out of it? You going to get me an early release?'

'Can't do that. But can give you the chance to put the record straight.'

Stojanović coughed as he laughed. He took a seat and gestured at the packet of Drina:

'They'll kill me so I might as well die a patriot.'

Marko slid over the cigarettes and lit one for him. Marko knew what he was getting into.

Stojanović was powerless in prison so had to gain control

where he could. Marko let him take his time inhaling and blowing out smoke. Stojanović gestured for Marko to start and asked:

'So what do you want to know?'

'Just interested in your arrest in 2003.'

'And why would you be interested in that?'

'Do you think anyone stitched you up?'

'You want me to grass on a grass?'

'Do you think there was a grass?'

'Do you?'

Marko and Stojanović stared at each other in silence, until Stojanović burst into a rasped chant:

'Who is from Zemun is not a pussy. We from Zemun love to fight pussies!'

Marko guessed he was wasting his time. Stojanović smiled at him:

'I've been in here for twelve years. Either you go insane or you get very good at mind games. You play them with me, I'll win, so why don't you just say what you want?'

Marko shrugged and gave it a try:

'I'm looking into a dealer who somehow escaped arrest back in the clan crackdown. Trying to see if there was a connection. Can't imagine you'd be happy being in here all this time while the person who grassed you up is out free.'

Stojanović shrugged back:

'I was an informer for the clan while I was on the force. So for sure there was someone on the clan who was informing for the police. But do you think he would still be alive?'

While Stojanović took a painful drag of his cigarette, Marko weighed up weather he should just come out and say Dragan's name. Being vague was getting him nowhere. Stojanović beat him to it:

'Let me think, Šarić is locked up in here. Kristijan is on TV. That leaves Dragan as the only Zemun guy still dealing. Is that who you're investigating?'

'Well seems strange that he was released just before all of

you were arrested.'

Stojanović made a dismissive gesture:

'Not all of us. Šarić was out for years. Don't think you'd be calling him a grass. And Dragan was a minor street dealer. He was more lucky than clever.'

Marko wondered if that was true. Stojanović had stuck with his tribalism and ended up in prison. Dragan behaved like a patriot, but did deals with whoever to stay alive.

Stojanović sucked on his cigarette, made a pained expression as he exhaled smoke. He wagged his finger at Marko:

'Ah, now I get it. This is about your dad. You want revenge on the guy who killed him.'

Marko tried not to rise to the bait:

'I'm just interested in why Dragan was released while the rest of the Zemun clan got put away.'

'Look, even if Dragan killed your dad, and I'm not saying he did, he was just carrying out orders.'

'I'm not here about my dad.'

'Your dad wasn't innocent you know.'

'He was just trying to survive.'

'By stealing drugs that weren't his? You didn't know that did you? Thought it was just about the petrol. It was the stash he had in his car that mattered.'

Marko couldn't help remembering what his mum had told him about someone buying his dad's car after he died. Had his dad been involved in drug dealing? Was that why he was killed?

Was Dragan the killer, ordered to carry out the hit by the Zemun clan? Marko took a breath.

He couldn't let Stojanović fuck with him.

Stojanović pocketed the packet of Drina, rose from his chair and smiled:

'Of course I could be blowing smoke up your arse. Guess you'll have to check if I'm telling the truth. Am I a dying man revealing why your dad was killed? Or maybe I secretly bear a grudge against Dragan and am letting you think he was involved. Told you I'd win.'

Before he was escorted back to his cell, Stojanović winked at Marko:

'See you in the obituary.'

Marko left the prison none the wiser than when he'd entered. How had he thought he would get any answers? Instead of finding any indication of Dragan and the Chief of Police making a deal, Marko had been mind-fucked over his dad's murder.

He knew he shouldn't pay any attention to Stojanović's claims, but doubt nagged at him.

There wasn't anything he could do about it that night. The one good thing about his encounter with Stojanović was that it had tired him out. At least now he was ready to sleep.

Chapter 16

The next morning at work, Jovanović and Viktor were nowhere to be seen. Marko was called into the Chief's office and took a seat the other side of Ivan's desk. It was as if the night before hadn't happened – Ivan didn't even mention it.

Marko could hardly bring it up. Viktor could simply deny he had searched Marko for drugs.

Yes, Marko's wife and son had witnessed it, but was he going to drag them into court as official witnesses? To prove what? That his car and flat had been searched?

Ivan had two files on his desk, one thicker than the other, an ashtray in front of them. A Marlboro between his fingers, Ivan tapped the thinner file:

'Good report on the Panić murder. I got Nebojša to print it out so we have a hard copy.'

Marko snorted. If Nebojša was going to be Marko's ally, he had to keep it secret:

'Got to be some reason to have a rookie around. The kid spent the other day questioning my methods.'

'He's just young and ambitious. You were too at the beginning. Remember your first month?'

Ivan flicked his cigarette, ash dropping into the ashtray. He looked across at Marko, said:

'You caught those New Belgrade boys almost single-handedly. We had you down as one to watch. Then you sat on your arse for ten years. What happened?'

Marko shrugged:

'Was concentrating on my family.'

Though what Marko also thought was he'd been out of the loop for ten years because he hadn't joined Ivan's gang when he'd been offered the opportunity. And now he was sitting in Ivan's office with no-one mentioning that Marko's car and flat had been searched for drugs, that Marko had become a pawn in a game of intimidation. Or had Marko got it all wrong? Was Ivan not part of the corruption?

Ivan inhaled, blew out smoke, said:

'The way you solved the Panić case reminded me of the good work you can do when you put your mind to it. Which is why I want you to personally deliver the file to the Interior Minister.'

Marko wanted to shout that he'd solved the Panić murder because Jovanović, Dragan and Vesna had set it up. Maybe even Ivan. Instead he said:

'Can't the Minister read emails?'

'I also want you to get close to him.'

'Not in a sexual way I hope.'

'This is serious Despotović. The Minister has taken an unhealthy interest in the Panić murder. We're also concerned about his recent meetings with the German Interior Minister, where we suspect bribery is taking place. In light of this, we need to monitor him.'

Marko didn't get it. It wasn't his section:

'Shouldn't that be for the guys in financial or telecommunication investigation?'

'They're already on it. But I want to use your personal connection.'

'I hardly know him.'

'Both your sons go to the same tennis academy. This is your way in.'

Marko couldn't ever remember telling Ivan about which tennis academy his son went to. It wasn't difficult to find out, but did that mean Ivan was watching him and his family? Ivan slid over the thicker file to Marko, said:

'We've kept an eye on the Minister for awhile.'

Marko opened the file, saw a photo of the Interior Minister receiving his PhD. Ivan said:

'It's a "public secret" that he gained his PhD in a fraudulent manner. I'm no academic, but even I know it takes more than one year to gain a PhD.'

Marko turned the pages, saw photos and transcripts of various meeting the Interior Minister had attended. How much had been monitored? Was the Minister's car bugged? Had Ivan heard the conversations between the Minister and Marko? If so, he wasn't letting on. Nothing in the file about Marko, but that could have been deliberately left out. Marko knew with certainty he was being played. Just as the Minister had got Marko to suspect Ivan of corruption, his boss was now turning the tables.

Ivan pointed at photos of the Minister shaking hands with another suited man:

'That's the German Interior Minister, Marcus Hoffman. He's been in Belgrade for the last two days for government meetings. That's normal protocol. But the women procured isn't.'

Marko flipped over to photos of two silicon stunners getting out of the Minister's Audi, parked outside a residence in Dedinje, the Minister's driver holding open the car door. Marko was sure he'd seen one of the women before. Ivan carried on his commentary:

'That's where the German Ambassador resides. The German Minister and a tennis scout are currently staying there. The women were delivered by Dejan Tomić.'

Ivan tapped a photo of the Interior Minister's chauffeur, said:

'Former Red Beret. Had close ties with Arkan. The suspicion is that the Minister is somehow involved in the drug route through Serbia, maybe trying to get a hold on it for his own purposes.'

Marko looked at the photos to give himself thinking time. Ivan was throwing back at him exactly the same accusations the Interior Minister had made against Ivan. Marko kept his mouth shut as Ivan continued:

'The German Minister is meeting the Albanians tomorrow. He seems to have some hold over our Interior Minister. At the very least he is being bribed with the tennis scout to watch his son. If we can get that on record, it will give us leeway to carry out full scale surveillance. For all we know he might be spying for the Germans.'

Marko couldn't help being sceptical:

'Really? What are the Germans going to spy on us for? What do we have that they'd want? Our *ajvar*?'

'The Germans always want something. The EU is just their way of controlling Europe. Serbia isn't in the EU and is out of their control. I doubt they like that.'

Marko didn't want to get into a political discussion with Ivan, but his Chief had only just started:

'You can't trust the West. It was their spy who told Slobo that the Croats attacked us so that he started the fucking war. All part of their plan to break up Yugoslavia because it was too strong. They needed someone to fuck it up and Slobo was just the man. Then the West has the balls to tell us to get rid of him. It's not enough that Yugoslavia is carved up, so they bomb us. We fought two world wars against the Nazis and they bomb us. That's still not enough for them, so with the economy fucked, they tell us we have to stop the mafia clans before we get sanctions lifted. How were we supposed to do that when the mafia had more money than the police?'

Marko guessed Ivan's question was rhetorical. He closed the Interior Minister's file and slid it back towards Ivan. Marko wasn't surprised by the revelations. He knew what politicians got up to. He was doubtful that the Minister was really a German spy, but he was furious with the Minister because he'd got him into the mess in the first place. It was this shit he'd spent years avoiding and now he was right in the middle of it. Looking his boss in the eyes, Marko said:

'I'll do it.'

'I believe both your sons will be playing in the Pančevo Open. Use the time until then to find out what you can. Liaise with the guys in telecommunication.'

'What about the drugs angle? Should I talk with Viktor?'

'I'm just guessing about the drugs. Viktor hasn't looked into that yet.'

Marko picked up the report he'd written on the Panić murder, asked:

'You know where the Minister is now?'

'He arrived at the German Ambassador's residence ten minutes ago. You might catch him there.'

Marko made to leave the office, then popped his head back in:

'Have you got Nebojša on something today? I can use him to do research while I go to the Minister. New generation and shit, he'll be quicker than me with his computer skills.'

'Okay, but don't let him know we're monitoring the Minister. Like I said, he's ambitious. Who knows who he might side with. You know, it was the Minister who got him fast-tracked.'

This confirmed what Nebojša had told Marko and he realised why Ivan didn't let the rookie near any big cases. Nebojša wasn't trusted. Marko gave a serious nod, said:

'I'll just get him to do some background research.'

Marko left Ivan to finish off his cigarette and called for Nebojša:

'Got some work for you to do. Tell you on the way out.'

Marko waited until they were in the car park before explaining:

'Ivan's got me on a new case. While I'm looking into it, you can check if Ivan and Vesna went to school together. Ivan's information will be on the police website. You'll have to go to local council offices to find Vesna's info. Don't tell me anything concrete over the phone. It might be being monitored.'

'You think so? Did Ivan say something?'

'No, but I think Jovanović suspects it was me on his

houseboat. Last night, Viktor and two guys from anti-narcotics searched my car and house. I guess trying to find the heroin we took from Jova.'

'What did you do with it?'

'Threw it in a bin by the Intercontinental.'

Marko could see Nebojša eyeing him with suspicion. Maybe the rookie didn't believe him and thought Marko was on the take. It was the least of Marko's concerns.

Entering the German Ambassador's residence, the Interior Minister found the tennis scout scoffing *burek* and yogurt. The scout was unshaved and his t-shirt dishevelled. He looked like he hadn't slept and was eating as if he needed energy after an all-night orgy, which was probably true.

Željko glanced around and saw signs of the night before. Empty bottle of *rakija* on the side, cushions strewn on the floor and a shirt tied to a drawer handle. The two silicon girls had obviously done a good job.

After opening the door to Željko, the Ambassador had retired to his quarters. He'd looked ashen, presumably having spent the night listening to the sounds of fucking. The tennis scout looked up from his breakfast, yogurt dripping down his chin:

'Man, Serbian woman are something else. They didn't even want to be paid.'

Željko grimaced a smile. The two women didn't want money because they'd already been well paid and been given strict instructions not to accept any more. In this way, the German Interior Minister couldn't ever be accused of soliciting sex. Just as Željko had got Dejan to pay and deliver the women so that if it ever became an issue, he could deny any knowledge. Still keeping the smile, Željko said:

'So I hope to see you at the Pančevo Open.'

'I'll be there, don't worry.'

Željko left the tennis scout to his breakfast. Following the sound of an electric razor, he checked the bathroom.

The German Interior Minister finished his shave and gave himself a nod in the mirror. Clean-shaven and clean-shirted, Marcus Hoffman once more had the appearance of a respectable politician.

From the bathroom doorway, Željko said:

'Good night?'

'Very good.'

'I'm glad. So as your stay has been so satisfactory, I hope this smoothes the way for an agreement.'

Hoffman picked up his electric toothbrush. Željko wondered if the German Minister even had electric toilet paper. Hoffman said:

'I'm not sure I understand.'

'Do I have to spell it out?'

'Please.'

'The women.'

'I understood they came of their own accord, attracted to two handsome German men.'

Željko gawped at his German counterpart. Was that German humour? Hoffman squeezed toothpaste onto his toothbrush, said:

'You are aware that as part of my Balkan tour, I'm meeting the interior ministers of Greece, Turkey and Albania in the next few days. I have to see that the Balkan drug route is being cleared up before Serbia can make further progress in joining the EU. At present, Albania has more of a chance.'

Željko couldn't listen to the German Minister's shit anymore:

'This isn't about the EU. You have no interest in Serbia joining. All you are concerned about is the drug route. Albanians? They'll never join the EU while I'm alive. Unless you have a deal with them.'

Hoffmann was aware that the Albanians controlled most of the Balkan drug route, but Albania wasn't a country the Germans could control.

In fact, he thought it was necessary to keep some elements of society on drugs as it suppressed rebellion against the system.

He always thought that Marx had got it wrong. Opium was the religion of the masses, not the other way around.

It was the German pharmaceutical company Bayern that had first commercialized diacetylmorphine, giving it the brand name 'heroin'. It was from the Greek word 'heros', meaning heroic.

The Greeks certainly weren't heroic anymore. They had failed to pay their debts and would now be bought up and sold off. With their Orthodox churches and Balkan mentality, the Serbs were just as volatile as the bloody Greeks. Not like the Croats, who could always be relied on siding with the German view. If Serbia could be brought in line with EU regulations, the Balkans would be almost fully controlled.

The German Interior Minister turned to Željko, pointed his toothbrush at him and said:

'And this isn't about a tennis scout watching your son. The only reason you want Serbia to join the EU is so that you can say you did it. Next stop, Prime Minister. Who do you think you are, the new Tito?'

Željko stiffened. Yes, he wanted to be Prime Minister. 'The new Tito' was stretching it, but he had his career ambitions. As the German Interior Minister had seen through him, there was no point beating around the bush:

'What exactly do you wish to be resolved? Police corruption or the clearance of the drug route?'

'Both. I'll expect clarification by the time I'm back in Germany in three days time.'

The German Interior Minister turned back to the mirror and turned on his electric toothbrush.

Željko had an urge to shove the toothbrush down the German's throat, but he resisted. Play the long game, he told himself, play the long game.

On his way to Dedinje, Marko was sure he saw Jovanovic's BMW in his wing mirror. Was he being trailed? Or maybe Jova was part of the surveillance on the Germans. The BMW went out of sight and Marko shrugged it off as he parked across from the German Ambassador's residence. In the drive was the Interior Minister's Audi. Dejan Tomić, the Minister's chauffeur was leaning against the side of the car, cigarette in hand. Marko mirrored the former Red Beret, standing against his Ford, report in his hand.

Marko nodded at the chauffeur, then scanned the street. There were a few cars, but nobody in them. If someone from the telecommunication section was watching, they must have been doing it from the house opposite.

When the Interior Minister stormed out of the Ambassador's residence, Marko strode over to him. Dejan's hand went behind his back, a handgun presumably strapped there. Marko held up his file in peace:

'Easy Tiger, just delivering a report.'

The Interior Minister was impatient:

'Couldn't it have been emailed?'

'I was requested to deliver it in person.'

'Does it contain evidence of police corruption?'

'No. It shows Milan Panić was murdered by two drug-fuelled football hooligans and that the investigation was all above board.'

'Did you not understand what I asked you to do?'

'I understand, but maybe you don't. I heard you got a rookie inspector fast-tracked into headquarters. Why don't you get him to do your dirty work?'

'Because he won't get access to cases. It will take a few years before he has the trust of colleagues. Listen, can we discuss this in the car?'

'Better not. It might be bugged.'

'It's not. My driver checks it.'

'You mean Dejan, a former member of Arkan's Tigers? Bit strange a former Red Beret working for a pro-EU politician. Would have thought it went against his patriotic feelings. What's in it for him? Control over the drug route?'

No, thought the Interior Minister, Dejan had been promised a position as head of security when he became

Prime Minister. The Interior Minister said:

'You have done some research I see.'

'No, I was given the information by the Chief of Police. You're under surveillance. They know about your deal with the Germans.'

'What deal?'

'The tennis scout, the women delivered last night, your interest in the drug route.'

'Prove it.'

'That's what Ivan intends to do. I'm not telling you this because I'm on your side. I'm telling you this because I want out. I don't know if it's you or Ivan who is more corrupt and I don't want to know any more.'

'Do you not care about your son's future? You don't want to see him play tennis?'

'We've had this discussion already.'

'But maybe you do not understand. I'm talking about him not playing ever again. If you have looked into Dejan's past, you will know what he is capable of.'

Marko let out a laugh:

'So finally we get to the real deal.'

Marko stepped forward to the Minister. Dejan put his hand to his gun. Marko pressed the file into the Minister's hands:

'Here's the report. Pat me on the shoulder.'

'What?'

'Pat me on the shoulder. Make it look like I've done a good job. If anyone is taking photos, that's what they need to see.'

The Minister patted Marko on the shoulder. Marko said:

'I'll meet you at the Pančevo Open. I need to be seen as if I'm getting something on you.'

'Fine. And I need evidence of police corruption. That drug route needs to be cleared.'

'For your own purposes?'

'For the good of Serbia.'

Marko burst out laughing. That would at least look good on camera. He crossed the road to his car, still smiling at the Minister's words. By the time he was inside his Ford, Marko's smile had vanished.

His first thought was to tell Ivan everything. Side with his boss, no matter if he was corrupt or not, and get the Interior Minister's driver killed to eliminate the threat hanging over his son.

But that would be a deal he'd never get out of. As the saying went, he'd pay one *dinar* to get in and he'd pay a hundred *dinars* to try and get out of it.

There was no guarantee Ivan would even side with Marko. He might leave Marko to clean up his own shit. Marko had to play both sides. If he went one way or another he was fucked.

He didn't know what the answer was yet, but to buy himself time, he had to keep both parties at bay. He would do as Ivan had requested and monitor the Minister. And as the Minister wanted, he would gather evidence of police corruption. He had two days to come up with a plan.

Chapter 17

Sitting in his Yugo, Nebojša checked the police website on his Samsung smartphone. It was more private than using a pc in headquarters and a lot quicker than the old computers. As Chief of Police, Ivan's profile was available to view.

Ivan's current position was in bold at the top of the page. Underneath were a list of Ivan's previous positions, service in the army and education. Ivan had served during the Yugoslav War so who knew what he'd been involved in. He was well decorated and not a man to get on the wrong side of.

Nebojša hoped he was doing the right thing. He'd been tempted to go behind Marko and contact the Interior Minister, but felt he should trust his colleague. His first impression of Marko was as a slightly corrupt has-been, but Marko was the only person to give him responsibility. He was finally doing proper police work, even if it was checking on the Chief of Police.

Nebojša noted that Ivan had gone to Zemun High School. Next he had to check if Vesna had gone to the same school. Vesna would be registered in the council offices for Dedinje as that's where she lived and presumably got married. He checked and found out that Dedinje came under Savski Venac council. He guessed that was the kind of thing Marko would automatically know. As Nebojša wasn't yet married and still lived with his parents, he'd managed to avoid visiting council offices.

The Savski Venac council offices were located on Kneza Miloša in a typical communist era concrete block of a building. Nebojša grimaced as he parked up. If Belgrade was ever going to escape its past, the city could at least paint its buildings.

Entering the council offices, Nebojša felt as if he'd been transported to a time before he was born. Several people were sitting on a bench against a wall, looking like they'd been there for eternity and would carry on waiting. Behind a thick plastic partition, the receptionist was busy talking with her colleague. Nebojša attempted to get her attention:

'Hello?'

The receptionist saw Nebojša, but didn't stop her conversation. Both women were in their fifties and had probably been working there since Tito's time. Their once-attractive faces had aged grotesquely under garish make-up and bouffant hairstyles thirty years old. The receptionist glanced in Nebojša's direction, only to remember she still had something to say to her colleague. She eventually turned to face him:

'Yes?'

Nebojša held up his police ID and said:

'I need to find the educational history of a woman who married in Dedinje.'

The receptionist gestured at the group of people against the wall and said:

'Join the queue.'

Nebojša stood there perplexed. Had the woman not seen his police ID?

'Excuse me, this is a police matter.'

'And?'

'And I need to get someone's details.'

'Do you have a warrant?'

'I don't need one.'

'Neither does anybody else.'

Nebojša didn't understand her logic but he got the gist of it. He was being told to fuck off.

Didn't police have any authority or respect any more?

In that instant, Nebojša had a flash of realisation. He understood why Marko did things the way he did. Being honest and reasonable with people didn't get results. Coercion did.

Nebojša leant towards the speaking holes in the plastic partition and said:

'Do you want to be arrested?'

The receptionist snorted in derision, not taking him seriously:

'You're going to arrest me? For what?'

'I will wait for you to finish work, then I will follow you and arrest you in the street in front of everyone for possession of heroin.'

'What heroin?'

'The heroin I will find in your possession.'

The woman looked at Nebojša. He hadn't raised his voice or been aggressive, but his face was deadly serious. She relented:

'Whose information do you want?'

'Vesna Panić. She was married to Milan Panić.'

'The businessman who just died?'

'Just give me Vesna's education details.'

The woman tapped away at her ancient pc. She stood and started to walk off. Nebojša called after her:

'Where you going?'

'To look for the marriage certificate.'

'Don't you have the details on the computer?'

The woman rolled her eyes and walked off. She would do what the police inspector asked for but it didn't mean she had to show him any respect.

As he waited, Nebojša shook his head in disbelief. Was being rude an inherent part of the job?

The receptionist came back and shrugged:

'The only information on record is that she married in Dedinje.'

'Nothing else?'

'Not here.'

'So where would it be?'

'In the council offices of her previous address.'

'Which is?'

'Stari Grad.'

Nebojša suppressed a sigh. He couldn't say coming there had been for nothing, but now he had to go to another council office:

'What street are the offices on?'

'Makedonska.'

'And what was her previous address?'

The receptionist didn't bother suppressing her sigh as she went away again and came back with the marriage certificate. She held it up against the plastic. With his phone, Nebojša took a photo of the certificate. Police headquarters and council offices might have outdated systems, but he was using modern technology. He smiled at the receptionist:

'Thanks.'

'No problem.'

Her politeness was poisoned with sarcasm and Nebojša shook his head at the bureaucracy that still existed in Serbia.

Looking at the photo of the marriage certificate, Nebojša saw that Vesna's maiden name was Ivanović. Her pre-marriage address was a flat on Rige od Fere and she was born in 1960.

Quickly checking the police website, he saw that Ivan was born in the same year. That was one coincidence already.

In his old Yugo, Nebojša drove to the Stari Grad council offices on Makedonska Street. It should have been a five-minute drive, but the streets were clogged with traffic so it took fifteen.

Nebojša wished he had a BMW with a siren on the dash. He wanted a better car, but he wanted to obtain it through hard work and ambition.

The Stari Grad council offices were just as ugly as the Savski Venac building. Inside, there was no bench, so people milled around as they waited to be seen. Having learnt how to deal with council office workers, Nebojša went up to the dishevelled male receptionist behind the partition and got straight to the point:

'I need to know which schools this person attended.'

Nebojša showed the photo of Vesna's marriage certificate. The man started to protest that he was busy but Nebojša cut him off:

'I need it now. Unless you want to be hauled in for possession of heroin.'

'I don't have any heroin.'

'You will if you don't get me that information.'

The man got the point. He noted down Vesna's details and stumbled towards a side door:

'I'll have to check the files.'

By the time the man came back, the vestibule had filled with several more people. He said:

'There are hundreds of Vesna Ivanovićs, but none have that address.'

'Can't you cross-check it with the date of birth?'

'The files are only ordered in surnames. Have a look if you want.'

The man let Nebojša in through the staff door. The back room was lined with filing cabinets and shelves. Stacked on top of every surface, were piles of files. Nebojša couldn't believe council offices still operated in this way. He took the files out of the open drawer and looked through all the Vesna Ivanovićs. The council worker was right. None of them matched Vesna's date of birth and address. Feeling stumped, Nebojša called Marko.

Marko was still sitting in his car in Dedinje, lost in thought when Nebojša called him. He came to his senses and answered the phone:

'Any luck?'

In case Marko was right and he was being monitored, Nebojša was deliberately vague:

'No matches with her name.'

'Maybe her first name is fake.'

Nebojša silently eyed the filing cabinet in resignation. He knew Vesna had changed her surname on getting married but hadn't thought that she originally had a different first name.

That meant he would have to go through every 'Ivanović'. Marko asked:

'Where are you?'

'Stari Grad council offices.'

'I'll meet you there.'

Marko drove towards the city centre. As he neared Slavija, cars, trams and buses converged on the chaotic roundabout. Car horns blared and trolley-buses criss-crossed in a fizz of electricity.

At the bus stops and kiosks to the side, people stood in the shade, smoking or drinking as they waited for their mode of transport.

Marko remembered when nothing functioned. During sanctions, no petrol came in officially.

People sold it off the streets in canisters. Russia sent some over but that got siphoned off by criminals and soon ran out. Some days, all the buses didn't leave the depot. And if there was an electricity black-out, the trams and trolley-busses would come to a standstill wherever they were.

Negotiating his way into the city centre, Marko parked up on Makedonska Street. He grabbed a bag of *pogačice* from the bakery on the corner, ID'd his way past the council office guy and found Nebojša in the back room going through a file cabinet.

Nebojša looked up, gestured to the files and exhaled:

'Vesna's maiden name is Ivanović. I'm only half way through.'

Marko offered the bag of pastries:

'Lucky I brought provisions. What are her details?'

Nebojša clicked up the photo on his phone of Vesna's marriage certificate and read it out:

'Born in 1960, address on Rige od Fere. Once we've

found her, see if she went to Zemun High school. That's where Ivan went.'

The two of them munched as they worked through the files, trying to find who Vesna was originally known as. Between files, Nebojša said:

'I can't believe all this hasn't been put onto a computer system. It's the same at headquarters with all the old arrest records.'

'You volunteering? I'm sure the Chief would be happy to get you doing it.'

Nebojša took the next file. He slapped it and shouted in relief:

'Got her! Jelena Ivanović. Same address and date of birth. Officially changed her name to Vesna in 1980…'

Nebojša trailed off as his euphoria died. Vesna had changed her name the same year she registered in Belgrade. Vesna Panić née Jelena Ivanović had been born in Gračanica, Kosovo and gone to school there too. He looked up at Marko:

'They didn't go to school together. Vesna was brought up in Kosovo. She didn't come to Belgrade until she was twenty.'

'Where in Kosovo?'

'Gračanica.'

'The same village Ivan was born in.'

'What?'

'Ivan was brought up in Belgrade but he moved here as a kid. He's proud of his roots, so it's not something he hides.'

Nebojša regained his excitement:

'If they were born in the same village in the same year, they must know each other.'

'Yes.'

'So what does it mean?'

'I don't know. It doesn't prove anything, just that they probably know each other. But it does seem suspicious. Give me time to think about it. You okay to clear up?'

'Keep me in on this Marko.'

'As soon as I have a plan, I'll let you know.'

Chapter 18

Ivan took a stool at the breakfast counter while Vesna, clad in only a kimono, made Nescafe for both of them. It was a ritual that had begun when they were teenagers. Back then, Ivan had bought the counterfeit Nescafe off the bonnet of a car on Bulevar before he went to visit Vesna in Kosovo. These days, Vesna ordered it direct from Switzerland.

Ivan and Vesna had been childhood sweethearts, growing up as neighbours in Gračanica.

Ivan's family had moved to Belgrade when he started high school, but he came back to visit Vesna. As teenagers, they'd sat in the kitchen of Vesna's parents before moving to the bedroom. They'd fooled around but never had sex. When they became adults, they'd kept in contact as their paths separated then merged.

Ivan had done his time in the army, gone to police academy and worked his way up to Chief of Police. He'd married his secretary and once he'd made enough money moved into the neighbouring Senjak, Belgrade's richest area after Dedinje.

Vesna had moved to Belgrade when she was twenty, seeking her fortune in the capital. When Milan Panić was Minister of the Economy, she'd got a job as his secretary. The first time she hooked him was when she'd leaned over his desk to give him a celebratory *rakija*. Milan had just drafted the privatisation laws and had a list of companies he was thinking of buying out.

Vesna had caught him looking, stayed in the pose to let him get a good eyeful, then looked him in the eyes and said:

'*Ajvar.*'

That one word had set Milan up as a businessman. Vesna had married him and become his right-hand woman. Up until his murder, he'd still called himself a businessman even though *ajvar* was no longer their main income. Throughout his rise to prominence, Vesna was his main advisor. She'd told him not to even consider negotiating with the Albanians.

Ivan and Vesna had never had an affair, but had always been closer to each other than their respective spouses. They had kept their relationship discreet and their shared past a secret.

Officially, Ivan was in Vesna's house to inform her that her dead husband's body had been examined. With her permission, the limbs could be sewn back on to his torso before the funeral.

Ivan watched as Vesna stirred a spoonful of coffee and sugar with a dash of milk. He wanted a cigarette with his coffee but knew Vesna wouldn't let him smoke in her designer kitchen. He could see she was wearing nothing under her kimono because her breasts moved in sync with her stirring. To take his mind off his cigarettes and her breasts, he asked:

'Do you miss Milan?'

Vesna paused from her stirring and stared into the cup:

'I foresaw it in a vision, so I was prepared.'

Ivan rubbed his moustache. When Vesna went into her spiritual mode, he felt he didn't know her. Vesna went back to her coffee-making, adding the water. Back to the Vesna he knew, she said:

'It was Milan's own fault. I told him not to attempt a deal with the Albanians. He didn't listen. So what happened, happened.'

As they both knew, Milan's death wasn't a direct result of the Albanians, but it was true that Vesna had warned Milan.

So her reasoning had logic to it. Vesna placed a cup of Nescafe in front of Ivan and asked:

'Is this Inspector Despotović going to cause any problems?'

'I don't think so. He's been useful so far. Though that was because he didn't know he was being used.'

'It looks like now he's starting to realise.'

'It could make him even more useful.'

'The Interior Minister's not letting it go either. His driver was asking my security guard about your Inspector.'

'You don't need to worry about the Interior Minister. He's just a pawn for the Germans. I have plenty on him if I need to use it.'

'Good. And make sure you've got Inspector Despotović under control. He has a strange aura and was in the periphery of a vision. His persona might appear to be non-confrontational, but there is a dangerous side to him.'

Vesna checked her watch. She had an appointment with the head priest. She asked:

'When will Milan's body be ready?'

'I'm waiting to hear from forensics. Should be by this afternoon.'

'Good. I have to go to church and arrange the ceremony.'

Vesna needed to change into suitable attire, something black and solemn. She smiled at Ivan.

He was the one person who was close to understanding her. Though even he was sceptical of her visions. She'd kept Milan under her thumb with a combination of her all-seeing presence and sexual promises. Though she hadn't let him touch her new breasts. With Ivan, it was different. They were like a brother and sister. Sex was prohibited but she let him touch. Opening her kimono, she said:

'You may hold them before you leave.'

Chapter 19

Exiting the council offices, Marko crossed over to the Maxi supermarket on the corner. He'd grown up knowing it as 'C Market' with its big yellow 'C' and swirled blue 'market' sign. Like Vesna, the supermarket chain had undergone a re-branding. Who knew who owned it now?

Some conglomerate no doubt with a German CEO.

In the nineties, it was the biggest supermarket chain in Serbia. Basically stocked, it was where you bought cheap packets of Turkish coffee, sugar and milk. During inflation and then sanctions, the sugar was no longer on the shelves, the shops half empty while long queues extended into the street – soon turning into chaotic scenes as people tried to grab basic provisions.

Inside the shop, Marko checked the shelves and picked up a jar of Panić Ajvar. Who bought that shit? Only someone who didn't have *ajvar* made by a family member.

Marko studied the label. The peppers were grown down south. It was jarred in Macedonia.

This was slightly surprising, but not completely strange. Macedonia exported *ajvar*. Serbia didn't. So maybe it was easier to use the factories just across the border.

Marko put down the jar and clicked on his phone. It wasn't only Nebojša who could use modern technology. Connecting to the internet, he looked up Macedonian *ajvar* companies and saw that they exported to Germany.

Clicking a map of the Balkans, Marko traced the route

with his finger. The *ajvar* route matched the western branch of the Balkan drug route.

Marko wasn't an expert in anti-narcotics, but he knew that in the aftermath of the Yugoslav War the traditional Balkan route had been divided into three branches. The northern branch went through Bulgaria, western through Serbia and southern through Albania.

The conspiracy theories were that other countries had wanted Yugoslavia to be carved up so they could benefit from the route. Though Marko wasn't sure having a well-known drug route was something to be proud of.

For the drug cartels, the advantages of the northern branch was that as soon as the drugs were in Bulgaria, they could be transported easily though EU countries. The disadvantage was that the EU had to at least appear to be a legal jurisdiction so getting caught could have serious consequences.

The western branch through Serbia meant it took longer to get to an EU border. But then transporting through Serbia also had an advantage. Police and border control weren't likely to check very hard and could always be bribed.

As for the southern branch, Albania was Albania.

Marko wasn't sure the division of the route was important. What was interesting was there were now two coincidences. First, Ivan and Vesna were born in the same Kosovo village.

Second, the transportation of Panić Ajvar followed the Balkan drug route. Marko had found heroin in the *ajvar* jar on Jovanović's houseboat. The Interior Minister's initial claim that Panić Ajvar was a drug cover seemed to be true. It was increasingly looking like the Chief of Police and Milan Panić's widow were key players.

Exiting the supermarket, Marko left the car on Makedonska Street and walked to Kalemegdan. The clatter of the city centre was cluttering his thoughts. Maybe a walk would clear his mind.

He passed the old women selling hand-embroidered cloths

on the pavement and the old men playing chess on the benches. Outside the fortress walls, tanks were marooned from the Second World War. As a kid, Marko had played on the tanks while his grandfather played chess.

In the nineties, the fortress grounds at night were an orgy of hedonism, teenagers taking drugs and fucking in the semi-darkness. Couldn't he forget that period?

What angered Marko was that he was ready to forget, to live in present-day Belgrade. But his present situation was in danger of fucking up his life.

The walk wasn't helping him think productively. He stepped down to the tiny church inset into the old stone walls of the fortress. He wasn't about to suddenly convert and didn't expect divine intervention, but it was a place of peace.

He pushed open the wooden door and stepped inside, instantly feeling the chill of the barely-lit church. He was alone apart from the icons that covered the curved ceiling and glowered down on him. No, he couldn't believe that God existed. Not when he thought about the horror of the Yugoslav Wars, the bombing of Belgrade, his father's death, the inter-clan killings, the murder of Milan Panić. How did his wife believe?

People believed all kinds of things. Like Vesna Panić with her 'spiritual visions'. Vesna Panić, previously known as Jelena Ivanović, born in the same village as Ivan Radić, the Chief of Police.

Marko knew that Dragan was a dealer and that Jovanović was on the take. He didn't need confirmation of the obvious. Ivan was a prime suspect in the corruption, but proving his guilt was going to be difficult. Could he get something on Vesna? He couldn't do it because he couldn't even get past her front door anymore, but he knew a woman who could.

He didn't know if Milica would go for it, but he had an idea. Stepping out of the church's cold air back into the heat of the day, Marko phoned Milica:

'Hey, where are you?'

'Hey, just about to go into class, but I can go back to the flat. I was just thinking about you.'

'No, it's okay, I'll meet you at Trg. Ten minutes?'

'Okay.'

Marko ended the call. As he crossed over the tram lines to Knez Mihailova, he called Nebojša:

'You still in the council office?'

'Just about to leave.'

'Wait for me outside. I've got a plan.'

'That was quick.'

'Had divine inspiration. See you in thirty.'

Ending the call, Marko made his way to the horse statue where everyone met, especially girlfriends and boyfriends. It wasn't where Marko should be meeting Milica. He was old enough to be her father. He was friends with her father for God's sake. What would people think? Fuck, what would his wife think?

Milica beamed on seeing Marko stride towards her. She wanted to kiss him but knew she couldn't in public. Instead she stood on her toes, kissed his cheek and whispered:

'I'm excited just seeing you. Are you sure you don't want to go back to the flat?'

'I can't.'

Milica let her hand dangle by his groin, brushing his growing erection. She asked:

'Can't you?'

Marko took Milica by the arm and led her to a seat under a parasol in the nearest café. The midday sun was too hot out in the open. Marko gestured at the drinks menu and asked:

'What do you want?'

Milica pouted as she scanned the menu. She smiled:

'An ultimate orgasm.'

Marko shrugged:

'If that's what you want…'

Milica laughed:

'You asked.'

Marko ordered the cocktail for Milica and a Coke with ice for himself. It was a bit early for alcohol but he needed her to be relaxed for what he was going to ask:

'I'm on a case and I've got a favour to ask you.'

Marko paused while the waiter brought their drinks over. They saluted to life with their drinks, Marko letting Milica take a good sip of her cocktail before he explained:

'I need someone to get inside Vesna Panić's home. I thought you could do it, but maybe it's a bad idea.'

'I thought you were going to leave that case alone?'

'I can't. It's too big. Milan Panić's *ajvar* business was a cover up for drugs. At least one police inspector is on the take, maybe even the Chief of Police. Vesna is involved somehow, maybe in on it with the Chief. Turns out they've known each other since school. I want to put a bugging device inside her house.'

Milica downed her cocktail, said:

'I'll do it.'

'You don't have to. I've already put myself in danger. I don't want to put you in danger too.'

'If you're in danger, I want to be in danger with you.'

Marko didn't have a reply to that. He saw how Milica looked at him with love and felt frightened. Was he misusing her love? Couldn't he forget the investigation, take her back to the flat and make love?

Marko outlined the plan:

'I thought you could say you were a business student doing some research about Panić Ajvar.'

'Wouldn't that be too obvious? How about I'm writing an article for a student magazine about the lifestyle of successful Belgrade women?'

'Great. Remember that her husband has just been murdered. Even if she doesn't seem distraught, you still have to act with compassion.'

'When do you want it done?'

'Today. See if you can set up an interview and I'll come by tonight with a bugging device.'

Milica checked the time:

'I'm already late for the afternoon seminar so I might as well go now.'

'You're my angel.'

Marko gave Milica the address, telling her to look for the wedding cake and she couldn't miss it. As they walked across the road, Marko was sure he saw Jova's BMW pass by.

That was twice in one day. Coincidence? Or was Jovanović trailing him? The BMW was hardly discreet. Marko shrugged. All Mister Inconspicuous would see would be Marko meeting a young woman. Milica blew Marko a kiss and skipped towards a bus stop.

Chapter 20

Sitting at the back of the packed bus, Milica felt a double thrill. She was excited about her secret mission and she was excited about seeing Marko later that night. She could feel her thong rub against her clitoris.

She didn't really believe her coffee reading. It was just superstitious fun. But she did think Marko was heading into dangerous territory. And she was ready to go with him.

Life was short, she'd always thought that. It had nearly been very short with her heroin addiction and car crash. She'd been given another shot at life and she was taking it. She was aware that Marko was a father figure, but whereas her real dad had been an alcoholic, Marko had got her off drugs.

At Slavija, more people elbowed their way onto the bus. As the bus rattled off, it smelt of sweat. Milica could hardly breathe. She leant forward to open the window but an old woman glared at her:

'*Promaja!*'

Milica sat back and kept her eyes focused outside the bus in an attempt to block out the hot odour. By the time they passed the Red Star Stadium there were fewer people on the bus and by Dedinje, there were several empty seats. Only the rich lived in Dedinje and they didn't travel by public transport.

Milica stumbled out, straightened her skirt and went in search of Vesna Panić's mansion. It wasn't difficult to find.

As Marko had described, it looked like a wedding cake.

At the electronic gate, Milica got into character as an innocent student. She didn't have to pretend to be a student. It was the innocence that was difficult.

Milica pressed the intercom buzzer but there was no answer. If there was no-one home, she'd have to find a café to wait in. As she turned to leave, a black-windowed 4x4 pulled up. Milica waited and watched as a bodyguard came from the driver's side to open the passenger door.

Vesna Panić stepped out of the car.

Vesna was wearing a long black gown, perhaps in mourning for her murdered husband, though the style was more of a high priestess, huge Gucci sunglasses at odds with the image.

Milica asked:

'Vesna Panić?'

Vesna didn't deign to look Milica's way. The bodyguard gestured for Milica to move away from the gate as he gave an order:

'Step to the side miss.'

'I was hoping to speak to Vesna…'

'She's grieving.'

As the gate opened and Vesna passed through, Milica persisted:

'I'm sorry to call on you at such a time of loss, but I'm doing an article for a student magazine and wondered if I could arrange an interview with you.'

Vesna raised a hand to her bodyguard:

'It's okay.'

As Vesna had passed the young woman, she'd felt a strange aura, one that demanded to be examined. After Ivan had left, Vesna had changed into her mourning attire and been driven to make funeral arrangements for her deceased husband. If she had arrived back home a minute earlier, she would not have passed the young woman who would have been dismissed by her bodyguard via the intercom. All things were for a reason. Maybe it was destiny that they met.

Raising her sunglasses, Vesna turned to Milica and asked:

'What's the article about?'

'It's about the lifestyle of successful Belgrade women. I know it's a difficult time, but I was hoping you might like to speak about that.'

'Come on in.'

'Now? I don't want to intrude.'

'I think it is not by chance that you are here. A minute later and we would have missed each other. Let's use this providence.'

Milica hadn't expected to gain entry so quickly. She would have to find another way of returning. She followed in Vesna's wake, into the mansion.

Vesna sat across from Milica, a straight-backed, black-clad high-priestess with her white backdrop. Milica's instinct was to sit erect and not be cowed. Vesna's breasts were a lot bigger, but Milica was younger and more naturally attractive. But she went for meek and humble, slightly hunching her shoulders. Vesna asked:

'So my dear, what would you like to ask?'

'First I'd like to express my condolences.'

'It has not been easy, but life must go on. In fact, distractions ease the grief, so please continue.'

Milica took out a notebook:

'Your wealth and success is what many women aspire to. Can you tell me how you achieved it?'

'I married a rich man.'

Milica raised her eyebrows at Vesna's answer. Vesna gave the semblance of a smile:

'That's a joke. My husband used to joke that I was his right-hand woman. He was the face of the business, but I was behind it. Panić Ajvar was my idea. But ideas are not enough on their own. You must work hard to implement them.'

Milica gestured around at the mansion:

'Was the design of this house your idea?'

Vesna nodded:

'Like all girls, I'd dreamt of being a princess. This was my chance to live in a palace. It is all in white to bring a feeling of peace. The chaise-longues are arranged in the best position to create calm. And at the back is my spiritual retreat.'

'You seem to have an amazing strength in dealing with your loss. Has your spiritual retreat been helpful for this?'

'Without doubt. I will show it to you if you'd like.'

'Please.'

Vesna led Milica to the glass 'retreat' at the back of the mansion. Milica thought the place should have been used for growing plants. She said:

'I've never meditated. How do you do it?'

'It takes patience, but the rewards are infinite. You should try it.'

'I'd love to. I... I used to take drugs. I haven't now for a year and a half. But sometimes the need comes back. Maybe meditation could help me fight those cravings.'

Vesna looked Milica in the eyes:

'I will teach you.'

'Really?'

'I felt you were here for a reason as soon as you announced your presence.'

Milica smiled at Vesna. It made Milica want to run far away and never come back.

'That would be brilliant. When...?'

'Come tomorrow at dawn. Can you do that?'

'Uh, yes. And I'll write up the article to make sure you're happy before it goes to print.'

'Then before you go, I must show you my kitchen. Like all women, that is my real sanctuary.'

Chapter 21

Marko found Nebojša waiting in the shade of the council office doorway, a bottle of water in his hand. Marko didn't blame him. The early afternoon heat was at its most insufferable. Marko had tried to stick to the shade as he walked from Trg, but his shirt was still sticking to him.

Marko joined Nebojša in the doorway and got straight to the point:

'I'm going to bug Vesna's place.'

'How are you going to do that?'

'I've got someone who might gain entry.'

Marko could see the next question forming on Nebojša's lips, so cut if off:

'Doesn't matter who. Can you do surveillance on Vesna's mansion? I'll tell you when the bug is in place. If you see Ivan arrive, you text me and get out of there. Until then, stay out of headquarters and in the shade.'

'Won't the Chief want to know where I am?'

'I'll say you're still doing research for me.'

'On a case you haven't told me anything about.'

'Will you do the surveillance?'

Nebojša sighed. He'd already gone along with Marko so far, so couldn't back out now:

'Yes, I'll do it.'

'Great. I'll text you as soon as everything is set up.'

Marko left Nebojša in the shade and got in his hot car. With windows open and air con on, he drove to headquarters. He'd trusted Nebojša so far, but felt it was best not to tell him about the Interior Minister being checked. The rookie's ignorance on that matter could be useful.

Before checking in with the Chief, Marko wanted to see a couple of colleagues. At his desk in the drug smuggling section, Viktor looked up as Marko came over:

'Hey, if this is about last night…'

Marko raised his hands in peace. He didn't want any confrontation, he wanted information.

He joked:

'Not unless you're planning to search me again.'

'Just don't go matching descriptions.'

Marko wondered once again if Viktor was genuine or not. But he couldn't directly ask if Ivan had ordered the search. He said:

'Ivan's got me looking into the Interior Minister.'

'Yea, he told me.'

Had Viktor been told so he could keep an eye on Marko? Or was Viktor also being fooled by the Chief of Police? Marko explained what he wanted to know:

'So one of the possible angles is that the Minister is interested in the Balkan drug route. You think there's any substance in that?'

Viktor shrugged:

'Who knows?'

'Who's the kingpin these days?'

'Nobody knows that either.'

'What about Dragan Mladić?'

Viktor gave a dismissive wave:

'Dragan is one of the city's main dealers, but he's not the kingpin. He's clever enough to never be caught but he's not so intelligent to be the main man. That's someone who doesn't seem connected to drugs and who can finance huge shipments continuously.'

Marko thought how to broach the subject. Viktor was the narcotics expert. Did he really not know about the connection with Milan Panić's *ajvar* company? Marko appealed to Viktor's expertise:

'Last night you told me the story about crates of peppers encasing hundreds of kilos of heroin. What about jars of *ajvar*?'

'For sure. Jars of *ajvar* out of the country. Cans of olives coming in from Greece. It comes in whatever works. We can't check every lorry load of food that goes through Serbia. You know how many lorries go through the Balkan route each year? Five million. We can't stop every one. You think the border control guys are going to risk their lives for the pittance they earn?'

'You managed to break up the coke cartel.'

'Sure, we made a major dent in the coke run from Montenegro, but heroin has been doing the Balkan route from Afghanistan to Western Europe much longer. It's more complicated. With cocaine, we followed the money. We saw how it was laundered and got to the accountants, turned them into informers. It was also easier to seize, huge shipments from South America arriving in Montenegro.'

Viktor snorted:

'I'll tell you something else. Since Kosovo's 'independence', the Albanians took over seventy per cent of the route. We can't even infiltrate to get informers.'

Marko nodded. He had to try:

'I've got a theory. Ivan told me that the Minister was showing an unhealthy interest in Milan Panić's murder. You think his *ajvar* business was a drugs cover up? That the Minister was trying to get hold of the business?'

Viktor frowned:

'We never had any intel that Milan Panić's business was dirty.'

Marko scratched the back of his head in a mock thinking pose. Was it that Viktor really never had any intel on Milan Panić's business or that he'd been told to ignore it?

Viktor looked at Marko:

'Why, did you find something when you looked into his

murder?'

Marko couldn't help saying:

'No, I wanted to question the two killers but didn't get a chance before Jova shot them.'

Viktor bristled:

'What are you implying?'

Marko once again raised his hands in peace:

'Nothing, just stating a fact.'

He couldn't tell if Viktor was reacting out of loyalty to his friend or was part of a huge cover-up. But he wasn't going to get anything else from him. He said:

'Thanks Vik, that's been useful.'

Marko wasn't sure how useful it had been. All he'd confirmed was what he'd thought – that it was possible for Panić Ajvar to be a cover for heroin smuggling and that Dragan wasn't the kingpin.

From Viktor, Marko went up a floor to the telecommunication section. Miloš Kovač was a mixture of brain and brawn. His glasses and goatee made him appear intellectual but his muscled arms showed why he was in the police. Marko had no idea if Miloš was corrupt or not. He wasn't going to test it:

'Hey Miloš, Ivan told me to see what you've got on the Interior Minister.'

'He told me you'd be coming. Read the report?'

'Yea, anything else I should know?'

'Just what's there. We only stepped up the surveillance one day ago.'

'No chance of getting a bugging device inside his car?'

'No chance. You know who his driver is?'

'Dejan Tomić, former Red Beret.'

'Exactly. Checks the car before the Minister gets in.'

Marko had no way of knowing if Miloš was lying, but he was pretty sure the car hadn't been bugged. Marko asked:

'So what have we got to connect the Minister with the Germans?'

'Not much. Women were brought to the German

Ambassador's residence, but the Minister wasn't present. The Minister likes to carry out meetings in his Audi, which we can't get into.

And we can't gain easy access to the German Ambassador's residence.'

'We can try.'

'How's that?'

'Maybe I've got a woman who can gain entry. What bugging devices have you got?'

Miloš got excited:

'The budget is fucked, but I ordered personally online from Germany.'

Miloš held up a small black device that looked like a USB stick:

'A mini black box recorder. Records up to ten metres away and lasts for forty six hours before it needs recharging. Magnetized so you simply attach it to something metal. Once you've retrieved it, you attach it like a USB stick to your laptop or whatever.'

Marko smiled:

'Let's see what we can get on that Minister.'

Taking the device, Marko went up to see Ivan. He was supposed to be looking into the interior Minister, so would report what he'd found out so far. The Chief of Police was on the phone, but waved Marko in as he finished the call:

'That was forensics. Milan Panić's body is ready for the funeral tomorrow. I'll attend it as a representative of the police force. How was the Minister with the report?'

'Seemed fine with it. Didn't question anything.'

'Good. Did you manage to set up a further meeting?'

'I'll see him at the Pančevo Open on Monday. He's already suggested a scout could watch my son, in return for some favour no doubt. Guess he's open to corruption. But it could take time to find evidence. I've got Nebojša looking up old records. The rookie couldn't believe they weren't on a computer.'

'We should get him updating all our arrest records.'

'That's what I said.'

'How did you sell it to him?'

'I said we were monitoring the safety of the Minister and needed to check the Germans weren't spies.'

'Good. Did you talk with Miloš?'

'Just now. If I get the chance, I'll try to bug the German Ambassador's place. I think there's someone I can use. Have you got that photo of the women Dejan brought to the Germans?'

Ivan got out the file on the Interior Minister and opened it. Marko took the photo of the women. He remembered where he'd seen one of them before. She'd been with Dragan. Her name was Biljana if he recalled correctly. Marko tapped the photo:

'I know who she is. I'll try and work on her tonight. Okay if I take the photo?'

'All yours. See what you can do. And take tomorrow off, you deserve it.'

'My day off anyway.'

'Then take Monday off too. Watch the tennis, get cosy with the Minister.'

Marko nodded and left the Chief's office. His head was spinning from all the semi lies and half truths he was telling.

Jovanović's BMW was in the car park. It hadn't been there when Marko parked an hour earlier. Was he becoming paranoid?

As he got in his Ford, a text bleeped. A message from Milica that she was back at the flat. Marko texted back that he would be at least an hour. Milica replied that she would wait in Hotel Miloš. Marko felt the bugging device in his pocket. Ivan was going to Milan's funeral the next day. Marko thought there was a good chance the Chief of Police would also attend a wake at Vesna's. If Milica could bug the place before then, maybe he could get an incriminating conversation recorded.

Chapter 22

Marko stepped into the bar on the corner of Silicon Street and ordered a beer. Picking up a copy of *Danas*, he took a stool which gave him a good view. He could see in both directions if Biljana came to see Dragan at Café Insomnia.

Marko drank his beer and read the newspaper from back to front. To take his mind off things, he started with the sport. The eternal derby between Partizan and Red Star was the next night so he read the pre-match details.

Working towards the front of the newspaper, Marko read an article on the German Interior Minister's visit, alongside a discussion piece about the pros and cons of joining the EU. Milan's murder had been relegated to page two, with a mention of the next day's funeral. The front-page news was about how Belgrade city council had lost fifteen million euros meant to fund a new hospital.

The article was by his wife. Marko smiled in pride as he remembered the first ever article of hers he had read. He'd said to her:

'Might make you some enemies.'

Branka's reply was:

'I can't live in fear. Nobody should. So-called nationalists call me unpatriotic, but I think I'm the most patriotic woman in Belgrade. I love my country. That's why I don't want it destroyed by corruption.'

Marko let go of the memory and the newspaper as he saw Biljana sashay past, her breasts bouncing in time to her steps. Marko slid off the stool, exited the bar and caught up with her:

'Biljana?'

Biljana glanced at Marko, ready to be dismissive, then she recognised him as the police inspector who had been to see Dragan. It didn't change her attitude:

'What do you want?'

'I want to know what you were doing with the German Interior Minister.'

That brought Biljana to a standstill:

'What are you talking about?'

'The two Germans. Does Dragan know you were with them?'

'I'm not Dragan's wife.'

'No, but I don't think he'd be happy to know that you're also Dejan Tomić's girl.'

'I'm not.'

Marko took out the photo of Biljana and another girl getting out of the Audi by the German Ambassador's residence, Dejan holding open the car door.

Biljana looked nervously towards Café Insomnia fifty metres down the street. She didn't need Dragan seeing this and had to end the situation quickly:

'I was just doing Dejan a favour.'

'Do yourself a favour. Answer one question and I won't show the photo to Dragan.'

Biljana gave Marko a look of hate:

'How can I trust you?'

'Biljana, I get it. Once you're fucking a drug dealer, it's a dangerous situation. A girl has to be ready to go with whoever the main guy is. I have no interest in the girl, just the guy. Is Dejan planning to oust Dragan?'

Biljana sighed:

'Dejan told me he's going to be head of security. He'll have more power than a dealer. Does that answer your question?'

Biljana wanted confirmation that the police inspector wouldn't show the photo to Dragan, but he was too immersed in thinking about her answer. It seemed he really was more concerned with Dragan and Dejan than her. The police inspector was right. For now she was with Dragan.

But Dejan had come to her with a proposition for the future. She had to be ready to go either way. Without another word, she turned on her heels and trotted off to Café Insomnia.

Marko thought about Biljana's answer. If the Interior Minister was working with the Germans, it wasn't to take over the drug route, it was to gain power. Marko didn't know what deal had been done, but if Dejan thought he was going to be head of security, the Minister thought he was going to become Prime Minister. Who knew what the Germans wanted? Not having an answer, Marko went to find Milica.

Hotel Miloš had once been a grand establishment that was now run down. The top floors were closed but the basement had been turned into a bohemian bar. A young woman was reading from a book while the literati listened, drinks in hand. It was more Milica's scene than Marko's.

Milica took Marko to an alcove so they could have a private conversation and in a blur of excitement, she spoke rapidly about her encounter with Vesna:

'I'm going back tomorrow for a meditation session.'

'What time?'

'At dawn.'

Marko showed her the recording device, explained how it worked and asked:

'You still okay to do this?'

'I'm excited, though she freaks me out a bit. And those breasts. They're unreal.'

'I doubt they are real.'

'I think she really believes in her spiritual visions. Gives me goosebumps.'

Milica looked into Marko's eyes:

'But if you hold me I'll be okay.'

Marko held her. He was tired. It would have been nice

to sit there and fall asleep as the woman read her poetry, but he wanted his bed. And he didn't want to end up in the wrong bed.

He got up and left, Milica listening to the poetry.

It was midnight by the time Marko entered the flat. Branka was waiting up for him:

'You're working a lot.'

'Crazy case.'

Branka eyed her husband. Was he having an affair? Or was it something more sinister? He hadn't satisfactorily explained the night he'd been searched for drugs by colleagues. She hated herself for thinking it, but was he involved in drugs and corruption? It had been strange that he'd suddenly splashed out on taking them for a meal after coming home soaked. She couldn't believe her husband was corrupt. He was a good man. He'd even reacted angrily when she'd suggested he talk to the Interior Minister about the tennis scout. With Marko not replying, she asked:

'What's going on Marko?'

'What do you mean?'

'I mean it's not normal to be searched for drugs by your colleagues.'

'I told you, it was a misunderstanding.'

'You're hardly ever here and when you are, you're acting strangely.'

'It's just this case I'm on. It will be over soon. I'm really tired. Got to be up before dawn.'

Marko kissed his wife on the head and went to bed. He wanted to tell her everything, but knew he couldn't. With everything weighing on his mind, he was ready to sleep.

Branka let her husband go without pressing him for more information. She was sad he hadn't suggested they go to bed together. But it wasn't the lack of sex that was worrying her. It was that Marko was keeping more and more from her. She would go to church in the morning to light a candle for her husband and son.

Chapter 23

Marko picked up Milica just before dawn. As they drove off, Marko checked Jovanović's BMW wasn't parked up around the corner. The city was empty apart from the street cleaners, hosing away the dirt and dust at the start of another sultry August day. If Jova was following him, Marko would spot his colleague.

Milica leant her head against Marko's shoulder. This was the first time they'd gone for a drive together. She wanted to imagine they were on their way to the sea for a summer holiday.

Instead, Marko stopped at the edge of Dedinje.

Marko didn't want to be spotted by any watching police, so kept a safe distance from Vesna's house. He appreciated what Milica was doing. Taking her face in his hands, he kissed her on the lips, said:

'Thanks for doing this.'

'No problem. Just make sure you make it up to me in the bedroom later.'

Milica winked and sashayed off, although sadness pervaded her. She genuinely enjoyed her role as sexy mistress, but she wished they could also drive off into the sunrise.

Vesna greeted Milica at her mansion entrance, wearing only a kimono, her breasts almost bouncing free. Taking Milica's hand, Vesna led her into the spiritual retreat:

'I'm so glad you came.'

Vesna's happiness was genuine. She wasn't yet sure of the

reason Milica had appeared in her life, but she felt strongly that it was important.

In the glasshouse, filled with light from the rising sun, Vesna disrobed. Milica couldn't help staring. For her fifty something years, Vesna had an amazing body. Vesna said:

'You must take off your clothes.'

Milica started to think Vesna was into lesbian sex. Milica wasn't afraid of being naked. Her breasts were small but firm and her stomach was flat. But she had to play her timid role:

'My clothes?'

'Don't feel embarrassed. It is necessary to feel the full force of the spiritual energy.'

Milica had often stripped for Marko, but this time she fumbled with her clothes as she took them off. Vesna touched the scar on her arm. Milica explained:

'It was from a car crash.'

Milica turned her wrist, showed the other scar where she'd used her veins too often:

'And that was from heroin.'

'It is your inner spirit which is important.'

It was easy for Milica to play the estranged daughter with Vesna, who was mothering her in a strange, lesbian kind of way.

Vesna showed Milica how to sit cross-legged on the parquet floor. She reached out and ran a finger up Milica's spine:

'Keep your back nice and straight.'

Milica wanted to laugh at the surreal situation of two naked women sitting next to each other.

She'd done some crazy shit, including lesbian sex, but this was a first.

Vesna gave instructions:

'Focus on a point in the distance… Feel the light from the sky. Relax your body… Let the lightness of the air fill your soul. Do not try to think of anything, but let your mind drift…'

What Milica was trying to think about was where to plant the bugging device. Vesna wouldn't be having meetings with the Chief of Police in her spiritual retreat. Milica's interview had taken place in the white lounge, but that seemed quite formal. Vesna had said the kitchen was her real domain and brought Milica there once she felt at ease. If Vesna and the Police Chief were close, it would be the kitchen where they talked.

Vesna was still giving meditation instructions:

'Now close your eyes and focus your mind on the strongest feeling inside you… Go deeper.

'Sink into that feeling. See what you see…'

With her eyes closed and the rising sun on her face, Milica felt her mind get heavy.

Images flashed into Milica's brain. Her arm up as the car windscreen smashed. Lying in a hospital bed, the room white. Marko standing by her bedside. Vesna appeared on the other side of the bed, in a black kimono. She opened the kimono and gave one of her breasts for Milica to suckle. She felt a mixture of excitement and comfort. But then Vesna held her arm and injected a needle into it. Milica looked in desperation to Marko for help but he had gone. She turned to Vesna but she had also vanished. The whiteness of the room blinded her and turned into darkness.

Milica jolted awake. Her eyes wide, she gulped saliva to wet her dry throat. She turned and saw Vesna looking at her with concern. Vesna asked:

'Are you ok my dear?'

Milica nodded, unable to speak. Vesna smiled:

'Do you want to talk about what you saw?'

Milica shook her head. Vesna rose, put on her kimono and said:

'That's okay, it's your first session. Don't be afraid of what you see. You can learn to act on your visions.'

Milica picked up her clothes and got dressed. She wasn't surprised she'd been susceptible to the meditation. She'd taken smack for two years with all that entailed. But still, it had unnerved her. As she put on her jeans, she felt the bugging device in her pocket and remembered why she was there. She found her voice:

'Can I get some water?'

'Of course.'

Vesna led Milica into the kitchen. While Vesna poured a glass of water, Milica looked around for where to attach the device. With its minimalist design, there wasn't any clutter to hide the device. The best way to hide things was to be blasé about it. She held up the device:

'I've got the provisional article on a USB stick if you want to read it.'

'I'm sure it's fine.'

Milica took the water and gulped it down. Feigning dizziness, she fell against the cooker and dropped the glass onto the floor. Steadying herself, she said:

'I'm sorry.'

'That's okay.'

While Vesna cleaned up the spilt water, Milica stuck the device to the side of the cooker.

Vesna asked:

'Are you okay now?'

'Yes, but I think I need to go home.'

Vesna smiled serenely and showed Milica out of the mansion. Watching Milica leave, Vesna wondered about Milica and what her own visions had meant. Milica had the same strange aura as Police Inspector Despotović. Seemingly relaxed, but in fact dangerous.

Milica walked away from Dedinje in a dazed state. She didn't notice Marko's Ford until he pulled up beside her. He pushed open the passenger door and she got in. Seeing Milica's demeanour, he asked:

'Hey, you okay?'

'I guess so.'

'Did you manage to leave the device?'

Milica nodded. Marko sent a text to Nebojša: it's on. Turning back to Milica, he looked at her with concern:

'Did something happen?'

'Just that meditation shit. Had a strange smack flashback, that's all. I'll be fine.'

Marko drove Milica home, starting to regret what he'd asked her to do. When they reached her street, she asked:

'Will you come in and lie with me?'

'Sure.'

Marko had never seen Milica in this subdued mood. They lay on her bed, Milica with her head on Marko's chest. He stroked her hair until he heard her even breathing and knew she was asleep.

Recovering his arm from under Milica, Marko gently turned her on the bed. He felt great tenderness towards her, realising that their relationship had become more than passionate sex.

Yet he also knew it had to end. For his marriage and for her future. It was all part of the mess in his life that needed clearing up.

Milica had done her part. Nebojša would let Marko know if Ivan visited Vesna. And then they would see if they managed to get anything incriminating recorded. With the plan in place, Marko drove home. He would spend Sunday with his wife and son.

Chapter 24

Driving through New Belgrade, Marko passed his mum's block. For the first time since visiting Stojanović in prison, Marko had time to think about the former inspector's claim that his dad had been killed for stealing drugs.

Even if Marko had wanted to dwell on it, there hadn't been the time. Now that he had a spare few hours, he still didn't want to think about it. But maybe it would be good to take his mind off all the other shit that was going on.

Marko parked up by his mum's building. At seven in the morning, it was too early for her to be in church, but she would be awake. He wasn't sure what she actually did with her days, but she was always busy being consumed by the past.

Marko's mum opened the door as if she knew he was coming:

'Just in time my son. Come and see this.'

He repressed a sigh. Maybe visiting his mum was a bad idea. He just wanted to get information about his dad's car, not hear any of her prophetic dreams or paranoia. Out of sonly duty, Marko followed his mum into the hallway. She stopped at the telephone socket and pointed at the wall:

'Look.'

Marko looked. The phone had been partly taken apart and the socket removed from the wall.

A hammer and screwdriver lay on the floor amid bits if plaster that had come off. Marko attempted a joke:

'You should have called me if you needed help.'

'Can't call you, the phone's no longer working. Don't want them listening anyway.'

'Don't want who listening?'

'The police. They've been spying on us.'

'Mama, the police aren't spying on you.'

'Not on me, on your dad.'

'He's dead.'

'When he was alive.'

'So where's the bugging device?'

'They removed it while I was out.'

Marko knew there was no win against his mum's paranoid logic, but he tried to reason:

'Why would the police spy on him?'

'Because he stopped being a party member and started selling petrol on the black market. I told him not to. Look at how Vuk Drašković was bugged.'

'That was when Milošević was in power and Drašković was in opposition. Dad wasn't a politician.'

Marko knew bugging still went on because he'd just planted his own device. But he couldn't believe that his dad's activities would have warranted police spying on him. Unless Stojanović's claims were true, that Marko's dad had stolen drugs from the Zemun clan. That was why Marko had come. He said:

'Mama, have you got those car documents?'

'What documents?'

'You showed me the other day.'

She looked at him perplexed. Marko realised she had simply gone onto her next paranoid idea and forgotten the previous one. He explained:

'The receipt from the guy who bought Dad's car.'

'Oh, that.'

Marko's mum reached into the drawer, pulled out the papers and handed them over:

'So you're going to check it?'

'Yes, I'm going to check it.'

Marko looked at the papers. Most of them were just MOT certificates through the years. The 'receipt' was a handwritten note and scrawled signature. Marko asked:

'So who was this guy who bought the car?'

'The mechanic from the Dorćol depot, where your dad took the trolley buses for maintenance. Do you remember it?'

Marko remembered the place. His dad took him there as a kid. It was where all the trolley busses and trams got washed, maintained and scrapped. But why would a mechanic from there come for the car? He asked his mum:

'How did he know you wanted to sell it?'

'I didn't want to sell it. I wasn't thinking about anything. He just turned up, said he'd buy it off me, make sure I had some money. I was too devastated to think about anything so I agreed.'

'Do you remember his name?'

'Of course, he was your dad's friend – Aleksandar Mihajlović. He's retired now, but on Sundays he still goes to the depot.'

'How do you know that?'

'His wife goes to the same church as me. I asked where her husband was because I wanted to ask about the car. She said he goes to the depot instead of church.'

'So did you go and talk to him?'

'How am I going to get down there?'

Marko thought the whole thing was probably a wild goose chase. His mum reached out and gripped his arm:

'Why are you doing this now? You've found out something haven't you?'

Marko didn't know how much he should tell his mum. He shrugged:

'I don't know. I was talking with the inspector in charge of the case, Stojanović…'

'You talked to him without telling me?'

'He's in prison now, I was seeing him about something else.'

'Typical. You don't even put your family first.'

'Mama, do you want to hear or not?'

'Come on, tell me.'

'I don't know if there's any truth in it, Stojanović can't be trusted, but he claimed Dad was killed because he stole some drugs, which he hid in his car.'

Marko's mum let go of his arm and slapped him on the hand. He looked at her in surprise as she said:

'Shame on you! How can you say such a thing about your dad?'

'I didn't say it, Stojanović did.'

'But you believe it.'

'He sold petrol illegally, so it's not such a big step to steal drugs.'

'Go to your room!'

'My room?'

Did his mum really think he was still a little boy? He looked at her as she started to cry. He put an arm around her shoulders, but she shook him off:

'Leave me be.'

Marko's mum turned to the broken phone and started examining it. Had she finally lost the plot? Would finding out why his dad had been killed make her any better? Probably not. But what was the point in solving any crime? Marko left his mum to her broken phone. Should he forget it and go home or drive to the Dorćol depot?

As Marko drove down through Dorćol, he thought about Milan Panić's murder. The depot where his body had been found was just along the riverside. The area seemed to reek of death.

But he realised it was just the smell of sewage.

Post-sanctions, the whole transport system had been upgraded, but the depot remained as Marko remembered it. Carcasses of disused trams marooned in the scrubland and a trolley bus on a raised ramp, a mechanic at work on the engine. Marko turned off his own engine and got out of the car.

The mechanic was in his sixties. He was too engrossed

in his work to look Marko's way so Marko decided he would start by being official:

'Aleksandar Mihaljović?'

The mechanic turned around, a spanner in his hand as he asked:

'Who wants to know?'

Marko flashed his police ID, not letting the mechanic see his name:

'Got some questions about a Yugo you bought twenty years ago…'

'Twenty years ago? Fuck, I can't remember two weeks ago.'

'You might remember this. The owner, Zoran Despotović used to drive one of these buses. He was killed selling petrol on the black market. A week later you bought his car from his widow.'

Aleksandar scratched his stubble with oil-stained fingers:

'Fuck, that car. Crazy times. Terrible what happened.'

'So why did you buy the car?'

'Why? I was just trying to help out the widow, give her a bit of money.'

'That's not how she remembered it.'

'Long time ago. Maybe she's got a bad memory.'

It was true Marko's mum wasn't reliable, but he wasn't taking the mechanic's word for it.

He decided to go personal:

'Look, this isn't an official visit, so you don't have to hide anything.'

'Who's hiding anything?'

'I'm looking into it because he was my dad.'

Marko held out his ID again, this time letting the mechanic see his surname. The mechanic was silent for a second before he replied:

'I'm sorry. I liked your dad. But why are you digging this up now? Won't bring him back.'

'So why did you buy the car? Was it because of what was inside?'

'What? I never saw what was inside.'

'If it was Zemun clan guys who told you to buy it, you've nothing to fear. They're either dead or in prison.'

'Hey, I'm just a mechanic.'

'And I'm just a police inspector. I told you, this is personal not official. But if you don't tell me anything, I'll make sure your car gets pulled over. Maybe drugs get found inside. And then you can share a cell with Darko Šarić. How about that?'

The old mechanic looked at the spanner in his hand, weighed it up:

'Two guys came to me and told me to buy the car. Paid me double what it would cost. The guns they both had sticking out of their jeans made it clear – I got paid for doing the job or shot if I didn't. What else was I supposed to do?'

'Do you know who the guys were?'

'Never saw them before or again, thank fuck.'

'They didn't pick up the car?'

'I hardly had the car back here when a police inspector turned up and had it taken away, said he needed to check it for evidence. He also told me not to worry, no-one would be upset the car was gone. I didn't know if that meant the two guys had been arrested or if the inspector was with them. But I was never visited again, until today.'

'You remember the inspector's name?'

'Stojanović.'

'So you know he went to prison?'

'Yea, I read about it and got on with my job. The war was over and eventually sanctions were lifted. We got new buses and trams. I wanted to forget the nineties and do my job. For two years I did this job without pay. Any savings I had were worthless. But I kept fixing the buses and trams because it kept me sane. That's why I come here on Sundays. This is my religion.'

Marko nodded his appreciation of the mechanic's sentiments and walked back to his car.

What had he found out? That two guys had wanted his dad's car and that the car had been taken by Stojanović. It was suspicious, but not evidence of his dad stealing drugs. And the circle led back to Stojanović, which the corrupt inspector no doubt knew would happen.

Marko knew he should go home, but he felt compelled to pay Stojanović another visit.

Sunday morning was busy at the prison, with the inmates getting a lot of visitors. Marko badged his way in and found the warden overseeing proceedings. Marko had to hope the warden hadn't drunk all the *rakija*:

'I know it's busy, but any chance that bottle of *rakija* will get me another visit with Stojanović?'

'Not unless you're going to the cemetery.'

'What?'

'He died last night.'

'Was his cancer that terminal?'

'Well in a way. He choked on his cigarettes. Put a whole packet of them down his throat. Guess he'd had enough.'

Marko was incredulous:

'He killed himself by stuffing cigarettes down his throat?'

The warden shrugged:

'There will be an internal investigation, but looks like a clear case of suicide.'

Marko looked at the warden. The guy was either an idiot or deliberately turning a blind eye.

Or, more sinister, the warden was following orders. Marko made light of it:

'Well, guess it frees up a cell for Kristijan.'

Leaving the warden to his duties, Marko exited the prison. He would probably never find out who or why his dad was killed. But what concerned him more was that Stojanović had died within twenty-four hours of Marko visiting him. It was hard to believe that was coincidence.

Marko felt a sudden fear. He called his wife to say he would be home for breakfast. Branka replied:

'It's on the table. I'm on my way to church.'

Chapter 25

Vesna stood to the side of the open casket, regal and sombre in her long black dress. St Mark's church was full of black-clad mourners for her murdered husband.

The autopsy surgeons and embalmers had done a professional job in attaching Milan's limbs back to his body. With Milan dressed in military uniform from his short stint in the army, you couldn't tell that he'd been dismembered.

But even with Milan not looking too horrific, Vesna hadn't wanted a wake in her mansion. It bucked tradition and his family had been upset, but Vesna cited his brutal murder as being too upsetting. What she really felt was that his dead body would disturb the spiritual equilibrium in her home. She'd made up for the lack of wake by paying for the funeral ceremony to be carried out in Belgrade's biggest church.

Vesna stood in a vacant state, but she was aware of how many people had come to pay their condolences. Former politicians from Milan's time as Minister of Economy. Employees of Panić Ajvar. Family and friends. Ivan was standing in the crowd, there in his official capacity as Chief of Police.

Gowned in a long vestment, the bearded priest was shuffling around the casket, shaking the incense burner at the end of its chain as he uttered prayers about Milan's body and soul resting in peace.

With all her meditation, Vesna was able to stand still

and impassive. As far as she was concerned, Milan was done and dusted. He had played his part in her life, a long and important one, but it was over. Vesna's present concern was to do with Milica.

In Vesna's vision, Milica had appeared as a naked nymph flitting around Vesna on a throne.

Vesna was initially intrigued but when Milica pointed an accusatory finger at her, she wanted rid of the nymph. She ordered a guard to remove the young woman, but the guard couldn't get hold of Milica, who slipped out of his grasp and kept pointing her finger at Vesna. Infuriated, Vesna shouted at the guard, who took a knife and stabbed Milica. The guard carted Milica away. Vesna relaxed on her throne, only to tense up. With the guard gone, she was left alone and exposed. She tried to rise and saw she was handcuffed to the throne. She stared around wildly, panic in her eyes, cursing Milica.

Looking pained, Vesna allowed the priest to guide her outside to the cemetery. Surrounded by mourners, Vesna watched as Milan's coffin was lowered into the earth.

Inspector Jovanović snorted a line of coke in the cemetery toilet, felt the burn turn into numbness. He wiped his nose, licked his gums and gulped saliva. He was alive in the land of the dead. He smiled at the irony.

Strutting out of the toilet, Jovanović waited for the funeral to finish. As the mourners departed, he walked jauntily over to the Chief of Police standing by a gravestone – Jovanović noticing how Ivan's white hair contrasted with his black suit.

Ivan gave Jovanović a disdainful glance through his dark sunglasses. He could tell Jovanović had just taken some coke, but he was tired of nagging. It was like telling off his teenage son.

Ivan asked:

'Well?'

'Well he hasn't been making any enquiries about Dragan or Vesna.'

'So it seems he has realised it is best not to rock the boat.'

'Seems he's doing what you told him to. He asked Miloš about getting a bugging device to listen in on the Interior Minister's conversations. And asked Viktor if he thought the Minister might be trying to get a part of the Balkan drug route.'

'I've already spoken with those two. Tell me something I don't know.'

Jovanović clicked his jaw left and right, feeling the pulse of cocaine in his brain:

'Apart from that, Marko spends half the time with his mistress. Not bad, I'll give him that. Though he's old enough to be her father. Cheeky fuck. I arrested her two years ago for heroin possession. Milica Vidić. He got her off as a neighbourly favour. Looks like he's been fucking her ever since. He was with her last night so I left him to it.'

'Looks like he won't be a problem. Take the rest of the day off.'

Leaving Jovanović to it, Ivan strolled to his car with the thought that Despotović was a dark horse. Having a mistress was good. It meant there was more Ivan could use if necessary. He would wait to see what Despotović brought him on the Interior Minister.

Ivan had told Vesna he would pop in after the funeral, assure her there were no problems with Despotović and the Interior Minister. If anyone ever questioned his visit, he'd say he was there as the Chief of Police giving his condolences. Ivan lit up a Marlboro, put his Audi in gear and set off to Dedinje.

Even though Ivan knew Vesna wasn't really grieving, he didn't think she should be alone. In her kitchen, they clinked glasses of *rakija*. Ivan said:

'To life.'

'And death.'

Vesna didn't drink alcohol, but it was the right occasion.

They had to mark the passing of her husband and the rebirth of the business. She said:

'Is Dragan coping with the extra responsibility?'

'Seems to be. The route is fully operational and with Dragan there's no chance of the Albanians trying anything. Just have to make sure he doesn't get too big for his boots.'

'He knows his place. He doesn't have the brains to ever try and takeover.'

'Could be the lack of brains that leads him to try.'

'He's all bravado. And that's good for us – keeps the focus on him. What about the Interior Minister and Inspector Despotović? Have they been sorted?'

'Will be. I've got Despotović digging dirt on the Minister, playing them against each other. And I had him searched for drugs in front of his family. I think he got the message. Jovanović has been trailing him. He reported that Despotović hasn't stepped out of line.'

'Let's hope Inspector Jovanović did his job properly.'

Vesna was scornful of Inspector Jovanović. She could respect a person who was strong enough to get off drugs but not someone who succumbed. It was a false high. People got what they paid for, which was addiction and death. Vesna checked:

'So no further action is required regarding Inspector Despotović?'

'Far as we can see, he does the job I tell him to do and spends any spare time with his mistress, who's some ex-smack addict.'

Vesna froze, Ivan's words making the hairs on her arms rise. She knew the answer before she asked:

'What's the mistress's name?'

'Milica Vidić. Why?'

'Early twenties, attractive?'

'Matches the description. How do you know?'

Vesna felt her breath get short. Fury rising inside her, she let out a burst of anger:

'I think this Inspector Despotović has made a fool of you.'

'What?'

'His mistress has been here.'

Ivan took a moment to process this while Vesna did a breathing exercise to keep calm. Ivan asked:

'Is it a problem we need to eliminate?'

Vesna didn't verbally respond, but Ivan got the answer he needed from the way she glared at him. He nodded and left the mansion.

Chapter 26

Nebojša was in Topčider Park with his girlfriend, on the pretence of having a picnic. It was in fact a beautiful day to be out and Ksenia appreciated the gesture. Things had been tense for the last week as he spent more time at work than with her. The picnic had made it up to her, Ksenia unaware that the real point of it was for surveillance.

From his position in the woods, Nebojša could only see the end of Vesna's street, but it meant he was out of sight and gave him a view of any cars turning into the street. He saw Ivan drive off and immediately sent a text to Marko.

Marko felt his phone vibrate in his tracksuit pocket as he waited for Goran to serve. Branka had returned from church and was preparing Sunday dinner so Marko and Goran had slipped out for a father-son bash in the local courts. Marko held up a hand to stop Goran from serving.

He checked the text from Nebojša and sent one to Milica, asking her to pick up the bugging device.

Marko picked up his racquet but hardly reacted as Goran smashed another ace past him. He raised his racquet in surrender and went to the net:

'Your match.'

'Wasn't much of a match.'

'What can I say, you're too good.'

'Come on Dad, you didn't return anything.'

'Sorry son, feeling a bit slow today. Let's go home, have

some food and watch the football later.'

It was the 'eternal derby' between Partizan and Red Star. Marko had always been more into basketball and Goran into tennis, but they'd both represented Partizan in their respective sports, so their allegiance lay with the gravediggers.

They packed up the racquets and balls. Goran was right. Marko had been too distracted to play. His son always beat him, but Marko usually won a few games. He couldn't concentrate.

Marko was worried on two fronts. More and more, he thought he shouldn't have got Milica involved. If Vesna and Ivan were behind Milan's murder, he was putting Milica in a dangerous situation. What if she was found out?

His other worry was what if there was nothing on the device? Maybe Vesna and Ivan hadn't said anything incriminating. Then he would have endangered Milica for no reason. He wanted to know she was safe and that bugging Vesna had been worth it.

Milica was trying to read the Ivo Andrić book she had to write an essay on, but she couldn't concentrate. It was irrational to be afraid of her meditation vision, but she couldn't help it. The other thing which niggled was her memory of taking heroin. Just the image of a needle had been enough.

She wasn't afraid of the needle itself, but of returning to her addiction. The blissful oblivion she still sometimes craved. Was studying literature worth it? What future was waiting for her?

It wasn't as if there were any jobs anyway.

A text from Marko interrupted her thoughts. She had to go back to Vesna's mansion and collect the bugging device. Milica wanted Marko to drive her to Vesna's but she knew he was spending time with his family. What did she expect?

As she sat on her bed, Milica felt like an idiot. She was twenty-three not thirteen. Yes, she loved Marko and she would get the device for him, but she knew in her heart the relationship couldn't last forever. She had to hope she was strong enough not to succumb to her first love – heroin.

On the bus to Dedinje, Milica passed the Partizan stadium. People were setting up stalls, selling scarves with the slogan 'gravediggers'. She didn't follow football, but guessed a match was being played later.

How was she going to spend her Sunday night? At home alone, with her bloody Ivo Andrić book. She'd kept apart from her university classmates, happy to be with Marko when he came around. But were books and Marko enough?

Once more, thoughts of heroin came into her mind. She decided she would go out that night, meet people, keep busy. Staying home alone in her own company was too dangerous.

Milica was greeted at the entrance by Vesna, who gave a slight smile but didn't say anything.

Seeing Vesna was dressed in funeral wear, Milica apologised:

'I'm sorry, is this a bad time?'

Vesna opened the door wider, gestured for Milica to go inside.

Milica wondered if Vesna had taken a vow of silence. She explained why she had come:

'I won't intrude. It's just that I can't find my USB stick and I wondered if I left it here. Maybe it fell out when I got undressed for the meditation.'

Vesna showed Milica to her spiritual retreat. The glasshouse was bare. Milica said:

'Maybe I dropped it in the kitchen when I was dizzy.'

Vesna led the way. Milica got on her hands and knees, looked under the kitchen unit.

Reaching to the side of the cooker, she said:

'Got it. Must have fallen out when I fell.'

Milica rose and found Vesna gazing at her. She felt like prey being sized up by a predator.

Did Vesna know what she was up to? Or was it all in Milica's imagination? Stumbling towards the front door, Milica said:

'So I'll be in touch about the article.'

Vesna gave a serene smile as she saw Milica out. She'd had to gather all her spiritual energy to remain calm and not kill Milica on the spot. She couldn't have a person murdered in her own home. Ivan would organise what needed to be done.

She had the same curiosity about Milica as she did with Milan when he had to die. Before her dawn mediation, she'd gazed at his face as he slept, knowing his breaths would be his last.

A death foretold.

As it was with Milica. It had to happen, but what would the consequences be? If her vision was correct, Vesna was setting herself up for exposure. Was she in control or had the visions taken over?

As soon as she got home, Milica sent Marko a text that she'd got the device and asking when he was coming to collect it.

She had waited until she was far away from Vesna before sending the message, just to be safe. It was stupid superstition, but until she was home, she didn't feel she'd escaped Vesna's gaze.

Milica lit a Lucky Strike and sat in the kitchen to wait. She had to change her life. She couldn't sit around waiting for Marko any more. Didn't she have any pride? It would break her heart to end the relationship, but it was for the best.

Her mobile bleeped with a text. She grabbed it up and read the message: 'Glad you're home safe. I'll come in the morning.' Milica chucked the mobile onto the table and spoke out loud:

'What the fuck.'

What was she supposed to do, wait all night? She'd said to herself she'd call her classmates and go out. But a night of drinking and clubbing could lead to drugs. And she could do that at home.

She put out her cigarette, fiddled with the bugging device. It really did look like a USB stick, so did it work like one?

She had nothing else to do, so she might as well listen to Vesna. Setting up her laptop, Milica plugged in the USB-cum-bugging device. With a few clicks, she was listening to Vesna speak with some man. The man had to be the Chief of Police.

Milica was riveted. Her old dealer Dragan was mentioned. Marko had been right. There was a connection between Vesna, the police and drugs. The Police Chief said he'd set Marko up against the Interior Minister and had him followed by another inspector. Marko had to hear this, to know what was going on. And then Milica heard her own name mentioned.

The hairs on her arms rose. Milica's cover had been blown. Vesna had known who she was, which explained the silent treatment. But why hadn't Vesna taken any action?

Milica heard the word 'elimination'. Her blood froze. She stopped the device, grabbed her mobile and called Marko. There was no answer so she left a message:

'Marko, you need to come here now. Vesna knows who I am. And they've been watching you. Another inspector, called Jovanović. And Dragan works for them too. She was talking to someone. I think it's the Police Chief. He asked if I should be eliminated. I'm frightened Marko.'

She lit another cigarette. As she smoked, she kept checking her mobile in case Marko replied and she somehow didn't hear it. Hearing the front door, she felt relief. Marko had come straight over. But then dread spread through her as she realised he couldn't possibly have got there that quickly.

Marko felt his phone vibrate in his jeans pocket. He was in the middle of tucking into a stuffed pepper, so couldn't answer it straight away. Finishing his mouthful, he took out his mobile and saw the missed call from Milica and that there was a voicemail message. He'd relaxed after getting her message that she was back home, but instantly felt tense. Giving his wife an apologetic smile, he got up from the table:

'It's work.'

He stepped into the hallway and listened to Milica's message. She was in a panic. How did she know Vesna knew? It didn't matter. He had to get over there. Before he could reply that he was on his way, there was a knock on the door.

Marko opened up to find Viktor on the doorstep. Viktor smiled:

'I haven't come to search you again. As way of apology I've got some information I thought you might find useful.'

Marko didn't understand. Wasn't it too much of a coincidence that Viktor turned up just after he got a message from Milica? He needed an excuse to get rid of Viktor so that he could get to Milica. He said:

'Uh, that's great Viktor, but I'm in the middle of dinner.'

'Sorry Despot, didn't mean to intrude. I was in the area and thought you'd like to see this.'

Viktor showed a photo of two men in suits shaking hands. One of the men was tall and clean-shaven, the other small and unshaved. Viktor said:

'That's the German Interior Minister and a top member of the Albanian mafia. We know the Albanians have been trying to get a grip on the Balkan drug route. If our Interior Minister is in cahoots with his German counterpart, then maybe your theory has some weight.'

It was potentially interesting, but why was Viktor telling him right then? Was it genuine? Or was it a smokescreen? Marko didn't have time to work it out:

'Okay, I'll look into it. I've got to get back to my food, promised the family I'd spend time with them. I'd invite you in, but not sure my wife's forgiven you for the search.'

'No worries Despot.'

Viktor slapped Marko on the shoulder and got the lift. Marko got on his mobile and called Milica. No answer. He texted that he was on his way, shoved on some trainers and grabbed his handgun. He shouted into the kitchen:

'Something's come up. I've got to go.'

'You don't have to shout.'

Marko looked up to see Branka standing in the doorway, with her arms folded. She asked:

'I thought I heard you say you had to spend time with your family?'

'I've got to go.'

'Just like that, in the middle of food? What about the match, will you be back for that?'

Marko didn't have time to explain things to his wife and son. Grabbing his car keys, he ran out of the flat.

Driving at high speed, Marko used his blue light on the dashboard as he weaved between cars. He crossed the bridge, veered left into Stari Grad. Parking up on Simina Street, Marko leapt out of his Ford as Dragan's Audi slowed down. With the window wound down, Dragan leant out and said:

'Not going to watch the gravediggers Despotović?'

Marko didn't bother replying as he slammed his door shut. Dragan winked:

'Too busy I guess.'

As Dragan drove off, Marko sprinted across the street, shoved open the gate and ran into the building. He called out:

'Milica?'

She didn't answer. He called her name again as he strode through the kitchen. Her laptop was open and a cigarette was unfinished. Was she resting or on the toilet?

Milica wasn't in the bedroom. Marko pushed open the bathroom door.

Milica was sat back on the toilet, her arms dangling and a needle on the floor. Her eyes were rolled back and froth dripped from her mouth. Marko slapped her face, shouted at her:

'Milica!'

Her head lolled. Marko put two fingers to the vein on her neck. No pulse. Her body was still warm, but it was past the time limit of when an adrenalin shot would revive her. Milica wouldn't be coming back alive.

Marko stood paralysed by conflicting emotions and thought processes. One part of him wanted to collapse and sob at Milica's feet. The police inspector side of him needed to investigate.

Marko took several deep breaths to calm down. He blocked out the grief that threatened to engulf him. As a police inspector he took in the scene in an objective manner.

The cause of death was an overdose of heroin. He didn't need an autopsy to tell him that. But Marko couldn't believe Milica had willingly done it. She'd been clean for over a year. He couldn't prevent personal knowledge from informing his judgement.

He scanned Milica's body. No bruises or cuts. Apart from her rolled up sleeve, her clothes were intact. He looked around the bathroom. The bathmat was in place as were the toiletries on the shelf. Nothing out of place to suggest any kind of struggle.

Had Milica really relapsed into her addiction? For the last year, Marko had never seen any evidence of drugs, but Milica had told him she could hide it if she wanted to. Was it his fault?

Had the pressure of what he'd asked her to do got to her?

Marko shook his head at his own thoughts. It didn't make sense. Milica had called him, left a message that she was afraid. She had said Vesna was on to her. How had she known that?

The bugging device. Milica must have listened to it, heard Vesna talking. Marko ran into the kitchen where he'd seen the laptop. It seemed cruel to abandon Milica, but she was dead.

Nothing could change that. He had to focus on finding evidence of how she'd come to die.

The laptop was on, but no USB stick was attached. Marko clicked up the download history. An unnamed media file had been looked at thirty minutes earlier. It couldn't be opened because the device it was on was no longer in the drive.

Marko nodded to himself as he made his deduction. Milica had listened to the device and someone had taken it. He couldn't prove it, but he was sure that Milica had been killed because of it.

He changed his mind. He had got Milica killed. Guilt ate at him. It was his fault.

He should never have got her involved.

Marko sank into the kitchen chair. The last time he'd been sitting in it, Milica was across from him, reading his coffee. She'd forecast a death to someone he loved. He bit his lip to stop the tears as it dawned on him. She hadn't just been his lover. He'd loved her. She'd trusted him. Her father had trusted him. His wife had trusted him. And Marko had fucked up. He had fucked his friend's daughter and brought about her death.

He shook himself out of his remorse, exhaled and called headquarters. No point calling an ambulance. Milica would be going to the morgue not to hospital. And no point claiming Milica's death as a homicide. He would never prove it. But he still needed to know who was responsible.

After arranging for a team to come for Milica's body, Marko listened again to her phone message. She mentioned Vesna, Ivan, Jovanović and Dragan. Had Vesna and Ivan given orders for Milica to be killed? Had Jovanović or Dragan carried it out?

Dragan had passed Marko right outside Milica's building. He'd previously made reference to her, knew where she lived and about their relationship. And he had access to heroin. He must have forced Milica to take it.

Red mist descended. Marko could no longer keep his feelings on a leash. It was bad police work to leave the scene, but he wasn't required. Milica's death would be officially recorded as an overdose by a relapsed heroin addict.

Marko rose from his chair and walked with slow purpose out of the building. He couldn't bear to look at Milica again. Starting his car, Marko set off to find Dragan.

Chapter 27

Marko got to the Partizan stadium a few minutes before the eight p.m. kick off. He knew Dragan would be there. Dragan wouldn't miss the eternal derby and had shouted he was going to watch the gravediggers when he'd passed in his BMW.

At the ticket kiosk, Marko flashed his police ID. The ticket seller shrugged and still insisted on payment. Marko felt like brandishing his Zastava handgun, but paid up the few *dinars* and went inside the stadium.

Making for the hardcore Partizan section, Marko felt the vibrations rise through his feet as soon as he reached the top of the steps. The whole crowd was jumping up and down as they chanted.

From his position at the back of the crowd, Marko could just about see the pitch. Dotted around it were men in helmets with buckets at their feet. The players came out and a roar reverberated around the stadium. From every side, supporters threw flares onto the pitch. The men in helmets dashed about, trying to put out the flares. But they weren't much use – red, blue and white smoke clouding the air and enveloping the players.

Marko scanned the crowd. The stadium was heaving, but he knew Dragan would stand out.

At that moment, a giant of a man clambered up a post that held a stadium banner. There were a few hundred people between the man and Marko, but even from that distance he knew it was Dragan – his rugged features caught in the floodlights.

There were no footholds on the post, so Dragan hauled himself up through sheer strength.

From his lofty position, he orchestrated a new chant:

'If you don't jump up and down you're a gypsy.'

'Gypsies' being the derogatory nickname Partizan fans had given to Red Star supporters. The crowd below obeyed their leader. Marko wasn't going to join Dragan at the top of the post, but he waded through the crowd in his direction. Supporters cursed Marko as he shoved past them, but he was immune to the insults. By the time Marko got to the proximity of Dragan, he had climbed back down. Marko's path was blocked by two of Dragan's gravediggers, big guys with shaved heads.

Marko moved to the side and one of the guys put his shoulder in Marko's face. Marko tried to go past him and felt a punch to his gut. Before Marko could get his breath back, he took another hit to the ribs. Bent over in pain, Marko was dragged backwards through the crowd.

He was too winded to shout for help. Even if anyone could hear him above the din, no-one would have helped. The crowd that had previously been difficult to get through parted with ease as Marko was hauled down the steps into the bowels of the stadium.

Dragan's two henchmen pinned Marko against a concrete pillar, frisked him and took his handgun. Emptying his pockets, they also removed his mobile and ID. Spittle hit Marko in the face as one of the thugs shouted:

'You think your badge gives you any rights here?'

Marko wasn't able to answer. The punch to his gut had made the bile rise inside him. If he tried to speak, he would vomit.

Over the shoulders of the two men, Marko saw Dragan march towards him. What had he been thinking? That he could simply take Dragan out? Instead, he was going to suffer the humiliation of a police inspector being beaten by a drug dealer and his thugs. Dragan shot out his arm and Marko couldn't help flinching.

Dragan waved away the two henchmen. Marko almost fell to the ground as they let go.

Dragan's men handed him Marko's Zastava, phone and ID. Dragan dismissed his men:

'You go back to the match. I'll deal with this.'

'You sure boss?'

Dragan waved Marko's gun:

'Don't worry. Everyone respects me. And those that don't, then they will.'

Dragan's men left. Marko steadied himself against the concrete pillar. Dragan asked:

'What the fuck is so important I have to leave the eternal derby?'

Marko stood his ground. Finding his voice, he had nothing to lose:

'How can you just watch football after killing Milica?'

'What are you talking about? I didn't kill Milica.'

'Really?'

'Really. This is the first I've heard about it.'

'Bit of a coincidence that you passed by her place just before I found her body.'

'Not really. I drive down that street every day.'

'She was killed because she found out about your connection with Vesna and Ivan. And you knew about Milica.'

'You're a police inspector. Haven't you heard of innocent until proven guilty?'

Dragan eyed Marko and said:

'I wasn't the only one who knew about Milica. Belgrade's a small city.'

'So who killed her?'

'I don't know. I respected her. Maybe you should look at your colleague. He arrested her.'

Marko wanted to go straight after Jovanović, but the energy was draining from him. What was he going to do, go after everyone?

Marko's mobile rang in Dragan's hand. Dragan saw who the caller was:

'Your boss.'

'Or is he yours?'

'No-one is my boss. Here, answer it.'

Marko took his phone and took the call, while he held eye contact with Dragan. At the other end of the phone, Ivan said:

'We need to meet. Where are you?'

'In the Partizan stadium, with a mutual acquaintance.'

Marko left it like that. There was a silence for a second as Ivan worked out who the acquaintance was before replying:

'Kalemegdan by the tanks in an hour.'

'Fine.'

Marko ended the call and looked at Dragan:

'You know what I think? I think you made a deal when you were arrested ten years ago. In return for setting up the arrests of Zemun clan members, you got to be the main dealer in Belgrade.'

'You know what I think? I think for someone who knows so much, you're lucky you're still alive. I didn't kill Milica. Why don't you meet your boss and find out who did.'

As they were trading accusations and truths, Marko had nothing to lose by asking about his dad's murder:

'I also heard your work for the clan included killing a civilian selling petrol.'

'Who told you that?'

'Stojanović.'

'Stojanović talks shit. Or he did until he died.'

Marko gave up. Would Dragan admit it if he had killed someone? Dragan handed Marko's gun back to him, said:

'What were you going to do, shoot me?'

Marko shrugged at the futility of it:

'Maybe. I don't know.'

Marko holstered his handgun. What was he going to do,

shoot everyone he suspected in a revenge killing spree? Dragan could be a mean bastard, but Marko believed him that he hadn't killed Milica. It was also true that Marko was still alive. There could easily have been someone at Milica's waiting to bump him off. Whoever had killed Milica wanted Marko alive. Why?

He didn't trust Ivan, but he would meet him.

Dragan ambled back to watch the match, acting nonchalant but thinking hard. Dragan respected the deal he'd made with Ivan. It had proved to be of mutual benefit. The problem was that all communication was through Jovanović.

Had Jovanović gone and killed Milica of his own accord? Or was it on order of Ivan, or even Vesna? Dragan didn't like being kept in the dark. He didn't need to know what wasn't his concern. But it was his concern if Despotović was coming to confront him about the murder.

A threat to Milica or Marko's family should have been enough. If Jovanović had killed her for no reason, he'd fucked up. If it was down to Ivan and Vesna, then Dragan should have been informed. He was starting to feel Ivan was being pussy whipped.

Killing Milan had been Vesna's idea or it wouldn't have been sanctioned. Dragan understood the reasoning. It was to show the Albanians that no deal would be considered. He wasn't complaining because he now had more responsibility about the route and more money. Even cutting off Milan's limbs had seemed to go to plan – planting evidence on the cousins. But if Ivan was becoming pussy whipped and Vesna's ideas were getting out of hand, Dragan had to rethink the whole deal.

Long gone were the days as a twenty-year-old openly dealing in the park. He'd been a street dealer for the Zemun clan until his brother was killed, a bystander in an 'Audi of death' chase.

He was told it was an accident and he'd said he accepted

it, but he harboured resentment.

Letting himself get arrested, he agreed to Ivan's deal.

With Dragan's inside information, the Zemun clan was broken up. And Dragan became Belgrade's main dealer, known and feared.

He'd mellowed during the last few years. He still put on a front as a Partizan hard man, but no longer got into knife fights. He didn't need to. Power could be more subtle.

Not that he was getting ahead of himself. He knew Ivan and Vesna pulled the strings from behind the scenes. But it was also a benefit for them that his role was known and theirs wasn't.

Milan had bankrolled the route through Serbia. Ivan had made it easy. If anti-narcotics police were on to something, Ivan knew about it. That way, he controlled who was caught and arrested. Now that Milan was dead, Vesna had taken over.

Dragan saw the method in Vesna's madness. Killing Milan had definitely put off the Albanians, who knew not to mess with the route. And Dragan wasn't complaining. He had more power and more pay.

But Milan could have been killed in another way. Now, there was a struggle between the Chief of Police and his inspectors. Ivan had sent assurances via Jovanović that Inspector Despotović was no longer a problem. Dragan was going to keep his wits about him.

Chapter 28

Day had darkened into night by the time Marko reached Kalemegdan. The old women had packed away their embroidery and the old men had closed their chess sets, vacating the park for young couples on romantic evening strolls.

Marko walked towards the outer fortress wall and saw Ivan leaning on one of the tanks from the Second World War. Ivan's shock of white hair was noticeable anywhere.

With the meeting out in the open, Marko tried to guess Ivan's intentions. It meant neither of them could be killed without possible witnesses. No-one else was lingering in the vicinity but an occasional couple passed by on their way to a view of the river.

As Marko neared the tank, Ivan took a final drag of his Marlboro and stubbed out the cigarette on the rusting metal hulk. Marko drew level with his Chief. It had the feeling of a showdown, but Marko didn't think there would be any shooting. For his part, Marko's need for revenge had dissipated since talking with Dragan. He wasn't even sure who deserved payback for Milica's murder.

Ivan nodded at Marko, said:

'Glad you could make it Despotović.'

'Not sure there was much choice.'

'There's always a choice. Just maybe not the one you want to make.'

Marko nodded at Ivan's philosophic words.

'You wanted to meet.'

'Yes, but first take a look to your left.'

Marko looked to his left. A red dot was lazered onto the tank. He watched as the dot moved across to his heart. He knew it meant a sniper had him in sight, but he felt calm:

'Are you really going to kill me in such a public place?'

'I wouldn't be so foolish. Jovanović on the other hand is another matter. He's still mad at you for breaking into his houseboat. And what with his coke habit, he can be trigger happy.'

Marko glanced up, wondering where Jovanović was positioned. Probably on the second-tier terrace behind the higher wall. He still didn't feel nervous. As Dragan had said, people wanted Marko alive or he'd be dead. By keeping his grief at Milica's death at bay, his emotions had also become numb.

Ivan said:

'Turn around and put your hands on the tank.'

Marko did as he was told. Not out of fear, but out of curiosity. What did Ivan want?

Ivan frisked Marko, feeling his gun but leaving it. He took out Marko's phone, checked it was off then put it back in Marko's pocket. He patted Marko's legs but didn't find anything else.

Marko couldn't help laughing, suddenly finding the situation funny:

'You know it's the third time in as many days I've been frisked. Either I must be suspected of being a big-time dealer or my body is irresistible.'

'Your problem Despotović is you don't take things seriously enough.'

'Life's too short to be serious, especially in Belgrade.'

'Okay, turn back around.'

Marko turned to face his boss, blinking as the red dot flicked across his eyes. Marko said:

'Viktor frisked me for drugs. Dragan's men patted me down for my gun. What are you after?'

'Just want to make sure we can have a private conversation without it being recorded. Don't want you telling tales to the newspapers. Or your wife. And I know you visited Stojanović in prison. Do you think a bottle of *rakija* will buy a warden?'

Marko realised he hadn't been paranoid. Ivan had eyes all over the city. Ivan waved a hand in the air and the red dot vanished. He said:

'Getting Viktor to check you was better than Jovanović going to your place with a gun in his hand. Although it would have been easier for me if he did. Two birds with one stone. I'd no longer have you fucking things up with your private investigations. And I could get that coke head arrested for murder of a colleague.'

Marko didn't know what Ivan's play was, but he strangely seemed to have more disdain for Jovanović, something Marko hadn't heard before. He waited for Ivan to continue:

'I know that you know about my connection to Vesna. We all have secrets. I guess your wife didn't know about Milica.'

Hearing Milica's name made the anger rise inside Marko. He contained it:

'And the point is?'

'The point is I'm sorry she had to die. Really. Jovanović has a way of going too far.'

Marko's desire to be violent battled with the information he'd been given. Wasn't it too easy that both Dragan and Ivan had fingered Jovanović as Milica's killer? Marko believed that Jovanović was capable but he wasn't sure he believed Ivan's word for it.

Did it matter who had killed Milica? Marko's anger once again subsided into sadness. Even if it was Jovanović, the order had probably come from Ivan. Killing either of them wasn't going to bring her back. And if he killed them then he had to kill himself. He was just as guilty.

Ivan couldn't tell if Marko believed him or not. In fact, he'd gone to Milica's flat himself.

He was planning to send Jovanović then Vesna had called

and told him about Milica coming for the USB stick. Ivan guessed that it was the bugging device Marko had obtained from the technology department. So Ivan had sent Viktor to delay Marko and Jovanović to keep watch while he did the deed.

It hadn't taken much to persuade Milica to inject heroin instead of taking a bullet to the head.

But she hadn't given up the bugging device and Ivan hadn't had time to search for it before Jovanović called to say Marko was almost there.

Ivan gestured at the fortress grounds:

'Let's sit over there.'

Ivan and Marko strolled over to a park bench, where they sat. Marko wanted to laugh at the situation. They weren't old enough to be chess mates. What did they look like? Gay lovers?

Ivan lit a Marlboro, exhaled smoke and asked:

'Where's the bugging device?'

Marko was surprised by the question and genuine in his answer:

'How do I know?'

'Really?'

'Really.'

'It wasn't in the flat.'

'Maybe you should ask Jovanović?'

The two men glanced sideways at each other, trying to gauge how much truth was being told.

Ivan flicked ash from his cigarette and said:

'Jovanović has become a bloody liability. You're a better police inspector than you pretend to be. I thought about getting you on board a long time ago, but you didn't seem serious enough.

With Milan's murder, you were meant to solve it, but not so quickly. I'm going to put my cards on the table. Dragan controls the city's main drug dealing. We control Dragan. You can't stop drugs or crime, but in this way, we at least maintain some control. Murders, arrests and crime are down.

Belgrade's a safer city.'

'At what cost?'

'At no cost. Only profit.'

'And making a deal with criminals.'

'The deal was of my making. There'd been internal fighting in the Zemun clan. Dragan had a grievance so I utilised that. He gave us the clan members on a plate. In return, I set him up as the biggest dealer in the city so that I could control him.'

'You think Dragan is under your control?'

'Control is maybe the wrong word. But it's a lot easier knowing who you're dealing with.'

Marko wanted to laugh at the warped logic. Only a few days ago he might even have agreed with it. In case Marko didn't understand, Ivan expanded his viewpoint:

'Let me give you some statistics. Since the American invasion of Afghanistan, opium production has doubled each year. The Americans made some deal with the Afghan drug lords.

'Opium for oil rights maybe. After the Yugoslav War, Serbia lost control of the Balkan route. Kosovo Albanians now control 70% of heroin entering the EU market. The two biggest markets are the UK and Germany. The West made a deal with the *šiptari*. For what, I don't know. What I do know is that Serbia is now a minor transportation route, but still an important one. If it gets into the hands of the Albanians, we're fucked.'

The whole conversation made Marko uneasy. It felt like the end of a movie when the bad guy revealed his plans and motives to the good guy before getting ready to kill him. But this didn't feel like the end, so why was Ivan telling him so much?

Ivan answered Marko's unspoken question:

'I want you on the team Despotović.'

'Which team is that?'

'I want you to replace Jovanović. We can have him arrested on drugs charges or killed in a bust gone wrong if you want revenge for Milica. Dragan respects you more than Jovanović.

'You'd liaise with Dragan to see who we arrest and who we don't. And we need the Interior Minister out of the picture. Viktor is already gathering evidence. The Minister is in a deal with the Germans who in turn made a deal with the Albanians. Everyone wants the same thing – the drug route. It's never going away. It's just a matter of who is in charge of it.'

'Who is in charge of it? You? Vesna?'

'Vesna's name isn't in this conversation.'

'Her husband being murdered was pure coincidence?'

'He was on the brink of doing a deal with the Albanians. A message needed to be sent.'

'By dismembering him?'

'It was a strong message.'

Ivan stubbed out his cigarette and looked at it in disgust:

'It's not enough that the Americans bombed us. Killing me with their bloody cigarettes.'

Marko knew the answer to his next question, but he asked it anyway:

'And if I don't join the team?'

'With what you know now, you're with us or against us. You saw what happened to Milica. Do you want the same to happen to your wife and son?'

Ivan stood up and said:

'It's your choice. I know what I'd choose. You've got twenty-four hours to decide. I will take Jovanović off your tail. Leave you time to inform Milica's father, attend your son's tennis match and bring me something on the Minister.'

Ivan left Marko on the bench. As he walked off, Ivan was unsure if he'd convinced Marko but either way it was sorted. The best option was for Marko to replace Jovanović. But if Marko didn't go for the deal, he knew too much to keep on living.

Marko's thoughts grew as dark as the night enclosing the park. In a way it was simple. Milica had been killed. Marko and his family were alive. If he wanted it to stay that way, he had to join his boss in corruption, drug dealing and murder.

Chapter 29

Marko sat paralysed on the bench. He'd been put in an impossible situation. He felt like Joseph K in *The Trial* – caught in a deadly labyrinth that didn't end well. At least Marko had a choice.

If he wanted his family to stay alive, he had to join Ivan.

Would it matter if he did? Did anything matter? It was hardly as if Marko was the most moral guy in the world. He'd been unfaithful to his wife. He'd used his mistress to get information which had resulted in her murder. He'd taken part in corruption on a small scale to make arrests.

So what was the problem in taking a step up?

He couldn't fight against Ivan, Jovanović and Dragan on his own. Ivan could turn the whole force on him, Jovanović in particular. Dragan had his own men. Marko was on his own. He had always been gregarious, joking with everyone, but who were his real friends? Who could he count on?

Gojko? Apart from the fact that Marko had fucked his friend's daughter, Gojko was an ex-alcoholic who had vowed never to use a weapon after what he'd witnessed during the Yugoslav war.

Nebojša? The rookie was ambitious and eager to fight corruption, but he didn't stand a chance. Marko wasn't going to ruin Nebojša's life.

The Interior Minister? He wouldn't be able to prevent Ivan, Jovanović or Dragan getting to Marko's wife and son. Marko now had it first hand that Ivan and Jovanović were corrupt, but he still didn't have any evidence. Even if he did, what could the Minister do with it?

The Interior Minister had made his own threat. Any possible tennis career for Marko's son would be over, but that was preferable to being killed. The Minister's bodyguard was outweighed by Ivan's police and Dragan's crew. Marko had seen what Ivan, Jovanović and Dragan were capable of.

Milan's dismemberment, the cousins' execution, Milica's staged suicide. The police c h i e f and drug dealer carried out their threats. The politician was all talk.

Marko's nihilistic thoughts were getting him nowhere. He didn't know how long he'd been sitting on the bench, but he was wasting his time. Nothing productive could come from thinking. There was only one choice to make if he wanted to keep his family alive.

He couldn't face his wife just yet. And he wasn't ready to inform Gojko about Milica's 'suicide'. He needed a drink first.

Marko rose from the bench and walked zombie-like through Kalemegdan to the terrace bar.

Groups of friends and cuddling couples sat at the dimly lit tables, chatting with animation and romance. People enjoying life while Marko's had turned into a path of darkness.

Milica should have been there, not with Marko, but with friends. Marko should be there with his wife.

At the bar, Marko ordered a glass of *rakija* and downed it in one go. The burning sensation in his chest brought welcome relief. What he needed was to get drunk, escape for a few hours into oblivion before facing the next day.

For the first time, Marko understood Milica's heroin addiction. He'd always thought that her life hadn't been that bad. Marko had been through worse than she had. So had a million other Serbs. But he realised it wasn't about how bad your life was. There were all kinds of reasons for not wanting to face reality. And they were all as valid.

Marko took out his wallet and asked the young barman

for the whole bottle of *rakija*. The barman laughed:

'We only sell by the glass.'

'I want the bottle.'

'We're a bar not a supermarket.'

'How much is a glass?'

'Two hundred *dinars*.'

'How many glasses in a bottle?'

'How do I know?'

'Have a guess.'

'Fifty glasses.'

'Fifty times two hundred is ten thousand *dinars*. That's quite a profit.'

'I just work here.'

'Let me see the bottle.'

'Come on man.'

Marko took out his ID:

'Give me the bottle.'

The barman hesitated. Marko was tired of being fucked off. He slammed his Zastava on the table:

'Give me the fucking bottle.'

The barman handed over the bottle. Marko left a thousand *dinars* on the counter:

'That's what it costs in the supermarket.'

Marko pocketed his ID and grabbed the bottle. Turning to leave, he saw half the people in the bar were looking his way. Brandishing his gun and the bottle of rakija, he shouted:

'You want to call the police? I am the police!'

Marko knocked back a hit of *rakija* from the bottle and went off laughing. He used to be a funny guy. Maybe he'd regained his humour.

Ivan had said he wasn't serious enough, implied that's why he'd never been vetted to join the 'team'. In which case, Marko's humour had saved him from that fate. In fact, it was only once he'd started being serious in his investigations that he'd got into this fucked up situation.

Marko thought about how he'd just used a gun on the barman. Of course, he'd crossed the line before. He'd planted drugs on junkies and made deals with informants. But it was small scale and the victims were always criminals. This was the first time he'd threatened an innocent person with a gun.

It wasn't so difficult to abuse his power. Maybe he was ready to become corrupt on a major scale. He could make more money and get a bigger flat for his family. Get a houseboat like Jovanović to use for a new mistress, one of the silicon stunners from Café Insomnia. He'd form a working partnership with Dragan and do Ivan's bidding.

Sitting on an outer wall and facing the Danube down below, Marko took another swig of *rakija*. The alcohol was making him sweat, or perhaps it was just the humidity. It was past eleven and still over twenty degrees.

The drink was giving Marko increasingly darker thoughts. If he accepted Ivan's deal, his boss had said that Marko could enact revenge on Jovanović.

Marko envisaged going over to Jova's houseboat and setting it on fire with Jova inside. Stage a suicide to outdo Milica's death. But doubts surrounded Milica's murder. Was Marko sure Jovanović killed her?

Jovanović was capable of it, but the suicide had been too poised to be his work. Jova would have lost his temper and hit her or got aroused and tried to fuck her. In all probability, it was Ivan who had killed Milica. Marko's boss both as Chief of Police and soon to be drug kingpin.

Although the more Marko thought about it, the more he was convinced Vesna was the real boss. Ivan had shown the love note to Marko in pretence at making Marko know too much. But it was what wasn't said that was just as important. For the Chief of Police to keep a love note from forty years earlier showed how much he was in thrall to Vesna. Milica would have been proud at how Marko read between the lines.

Marko stood unsteadily and drank more *rakija*. He wanted to roll down the hill, like he used to as a kid. His childhood had been poor but he'd been happy as long as he was out on some adventure or on the basketball court. His mum made stuffed cabbage everyday but he didn't complain. His dad didn't have a big income as a bus driver. During inflation, he didn't have any income so he turned to selling petrol on the black market. Maybe even stole a cache of drugs. Whatever way he supplemented his income, it brought about his death.

Drink was making Marko emotional. Tears welled up. He blinked away the image of his dad burning to death. He'd buried his dad's murder the day he received the news. There were other horrific images in Kosovo at the time.

For several weeks, rumours had swirled about 'the red barn'. The story was that on a remote farm, a barn was being used by Albanians as an operating room for organ harvesting. Marko thought it was probably just propaganda, told to make the Albanians appear evil. Who knew if it was true?

In a routine patrol, Marko's regiment came across an isolated red barn, half hidden by trees.

The Serbian soldiers went into stealth mode. Two KLA soldiers were on guard outside the barn, although one of the Albanians was asleep inside a van. The Serbs crept out of the trees, silenced the Albanians with a gun to the head. The officer in charge opened the barn door.

Inside was a makeshift operating room. A Serbian farmer was strapped down, half dead. An Albanian 'surgeon' backed off, scalpel in his hand. The farmer's kidneys had already been taken, an Albanian woman acting as nurse in the middle of bagging the organs.

It was too late to save the farmer, but there was plenty of time to kill the Albanians. The 'surgeon' was tortured first, his ears cut off followed by each of his fingers. Marko had watched *Reservoir Dogs*, but Tarrantino's film was nothing compared to real-life butchery.

Marko understood the desire for revenge, but didn't take part in it. Nor did he try to stop it.

He stood guard while the nurse was repeatedly raped and

sodomised. Did that absolve him?

No, he was as guilty as anyone else. But life was full of non-choices.

Did his dad have a choice? He'd sold the petrol even though he'd been warned off. But it was the only way he knew how to make money so he could feed his family.

Marko took another gulp of *rakija* and staggered down the slope towards the Danube.

Midnight mist rolled off the river and enveloped Marko. Figures seemed to appear. Squinting, Marko saw a line of Serbian Partizans at the water's edge. German Huns aimed their rifles and fired, the Partizans falling backwards into the Danube. Marko blinked in disbelief, the mist evaporated and the riverside was empty. His granddad had told him about Germans murdering Serbs during the Second World War. It must have been a drunken vision.

How much blood had flown through Balkan history? Marko envisaged images stretching back and forth through history. The Turks conquering the area in 1120. The First World War set off by a Serbian assassinating Archduke Ferdinand in Sarajevo. Fighting the Germans again in World War Two. Serbs, Croats and Bosnians killing each other in the Yugoslav War. The Kosovo war with the Albanians. Marko had no patriotic illusions. The Serbian people were as guilty as those around them.

The whole region was seeped in bloodshed and violence. Why, when a region had such great food and beautiful women, did they spend so much time killing each other?

Marko's vision made him think of Vesna. Was she really behind it all? If he killed Vesna, would that bring peace?

It wouldn't solve anything. Ivan was so in thrall he'd seek revenge. Besides, Jovanović and Dragan would still be at large. If Ivan and Vesna thought they had Dragan under control, they were deluded.

If the drug kingpin was taken out, another person would take her place. Ivan and Viktor had both intimated that the Albanians were waiting for the opportunity to take over the drug route.

The Interior Minister was in league with the Germans who in turn had made a deal with the Albanians. Marko didn't know how much truth there was in the theory, but he wouldn't be surprised if it was true.

Someone had to be in charge of the route. So was Ivan so wrong in trying to control it?

Marko didn't want to think about it any more. He wanted to go home. He wanted to quit the police. He would get a job as a street cleaner, make just enough money to survive. And be satisfied that his family were alive.

But he wasn't even allowed to do that. In self pity, Marko finished off the *rakija*. At least he was ready to tell Gojko about his daughter's 'suicide'. If he could get his words out.

Chapter 30

Marko leant against Gojko's door for support as he knocked on it. He'd been tempted to head straight up to his own flat, but he owed it to his old friend.

Maybe Gojko was asleep. Marko didn't check the time, but knew it was around about midnight. He k n e w h e w a s d r u n k. Without the drink inside him, he wouldn't have had the courage to inform Gojko about his daughter's death.

Marko had given bad news to parents before, but it was different telling a friend. Not to mention that the friend's daughter had been Marko's lover.

The door opened and Marko almost fell into Gojko. Marko made a vague gesture, asked:

'Can I come in?'

'Think you already have.'

The two old friends smiled. Gojko closed the door and Marko followed him into the living room, the sofa-bed pulled out. Marko said:

'Sorry, were you asleep?'

'Reading. Are you drunk Marko?'

'Just a bit of *rakija*.'

Marko held up the bottle:

'Still got some left.'

Marko swayed in the middle of the room as he pointed at Gojko:

'I need to talk to you.'

'Okay. Sit here.'

Gojko eyed Marko. He'd never seen Marko drunk. Something bad must have happened.

Maybe Marko had witnessed a terrible murder. Or Branka had left him, though he couldn't believe she would. Whatever it was, Gojko was ready to listen. Marko had more than helped with Milica, so he was there to return the favour.

Sinking into an armchair, Marko offered the bottle of *rakija*:

'Can you get us two glasses?'

'You know I don't drink anymore.'

'You'll need it.'

Gojko frowned as he took the bottle and went into the kitchen to get two glasses. He poured water into his own glass and watered down Marko's *rakija*. He smiled at the irony of him taking care of a drunken Marko. It had been the other way around plenty of times. But why had Marko said Gojko would need a drink?

Gojko brought in the drinks and handed Marko his watered down *rakija*. Marko looked around the room, trying to focus on anything else apart from what he had to say. His eyes drifted from the bookshelves to the floor. Next to the sofa-bed was a box of hardbacks. Marko made a drunken gesture at the books:

'What you got there?'

Gojko picked up a book:

'*The Myth of the Heavenly Serbs*. Five volumes. A history professor died and his widow didn't want to keep them. Some beautiful illustrations. Tempted to keep them for myself, but they'll get a good price.'

Gojko took the opportunity to talk. Fear nagged at him and he wanted to put off whatever Marko had to say. Flicking through the book, he said:

'Serbia is unique in that we are a highly educated nation that believes in myths, especially when it comes to national mythology. Serbian history is full of alternative versions. It started in Kosovo with legends of rebellions against the

Turkish during the Ottoman Empire. The Serbs lost the military battle but claimed a spiritual one and called themselves 'heavenly people'.'

Gojko put the book down, shrugged and said:

'Milošević used exactly the same phrases in the Yugoslav and Kosovo wars. He took propaganda to another level, state TV only showing Serbian victories. Atrocities were solely committed by Croats and Albanians. And the West was against us. I guess the last part was true.'

Marko downed his rakija, too drunk to notice it had been watered down. He hadn't really been listening to Gojko. He couldn't let his friend carry on talking:

'She's dead Gojko.'

Gojko swallowed, afraid of the answer to his question:

'Who?'

'Milica.'

Gojko started to laugh at Marko's drunken words, cut himself short. He knew that although Marko was drunk, he was telling the truth. That was why Marko was drunk. That was what he had come to say.

Gojko didn't cry or shout. His daughter had been a heroin addict and had survived a car crash.

Gojko had always known Milica might die before he did. He asked:

'How?'

'Overdose.'

Gojko nodded, accepting the cause of death. Marko shook his head in apology:

'I'm sorry. It was my fault.'

'How can you say that? You couldn't have done any more than you did.'

Marko glanced at Gojko, then looked away. Was he going to tell him everything? Would it help? Was Marko's self-pity helping Gojko now? Marko said:

'Maybe I could have gone there more often than I did. I went when I could.'

'I know.'

Marko stood, embraced Gojko and headed out of the flat. He couldn't carry on with any more deception.

Gojko let Marko make his own way out. He needed to digest the news. He went into the kitchen and poured away the rest of the *rakija* before he was tempted. If he didn't resist, he'd never stop. He went back into the living room, picked up a framed photo of Milica as a little girl sitting on his lap, Gojko reading to her from a book of Hans Christian Anderson tales. Tears ran down his cheeks.

Marko didn't remember getting in the lift or pressing any buttons, but the doors opened and he was on his floor. He stepped out and dug in his pockets for his keys. He dropped them, picked them up, tried until he found the right one. Entering the flat, he heard Branka's hushed voice:

'Marko?'

Marko shut the door as quietly as he could, squinted as Branka turned on the hall light. Seeing him, Branka asked:

'Are you drunk?'

'Just a bit.'

Marko made for Goran's room. Branka tried to stop him:

'What are you doing? Don't wake him. He needs to sleep before the tournament.'

'Just to check.'

Marko peeped in, saw his son's sleeping form, turned and hit his head against the door:

'Fuck.'

'Dad?'

'It's okay son, go back to sleep.'

Marko put his hands out to balance as he made his way down the hallway. From behind him, he heard Goran ask:

'Is he okay?'

Marko didn't hear his wife's answer as he crashed onto the sofa and his eyes closed.

Chapter 31

With her eyes closed, Vesna was sitting cross-legged, straight-backed and naked as she meditated at dawn. In her vision, she saw how opium went from the farm to the arm.

She envisaged a poppy seed being planted in the earth, taking root, green shoots growing into a red poppy. Her view expanded, taking in the fields of colourful poppies that filled the valley.

But sadness pervaded. The poppies were crying, white tears oozing out of their pods.

The opium fluid seeped out into a stream that ran through the mountains into Iran. As if on a map, the white stream of opium followed a route through Turkey and Greece to Macedonia.

Here, the liquid split into three streams. The thickest stream ran west into Albania, while two smaller streams trickled into Serbia and Bulgaria. White Balkan veins.

Vesna focused on the Serbian stream as it meandered north to Belgrade, pausing there before crossing borders and making its way to Germany.

The opium liquid dripped off the map onto a man's arm, tracing a vein, seeping into his skin and leaving a scar. The arm turned blue and lifeless.

A hand picked up the map and folded it. The hand belonged to a suited German politician who shook hands with a bearded Albanian.

Anger rose through Vesna. Since Kosovo had gained independence, the Albanians had taken over most of the Balkan route.

Kosovo had been Serbian since the fourteenth century. It had the oldest Orthodox church. It was where Serbs had lost the battle against the Turks but won the war to become heavenly people. It was where the first golden fork had been used. During the Kosovo war, her parents had been killed by the KLA.

It was Vesna's duty to keep the Serbian route open. It had become more than just about money. That was why Milan had to die. Her own husband had dared to enter into negotiations with the Albanians. Killing him had delivered a message. If a traitor could die, imagine what would happen to an enemy. And it had worked. The Albanians had gone quiet.

Milica's murder was more complicated. Had it been necessary? Were Vesna's visions pure or influenced by her thoughts?

In her meditative state, Vesna frowned. She was thinking too much, letting her thoughts disturb her equilibrium. Unable to meditate, she opened her eyes.

Chapter 32

Marko blinked in the sunlight flooding though the windows. He could smell coffee and home-baked *projica*. Marko smiled. He was alive and awake after a bad dream.

As he tried to rise, pain exploded in his head. His smile evaporated. Fuck, it wasn't a bad dream. It was reality.

He really had been drunk. Milica really had been killed. Marko really had been given an ultimatum by Ivan: take part in drug dealing corruption or his family would die.

The world was still turning, but nothing had changed. Marko had to get up, but he couldn't face anybody.

Branka appeared with a cup of Turkish coffee and a plate of *projica*. Sitting up on the sofa, Marko grimaced as he sipped his coffee. He couldn't eat. It would come straight back up.

Clearing his throat, he asked:

'Did Goran get off to Pančevo?'

'Yes, his coach picked him up. They'll have a final training session before his match. I said we'd be there to watch him and take him home after.'

Marko nodded and took another hit of coffee to clear his head. His son and wife had to carry on with their lives. There was no immediate danger. Marko had until the end of the day to join the Chief of Police and bring down the Interior Minister.

Branka took a breath and said:

'I spoke with Gojko this morning. He told me about Milica.

I'm so sorry for him. And her.'

'Yea, I didn't know how to tell him.'

'Turning up drunk probably wasn't the best way.'

'No, I should have waited until this morning to tell him. I'll have to take him to the morgue. Is he at home?'

'Yes, he's waiting for you.'

Marko rose from the sofa, felt dizzy and steadied himself in the doorway. Branka said:

'Marko?'

'Yea?'

'Were in you in love with her?'

'What?'

'I'm not stupid.'

'I know.'

'So be honest with me.'

'What do you want me to say?'

'The truth. Why did she overdose?'

Marko looked at his wife, said:

'She didn't overdose.'

'So why did you tell Gojko she had?'

'It's complicated.'

'Too complicated for me to understand? I understand. You fucked her. She fell in love with you. You wouldn't leave me. She overdosed. How's that?'

'You want to know the truth? The overdose was staged. She was murdered to get at me because yes I had sex with her. I found out something I shouldn't have. And if I want to keep you and Goran safe, I need to keep it secret.'

Branka's face drained of colour. Her journalistic instincts battled with preservation of her family:

'Is Goran in danger?'

'I'll make sure he isn't.'

'If you need to keep him safe, why are you letting him go around without protection?'

'What do you want me to do, lock us in and keep guard twenty-fours hours a day?'

'You're a police inspector. Can't your colleagues help?'

'It's my boss and colleagues who did it.'

Branka tried to comprehend the situation. There was too much to take in. She was deeply hurt by Marko's affair, but there was time to deal with that. If something happened to Goran, her heart would break:

'What have you got us into?'

'I didn't get us into anything. I was put in the situation. I was just doing my job. The Interior Minister came to me, asking me to look into police corruption. The Chief of Police has made it abundantly clear if I don't join in with the corruption, my family won't be alive for very long.'

'Can't the Minister do something?'

'The Minister is just as corrupt. He's in league with the Germans and Albanians who want the drug route for themselves. He even threatened Goran's tennis future.'

'What?'

'He's just talk, unlike my colleagues.'

'So what can we do?'

'I don't have a choice. Do you understand now?'

Marko walked off before Branka saw his tears. He shut himself in the bathroom and took deep breaths as he tried to shower away his pain. He'd been beaten in every sense. Dragan's men had used brute force. Ivan had killed Milica and left Marko no choice but to become his corrupt dogsbody.

Marko stepped out of the shower and looked in the mirror. He hadn't shaved for three days and stubble covered his jaw. A glimpse of white caught his eye and he examined himself closer in the mirror. His stubble was flecked with white hairs. In panic, he shaved it all off. It was the least of his problems but hit him hard all the same. He was getting older. Time waited for no-one. Was he going to grow old as a corrupt cop or die in his forties as a man who made a stand?

Marko brushed his teeth and changed into clean clothes. He no longer smelt of sweat and *rakija*. But his soul was still heavy. He stood in the kitchen doorway, said to his wife:

'I'm going to see if Gojko's ready to go to the morgue. Do

you want me to pick you up after?'

'No, I'll get a bus to Pančevo.'

Branka faced her husband. She loved him, even if it was difficult to get over his betrayal. She knew he loved her and Goran, that he would do all he could to protect them. She had to support him. Branka reached out and adjusted the button on his shirt.

Marko didn't dare try to kiss his wife. He gave her a sad smile and left the flat. He found Gojko outside, loading his battered old Yugo with boxes of books. Red-eyed from crying, Gojko was trying to carry on with life. Marko said:

'Sorry about last night. It was the only way I could tell you.'

'I understand.'

'We need to identify her.'

'I'll follow you.'

They drove to the morgue, Marko's mind blank. At the morgue, Marko and Gojko waited in silence as Milica's body was brought out. Marko avoided looking as Gojko confirmed it was his daughter, Gojko openly crying and kissing Milica on the forehead.

Outside, Gojko said he'd like to see where Milica had been living. Marko had told him about the place, but Milica had never invited her father. Marko showed the way to Simina Street.

They went into the old building and Marko opened up. Gojko asked:

'You had your own key?'

'Milica told me to keep a spare in case anything happened.'

'How did you find her?'

'She'd left a message that she was fed up of everyone thinking of her as a junkie, so she might as well be one. I didn't see the message until too late. I drove over as soon as I could.'

Marko felt sick with his lies, but he couldn't tell the truth to Gojko. It wouldn't help.

Gojko nodded. He wanted to see how Milica lived, maybe take home a memento of her life as a young woman.

Leaving Gojko to wander around, Marko stayed in the kitchen. The laptop was still on the table. The police inspector inside him kicked in. If Ivan hadn't found the device, where had Milica hidden it?

She hadn't had much time between her call to Marko and her killer entering the flat. If she had deliberately hidden the device, it would have been somewhere for Marko to find.

Looking around the kitchen, Marko's eyes took in the coffee tin. What connected Marko to Milica? She had predicted that a person close to him would die in her coffee reading. Marko took off the lid and emptied the tin. Coffee powder poured onto the table. Sticking out of the heap was a USB stick.

Marko pocketed the device, his heart beating fast. He didn't know if anything was on it that could help his situation. He'd find out.

Gojko came into the kitchen carrying several books. Marko was surprised by Gojko's question:

'Were you sleeping with her?'

'What?'

'Were you fucking my daughter?'

'What are you talking about?'

'It's a simple question.'

'It's not so simple.'

'I guess she loved you more than me.'

Gojko placed the Ivo Andrić book on the kitchen table. Marko remembered the inscription Milica had made him write, Milica drawing a heart around their names.

Gojko tried to find the energy to hate Marko. He was too sad to do so. Clutching Milica's books, Gojko left the building.

Marko didn't go after Gojko. Nothing could immediately repair their friendship. There probably never would be. The reverberations of Milica's death were going to have lasting effects.

He wanted to leave the building himself, but the USB device was clenched in his fist. Milica was dead. Marko's friendship with her father was over. His wife might or might not forgive the affair. The safety of Branka and Goran was what he had left to protect. Could there be anything useful on the USB?

Marko had to get to the tennis tournament, but first he needed to check the device. He opened Milica's laptop and turned it on. He inserted the USB and clicked for it to play.

Listening to Ivan and Vesna's conversation, Marko heard Dragan named and dismissed.

Marko already knew Dragan was the main dealer and had taken over Milan's role. He thought Ivan and Vesna underestimated Dragan, but that wasn't his business.

He heard how Jovanović had been following him under Ivan's orders. But again, he'd already had that confirmed to him by Ivan.

And then he heard Ivan asking what should be done about Milica. Vesna didn't reply, but Marko knew what the silence meant. Milica had listened to the recording, had heard her own death sentence.

A swirl of emotions stopped Marko from thinking clearly. Guilt, sadness and anger all mingled. He had to focus. Milica couldn't be saved. He had to concentrate on his wife and son.

Marko tried to work out how useful the recording was. It didn't tell him anything new. Ivan had already given the game away, deliberately to put Marko in a bind. Ivan and Vesna were the kingpins of the Balkan drug route. Marko changed his thought. He'd previously guessed, but it was obvious from the recording, that Vesna was the kingpin, or the queenpin. Dragan was the city's main dealer and now in charge of the route.

The recording wasn't enough to convict either Ivan or Vesna. It could lead to arrests and investigation but who was going to investigate the Police Chief?

Even if the Interior Minister managed to get non-corrupt police to carry out the investigation, Marko's wife and son would be dead before the case got to court.

The only advantage was that Marko had the USB in his possession. Maybe it could be used as a bargaining tool somehow.

It didn't offer Marko much hope, but it meant he hadn't completely given up. He pocketed the device and gave the flat a final glance before heading out to his car.

Chapter 33

Goran was warming up on court as Marko took his seat. Branka had arrived earlier and saved a place next to her. They grimaced a smile at each other. Their son's tennis match was respite from the danger they faced. Marko was sorry he hadn't been in time to wish his son good luck, but Goran was almost a young man. He would cope. He had his coach.

Goran started erratically, an ace followed by a double fault. He hit a backhand winner then a forehand into the net. The other player, a Bulgarian, hardly had to do anything. Goran was winning and losing the points all on his own. The whole set followed the same pattern, Goran winning one game then losing one.

Marko hoped his drunken behaviour the night before hadn't had an adverse effect on his son, disturbing Goran's focus. He dismissed his thoughts as vanity. Goran's temperament wasn't ruled by his father's actions.

With the set at five games each, Goran lost control of his temper. Angry at himself for missing a simply volley, he managed to lose his service game. He gripped his racquet to stop himself from smashing it into the ground.

Watching his son, Marko couldn't help but smile. When Goran was a kid he'd never been able to control his temper if he lost.

Branka and Marko had constantly disagreed about how to play tennis with Goran. Branka thought Marko should go easy, let Goran win every time. Marko thought the opposite. How would Goran ever improve or learn how to deal with winning and losing if he was always given an easy ride?

By the time Goran was thirteen, Marko had to play to his maximum to win. A year later it was even. And now Marko didn't stand a chance.

Next to Marko, Branka was biting her lip, ready to cry if her son lost the set. Marko wasn't nervous. Maybe with a death threat looming over his family, a tennis game didn't seem so important. Or maybe he believed in his son.

On court, Goran smacked the Bulgarian's serve right back at him to win the first point. He did the same for the rest of the game. With the Bulgarian thrown of balance and Goran having regained his focus, Goran went on to win the tie break seven points to one.

For the rest of the match, the Bulgarian didn't know what hit him. Goran served one ace after another and returned serves with unnerving accuracy down the line. The match ended 7-6, 6- 0, 6-0.

Goran turned to face the seats where Marko and Branka had stood to applaud. His game face on, Goran simply nodded, before breaking into a grin. Marko seeing both his young son and the young man he would become.

While Goran warmed down and changed, Marko and Branka waited in the court's café.

Branka had cried anyway, despite Goran winning. Without thinking, she kissed Marko on the lips. For a second, the two of them were in proud parent unison, as they had been for fifteen years. Until the last few days.

In a flash, it all came back to Branka. Marko's affair. Milica's murder. The death threat hanging over their family. She couldn't stop the tears coming again, out of helplessness this time. She turned and fled to the toilets.

Marko exhaled. Like Branka, for an hour and a half, he'd managed to forget all his problems as he watched Goran play. But they hadn't gone away. As if to make the point, the Interior Minister was walking over to him, another man ambling next to him. The Minister did the introductions:

'Inspector, this is Karl Babel. He's a scout for Pilić Academy.'

Marko got a firm handshake from the tennis scout. The man had obviously been athletic at one point and still had a firm grip. But his red cheeks betrayed a fondness for alcohol and his wandering eye suggested his attention was more on women than tennis these days. He smiled at Marko, said a sentence in German. The Minister asked Marko:

'You understand German?'

'Tell him to speak Serbian so the whole world can understand.'

The Minister smiled:

'I'll translate. He said he saw the end of your son's match and was very impressed. Only the first round of course, but if he carries on maybe he'll meet my son in the final.'

'He said all that?'

'It was a liberal translation.'

The tennis scout had lost interest, his eyes roaming to a bargirl. He motioned that he was going to get a drink and left the two other men.

The Minister asked:

'So, any news for me?'

'Nothing you don't already know.'

'You understand the urgency?'

'I understand.'

'And you understand the consequences of not providing evidence of corruption?'

'I understand that too.'

Marko gripped the USB bugging device burning a hole in his pocket. The Interior Minister would love to get his hands on it. The recording would be enough to set up an investigation into police corruption. But Marko had no intention of handing it over. Unless he came up with some new plan, he was siding with Ivan. His boss had proved he could order a murder of someone close to Marko. The Minister just bluffed. Marko shrugged:

'As soon as I have anything, I'll let you know.'

The Minister didn't like Marko's dismissive tone. As his wife and son joined at his side, he realised it was the same contempt he'd often been shown at home. And by the German Interior Minister. Hoffman had called that morning with an ultimatum. If the route wasn't under control within twenty-four hours, the Germans would no longer back him. It was time to show Inspector Despotović that his words were backed by action. The Minister left, got out his phone and called Dejan Tomić.

Chapter 34

As the Minister and his family walked out of the tennis centre, Marko was joined by his wife who asked:

'What did the Minister want?'

Marko shrugged:

'He introduced me to the German tennis scout.'

Marko gestured at Karl Babel, who was attempting to chat up the bargirl. Marko said:

'The guy is more interested in scouting females than spotting tennis talent. The Minister is full of shit.'

Branka had resigned herself to the situation. She had to trust Marko. If he said the only way to stay alive was to side with police corruption and go against the Minister, then this was this.

She said:

'I checked the Minister's university records. He did a semester in Bonn University as an exchange student back in the nineties. A quick internet search showed the German Interior Minister was there at the same time. I made some calls and got confirmation they attended the same course. Obviously, that's nothing in itself, but odd that their shared past has never been made public.'

Marko thought about the information Branka had given him. It further suggested that the Minister had some deal with his German counterpart, but wasn't hard evidence of any wrongdoing.

Branka smiled:

'Goran was amazing, wasn't he?'

'Yes, he was.'

For a few minutes, shared parental pride overcame any death threats hanging over their family. Marko frowned:

'Taking his time to get changed though.'

Marko looked towards the changing rooms. He saw Dejan Tomić striding from that direction, Dejan glancing Marko's way as he exited the tennis centre. Marko thought the Minister had already left, but he wouldn't have left without Dejan. Fear grabbed Marko.

Without a word to his wife, Marko set off to the changing rooms. Yanking open the door, he told himself it was probably just paranoia. His fear was that Dejan had harmed Goran. But maybe the former Red Beret had been there for another reason.

The changing rooms seemed to be empty. With the afternoon session in full swing, all the players were on court. Marko called out:

'Goran?'

No answer. Marko told himself he was being stupid. Goran must have left the changing rooms without Marko noticing. Maybe he was with his coach, going over the match.

Checking the showers, Marko froze.

Goran was slumped on the floor. Marko's blood went cold. No, his son couldn't be dead. He hardly dared take a step forward. Almost unable to speak, he whispered:

'Goran?'

Goran's head slowly lifted. Marko exhaled. His son was alive. Their eyes locked.

Marko couldn't read his son's look. He saw pain and bewilderment, but didn't know what it meant. Marko's eyes lowered to see Goran was cradling his right arm, which was swollen and disjointed at the wrist.

Marko knelt by his son, gently took the arm. Goran grimaced in pain. The wrist was clearly broken, the hand hanging at an unnatural angle. Marko had to ask:

'What happened?'

As he sat there, Goran felt pathetic. He'd been so easily overpowered. In one swift movement, the Minister's driver had snapped his wrist and put him on the floor. His self pity spread as he realised that any possible tennis career was over. It wasn't just the Pančevo Open. He wasn't going to recover from a broken wrist.

Goran looked up at Marko. He was a child and his dad couldn't help. He'd looked up to his dad all his life. But now he knew there were people who could hurt and that his dad couldn't protect him. What was his dad involved in? Goran spoke through the pain:

'He said to tell you this is a warning, so you take it seriously.'

Marko clenched his jaw in fury. He was pretty sure he knew, but he still asked:

'Who did this to you?'

'The Minister's driver.'

Marko wanted to run out of the tennis centre and shoot Dejan Tomić in the head. But the Interior Minister's chauffeur would already have driven off.

Marko put an arm around Goran and lifted him to a standing position. He had failed as a father to protect his son. He wanted to lash out, to cry, to be sick. But he had to at least show his son he was still there for him.

As they made their way out of the changing rooms, Branka rushed over.

'What happened?'

Goran was too distraught to talk. He wasn't crying, just silently devastated.

Marko couldn't face explaining to his wife. He focused on what they needed to do:

'We need to get to a hospital.'

Branka wasn't stupid. She understood what Marko's answer meant:

'You said nothing would happen to him!'

People at the bar looked around. Branka turned to attend her son. The German tennis scout grimaced as he saw

Goran's arm, said something in German. It was probably sympathetic, but Marko didn't care. In one stride, Marko reached the tennis scout and punched him full force in the nose. Karl Babel fell back against the bar, blood spurting from his nose and glasses flying.

Marko turned back to his wife and son, who were making their way to the exit. It had been pointless to hit the tennis scout, but it had at least released some fury.

Marko drove on autopilot into Belgrade, unaware of the route he took. The car was full with silence. Branka sat in the back with Goran, but he was oblivious to her comfort.

Marko pulled into the hospital, the same one where Goran had been born. And where he had talked with Milica after her car crash.

At the reception, Marko told Branka to wait with Goran while he sorted getting the wrist seen to. He knew they would be made to wait. A broken wrist wasn't life threatening. It had to be x-rayed, put in the right position, set in plaster. With the bureaucracy in Belgrade, that would take all night and Marko wasn't prepared to wait. He took out his police ID and his gun.

A few minutes later, Goran was taken to have his wrist looked at by a doctor. As Branka went to go with Goran, Marko held her back for a second:

'I have to sort some things out.'

'You're leaving us here?'

'Nothing else will happen. I'm going to make sure of it. Call me when you're home.'

Marko didn't wait to see his wife's reaction. He exited the hospital and got his car in gear.

He had underestimated the Interior Minister. It should have confirmed to Marko that he needed to join the Chief of Police in taking down the Minister. Eliminate one threat with another. But Marko had had enough of threats from all angles.

Chapter 35

Dragan was sitting in Café Insomnia with his third espresso in front of him and a smouldering Davidoff between his fingers. The café was the right place to be as he hadn't slept the previous night.

Partizan had drawn with Red Star, which was an anti-climax. You couldn't celebrate the win or express anger in defeat. After the team's midweek exertions versus Spurs, the players didn't have enough energy to beat their rivals. Dragan should have gone into the changing rooms at half time and given them all a line of coke.

Back in Arkan's day, when he'd bankrolled Obelić FC, Serbia's national hero would have just gone on and ordered the opposing team to lose or be shot. But times had changed.

And if Dragan was honest, he didn't care as much as he used to. Maybe he was becoming more responsible. After the match, he'd stayed up for the dawn pick up in the Dorćol Depot.

Jars of *ajvar* containing heroin being unloaded and stored while the rest went on to Germany.

Milan was dead, but the route continued working.

Unable to sleep, he'd called Biljana. But even fucking her hadn't been enough. She'd suggested they do some coke, but Dragan had resisted. He wanted to be alert, but not cocaine-induced. So he'd come to the café and waited. Because he knew someone would visit him. It was just a matter of who.

Dragan wasn't surprised when Despotović walked through the door. It was either going to be him or Jovanović. The only surprising thing was that the he was carrying a laptop not a gun.

Marko strode up to Dragan and set the laptop on the table. He'd been home to take the heroin from its hiding place under the pepper plant, but that was in the car for later use. He said:

'You got somewhere we can talk?'

Dragan asked:

'Straight down to business eh. You don't want a coffee?'

'We can do it here, but didn't think you'd want other people hearing what's on this.'

Marko held up the USB stick.

Dragan looked at him, trying to work out if he had something worth listening to.

There weren't many people in the café and they'd do what he told them, but he was ready to be cautious. He downed his espresso, stubbed out his cigarette and said:

'As you want. Let's go in the back.'

In the backroom, Dragan gestured for Marko to take a seat, ever the host. Seated across a table from each other, Marko started:

'Ivan wants me to take over as go-between.'

'I guessed. And I guess Jovanović will be eliminated.'

'You guessed right. But I don't want to do a deal with Ivan.'

'No?'

'No. I want to do a deal with you.'

'Yea?'

Dragan was ready to laugh. The night before, Despotović had been humiliated by Dragan's men, but he showed no sign of it. He just kept coming back with his direct approach.

Marko set up the laptop, inserted the USB stick and said:

'Listen to this.'

Dragan indulged the Inspector and listened to the recording. He heard how Ivan and Vesna were dismissive of him, how Ivan had ordered Jovanović to follow Despotović and how Vesna and requested Milica be eliminated.

When the recording finished, Dragan lit up a Davidoff. He wasn't surprised by Ivan and Vesna's attitude, but it wasn't good for other people to hear him being dissed like that. Sure enough, Marko said:

'Doesn't look like they think much of you.'

Dragan looked across at Despotović. He could simply shoot the Inspector in the head and keep the recording. Then no-one would know he'd been disrespected. But Despotović didn't seem to be disrespectful:

'I think they're making a mistake. That's why I want to do a deal with you.'

Dragan was still thinking if he should take out his gun or not. He said:

'I guess you've got another recording?'

'No, that's the only one.'

Dragan eyed Despotović. Was the Inspector telling the truth? Dragan decided to hear what Despotović had to say:

'So what's the deal you want to make?'

'We kill Ivan, get Vesna arrested and you take over the business.'

This time, Dragan had to laugh. He regained his composure and said:

'Man, you crack me up. How do you know I won't go to Ivan and we kill you?'

'Guess I trust you.'

'Really?'

'Okay, not trust. Maybe respect.'

Dragan raised an eyebrow in doubt. Up until now, the Inspector had been honest.

Marko shrugged:

'Fuck it. You and me doing a deal has advantages for both of us. This is this.'

Dragan nodded:

'Okay. Go on.'

'If I don't team up with Ivan, my family are in danger. If I do team up with him, the Interior Minister's threatening to kill them.'

'The Interior Minister?'

'Not him personally. His driver. Dejan Tomić. Guess you know who he is.'

'Former Red Beret.'

'That's him. He broke my son's wrist an hour or so ago. A warning. Like when Jovanović killed Milica. If it was him. Doesn't matter. I'm fucked either way. So my only choice is to get rid of Ivan and Jovanović. And Dejan while I'm at it.'

'That's quite a bit of killing.'

'That's why I need you. In return you get to take over the heroin route.'

'I can see how getting rid of Ivan and Vesna helps me, but why do I need to kill Dejan?'

Dragan wasn't afraid of anyone, but there was no point risking his life for no reason.

Marko showed the photo of Biljana getting out of the Minister's Audi, Dejan holding open the car door in front of the German Ambassador's residence. Being mostly honest, Marko explained:

'The Minister and Dejan want to take control of the route because they've made a deal with the Germans. Biljana was used in the deal. It wasn't her fault. Dejan threatened her family so she had no choice. After I saw the photo, I made her tell me. If we get rid of Ivan and Vesna but not Dejan, you'll have an enemy and no backing.'

'You've got a lot of balls telling me all this shit.'

'I've got nothing to lose.'

'So what's the plan? We just round everyone up and kill them?'

'Pretty much. I go to Ivan, say we're all meeting to agree that I'm taking over from Jova. Apart from Jovanović, we all know he's a goner so that won't be a problem. While Ivan is there, we take him out. And I'm going to do my best to get Dejan there too.'

'What about Vesna?'

'She'll be arrested.'

'How's that?'

'With the recording and the heroin that's found in her place.'

'The heroin you stole from Jovanović no doubt. I heard about that. But I'm hardly going to let you use the recording with my name mentioned.'

Marko gestured at the laptop:

'Delete the first part of the recording, give me back the USB and we've got a deal.'

Chapter 36

As soon as Nebojša received Marko's text, he got ready to meet his colleague. The message was simple: 'Hotel car park. 1 hour.' Nebojša knew Marko meant Hotel Intercontinental and was being vague in case their phones were being monitored. He'd been waiting twenty-four hours for news from Marko. Had Ivan and Vesna been recorded saying anything incriminating?

Marko was already parked up outside the Intercontinental when Nebojša pulled in. Marko thought it was as good a place as any to meet. He just hoped he wasn't going to follow in Arkan's footsteps and be killed. In case Jova was still trailing him, Marko could see any approaching vehicles. Ivan had said he'd called Jova off, but Marko wasn't taking any chances.

As Nebojša parked next to him, Marko gestured for the rookie to join him in the Ford. With the air con on, they wouldn't sweat to death as they nearly had in Nebojša's old Yugo. Marko was already getting the sweats as his hangover kicked in anyway.

Nebojša got in, eager to know what was happening. Before he'd even shut the door, he asked:

'Did you get anything? I was waiting to hear from you.'

Marko nodded. The rookie was unaware of Milica's murder or Goran's broken wrist. He didn't know of the threat to Marko's family and the predicament he was in. Marko wasn't about to fill him in. He opened the laptop and played the recording from the USB device.

Nebojša listened, whistled and said:

'Can't believe it. So surely we have to go to the Interior Minister now.'

Marko put the laptop away and handed the USB stick to Nebojša:

'Yes, you can take it to him.'

'Me?'

'He trusts you.'

'Why not you?'

'Better from you. Take it to him and he can get a judge to sign off a warrant to search Vesna's place. Tell the Minister the search has to be done at dawn. The Minister can go to the judge's house, take him from the dinner table or bed or wherever he is. Then you go to Viktor, get the drugs squad boys to go with you and arrest Vesna.'

'Viktor's not going to take orders from me.'

'That's why you have the Minister and warrant with you. With Ivan not around, Viktor won't have a choice.'

'Why won't Ivan be around?'

'He'll be busy with me.'

'What about Jovanović?'

'Jova will be with me too.'

Nebojša wasn't stupid. He squinted at Marko, asked:

'What does that mean?'

'It means what it means. Ivan and Jova will be with me. We need to separate them from Vesna and Viktor. I don't know if Viktor's corrupt or just loyal to Ivan. Either way, he won't want to go against the Chief. But if Ivan's not around, Viktor will want to make a major drug bust.'

Nebojša wondered if he was being stupid:

'How do we know there's going to be a bust? We've got the recording, but what if there's no drugs as hard evidence when we search Vesna's place?'

Marko reached under his seat and took out the packet of heroin. He said:

'Here's the evidence you'll find.'

Nebojša wasn't happy. His first reaction was:

'I thought you said you threw it away?'

'I retrieved it. Thought it might be useful.'

Nebojša shook his head. Ivan and Vesna had incriminated themselves as drugs kingpins, but that didn't mean evidence could be planted on them:

'We can't do that.'

'Then we can't arrest Vesna. You make the arrest, you'll make a name for yourself.'

Nebojša was feeling more and more uneasy:

'Why are you ready to let me be the face of the case?'

'I told you, I'll be dealing with Ivan while you arrest Vesna. And I'll be honest with you. You'll make a name for yourself, but you'll make enemies too. Even with Ivan being found out, no police are going to be happy about it. Me, I want a quiet life with my family. You've got a career ahead of you.'

Nebojša needed time to take it all in. Yes, he was ambitious and he wanted to root out corruption. But planting evidence was corrupt itself. How would they even manage to do it?

He knew he shouldn't ask, but he did:

'Not that I'm agreeing, but how would the heroin be planted?'

'Distraction technique.'

'What's that?'

Marko suddenly looked over Nebojša's shoulder and shouted:

'Fuck, they're coming.'

Nebojša turned to look and Marko dropped the packet of heroin on his lap.

Nebojša turned back around. He looked down at the heroin then up at Marko:

'Fuck, I thought you were serious.'

'I am. You go into Vesna's with the Minister and Viktor's men. While everyone is looking in one place, you plant the smack and let someone else find it.'

'And where exactly do I plant it?'

'Improvise. Try the kitchen. Put it in a jar of Panić Ajvar if there is one.'

Marko took the heroin and wiped off his fingerprints. He took out some plastic gloves and wrapped them around the packet.

Nebojša watched Marko. He didn't know if he could do this. He'd threatened the council office receptionist, but that was just an empty threat. Actually carrying it out was different. But this was a chance to clean up corruption and make a name for himself.

Marko held out the packet of heroin:

'So?'

Chapter 37

Ivan stubbed out his Marlboro and stood up to leave. It was the end of the working day. He'd given Despotović time to agree to the deal. He could give him another hour or so, but decisions had to be made. Despotović or Jovanović? One of the inspectors would have to die by the end of the night. That was easy to solve.

More troubling was the missing bugging device. Nothing had been found at the flat of Despotović's mistress. Had it really just vanished? And what was on it? If any of his conversations with Vesna had been recorded, they couldn't be made public.

The Interior Minister was also proving to be stubborn. Having German backing and a former Red Beret as his driver was making the Minister cocky. Ivan and Vesna had put off the Albanians. They couldn't let the Germans get hold of the route. Ivan in fact hoped Despotović would come with something on the Minister and join the team. As Ivan stared out of the window, he saw Despotović's Ford pull in to the car park down below.

Marko parked his car next to Jova's BMW. So his colleague was in work and hadn't been following him. Ivan had kept his word so far. Either Marko or Jova would be killed that night.

It was a strange knowledge to have.

As Marko got out of his car, the strangeness stayed with him. It felt like he didn't know his workplace for the last ten years, as if he was entering police headquarters for the first time. And maybe the last.

Marko had an urge to turn around and drive away. Go to his wife and son in the hospital, stay with them until the end. It would be easier to just stop and give up. Let Ivan or Jova or Dejan come and kill his family. He kept walking forward and entered headquarters.

Jova wasn't at his desk as Marko made his way to the Chief's office. Probably with his buddy Viktor. Ivan was waiting for him, newly lit cigarette in his hand as he gestured for Marko to shut the door behind him.

Marko took a seat across from Ivan, who said:

'Glad you could make it. I was just about to go home. So what have you decided?'

'I'm in.'

'Good. Got anything for me on the Minister?'

'Yes. You're right, he's trying to take control of the route. He's promised Dejan Tomić a job as head of security. My guess is he's aiming to be Prime Minister and gain power in that way.

They're even planning to take out Dragan.'

'Do you have evidence of this?'

'No. Just what Dejan told one of the silicon girls, who told me. She's caught between Dejan and Dragan.'

Ivan took a drag of his Marlboro. The second-hand tale wasn't anything that could be used officially to discredit the Minister. Yet Despotović was clearly better than Jovanović at digging up info. He felt vindicated about his decision to swap inspectors.

Marko had a headache from Ivan's cigarette smoke. Or maybe his hangover was hitting home. He made his next move:

'I've been to Dragan already. He knows I'll be the next go-between.'

'Really?'

Ivan was impressed by Despotović's initiative, but also on the alert. Would Dragan agree to this without word from

229

Ivan? As if to allay his suspicions, Despotović held out his phone. The message displayed was: 'All agreed. Dawn meeting. Dorćol.' It was Dragan's number. Ivan asked:

'What's 'all'?'

Marko put his phone away and explained:

'You, me, Dragan and Jova meet. As you said, Jova has to go. It's not revenge, but it won't work with both of us. The dawn meeting in Dorćol is to set us all up as bait. We appear to be doing a drugs deal. Dejan Tomić will be around on behalf of the Minister to catch us at it.

Instead, we take him out.'

Ivan nearly choked as he inhaled. He got his breath back and said:

'That's quite a plan.'

Marko shrugged:

'Dragan agreed to it.'

'How do we know Tomić will be there?'

'I tell him to come. Say I'm setting you and Dragan up.'

Ivan pointed his cigarette at Marko:

'You know if it goes wrong you'll be killed?'

'I know. Look, a few hours ago Dejan broke my son's wrist. He won't play tennis again. The Minister's getting tough. I've chosen my side. I want Jova dead. And I want Dejan dead. After that, I know the score. In return, my family are kept safe. That's the deal as I see it. I'm ready to do my part.'

Marko and Ivan looked each other in the eyes through the cigarette smoke that had filled the office. Marko was desperate for water. The heat of the day had got to him. Not to mention dehydration from his drunken night. He couldn't keep going on adrenaline forever.

Ivan took a final drag of his Marlboro. He had to admire Despotović's courage. The Inspector had been put in a no-win situation, had chosen the best option available and was standing proud.

As long as Despotović didn't become too brave and try something stupid. The Chief of Police stubbed out his cigarette.

Chapter 38

The Interior Minister was sitting in the back of his Audi, which was parked up on Nemanjina Street. Dejan Tomić was on guard outside. It was only a few hundred metres away from where Prime Minister Đinđić had been assassinated. That was twelve years ago and times had changed, but the Minister wasn't taking any chances.

The Minister already thought of Dejan as his right-hand man. When he became Prime Minister, Dejan's position as Head of Security would be the first appointment he made. Dejan's actions had made things happen.

Željko had never resorted to violence before, but it clearly worked. Within a few hours, Inspector Despotović had magically turned up evidence of police corruption. It had been delivered via the young inspector, Nebojša Vranac.

He hadn't had time to question why the younger inspector had been entrusted with the task.

As soon as he'd heard the recording, he'd gone straight to the law courts a few blocks down from his government office. The Chief Judge had already left his chambers, but Željko knew which bar to find him in. With Inspector Vranac at his side and the USB device in his hand, the Minister had got the judge's interest. A hushed promise of fine French wine had obtained the judge's signature.

Željko had the warrant for Vesna Panić's arrest in his hands. Now he was waiting for Inspector Despotović to come and explain how the Chief of Police would be apprehended.

Marko took in the sights as he drove along Nemanjina Street. To the left was where Đinđić had been killed. Marko hoped it wouldn't give him bad ideas. He felt like killing the Interior Minister, but he knew Dejan Tomić would be there. Marko wasn't a former Red Beret with connections who could shoot a politician in the head and walk away.

To the right was the former Army Headquarters that NATO had bombed. Fifteen years later and the building was still in ruins. Unlike Germany after World War Two, Serbia hadn't received any reparations. Even if they had, the money would just be 'lost' in politicians' pockets.

Up ahead was the Interior Minister's Audi. Dejan Tomić was standing nearby in the shade.

Marko pulled up and took a breath. As a father, how did he face the man who had broken his son's wrist? Marko checked his phone. Still no message from Branka. He'd asked her to phone as soon as they were ready to leave the hospital. Marko put away his phone and got out of the car.

Dejan stepped out of the shade. Marko was ready to eyeball the former Red Beret, but Dejan was all nonchalance as he opened the Audi's door for Marko to get in.

With Dejan in the driver's seat, Marko sat in the back with the Interior Minister. The Minister started with an apology:

'It is a great shame that we had to resort to violence. However, it does seem to have achieved the necessary results. I see you have entrusted Inspector Vranac with the case.'

'Did you get the warrant?'

The Minister was momentarily taken aback by Marko's interruption, but he understood. The Inspector was upset about his son. Željko tapped the warrant on his lap:

'I do indeed have it. Inspector Vranac outlined the arrest procedure, but perhaps you can explain in your own words.'

'It's just like Nebojša told you. The two of you go to Viktor Antić just before dawn. The drug squad raids Vesna's place and you'll find enough heroin to arrest her. Combined with the USB recording, she'll go down.'

'How can we be sure heroin will be found?'

'You'll find it.'

'I admire your confidence. A pity that you couldn't have delivered this earlier. It would have saved unnecessary harm. Now, I see how Vesna Panić can be arrested. But you haven't mentioned the Chief of Police.'

'At dawn, the Chief of Police, Inspector Jovanović and Dragan Mladić will all be in the Dorćol depot. I will be there with them. A deal is going down and I've got myself on board.'

'Do you propose to arrest them all?'

'We're not going to arrest them.'

The Minister was puzzled, but before he could ask anything, Marko continued:

'We're going to kill them.'

'What?'

For a second, the Minister's eloquence had vanished. Marko shrugged:

'You want corruption rooted out and you want the heroin route sorted. This is how you do it. You've already gone down the path of violence, so this is the next step.'

The Minister regained his politician's lexis:

'Obviously I cannot have any direct involvement in this matter. And while I admire your determination, I wonder how you're single-handedly going to overpower three men.'

'I'll need help.'

Marko turned and looked into the driver's mirror, meeting Dejan Tomić's eyes. Dejan stared back. Marko wasn't going to win the contest, so he turned back to face the Minister and said:

'You had my son's wrist broken. I won't ever forgive that, but I'm willing to eliminate police corruption and change who controls the heroin route. After that, my family are left alone.'

The Interior Minister nodded:

'Sounds reasonable.'

The Minister turned to his right-hand man in the driver's seat:

'Dejan, what do you think?'

Chapter 39

Branka was waiting for Marko when he returned to the flat. She'd texted him that they were back from the hospital. Marko checked in on his son. Goran was fast asleep, his arm in a cast.

Branka said:

'He took painkillers and went to bed as soon as we got home.'

Marko followed Branka into the kitchen. She made him coffee and he said:

'Here's the deal. I'm going to tell you everything I've been looking into. If I'm dead by tomorrow, you can print everything. If I'm alive, you have to forget it.'

'Marko, I don't want anyone to die.'

'Writing it down is what might keep you two alive. So do you want the story or not?'

'Tell me.'

Marko told her. Branka took notes as she listened to Marko's story of corruption. After Marko had told her everything, she asked:

'How much of this can you prove?'

'Not much. I've given a recording to the Minister. Sure if you ask him, he'll let you hear it.'

'I thought you didn't trust the Minister.'

'I don't. He's as corrupt as the Chief of Police. Far as I can see, he just wants the route cleared because the Germans have a plan for it. But I can't prove that either.'

Branka shook her head in dismay:

'Sometimes I don't understand Serbians. I love my country, but we do our best to fuck it up.'

'I was thinking something similar just last night.'

'You're a good man Marko.'

'Not really, I'm just a man trying to keep his family alive.'

Marko checked the time. They'd spent all night going over everything. Now it was time to go. He got up, went into the hallway and holstered his Zastava. Branka followed him, said:

'Don't go.'

'I have to. Will you have breakfast ready?'

Marko smiled at his wife. It was a sad smile, but genuine as he said:

'I love you.'

Branka sighed. She stopped herself from crying and said:

'I love you too.'

'If I'm not back for breakfast, run the story next to my obituary.'

As Marko left the flat, he wondered what would happen if he didn't return for breakfast. Had he been reckless? If he didn't succeed, would Dejan or Ivan or whoever survived come after his family? Surely if Marko was dead, Branka and Goran no longer needed to have their lives threatened.

With his Serpico sunglasses on, Marko zig-zagged out of New Belgrade. A feeling of déjà vu shivered through his body. Less than a week earlier, he had left his wife in the early hours a happy family man on the way to his mistress. Now, as the sun rose over the Danube, Marko was driving to someone's death. Maybe his own.

Marko drove over the bridge and turned left after Kalemegdan. He pulled up alongside the Minister's Audi. Alone in the driver's seat was Dejan Tomić.

Dejan lowered his window as Marko pulled up. For Dejan, it was all a matter of what operation worked. He didn't work for the Minister for any political reasons. It was simply because when the Interior Minister became Prime Minister, Dejan would become Head of Security.

Ever since the Red Berets had been disbanded, Dejan had felt ill at ease. As Head of Security, he could restore order. Arkan had been a great leader. Dejan aimed to be the same. But he recognised it would have to be done through official means.

He waited for the Inspector to lower his window, then gave instructions:

'I'll follow you then park out of sight. You have your meeting. Once the others start to leave, I'll take them out one by one.'

Marko had to laugh at Dejan's military precision. The guy had no feelings. Marko attempted a joke:

'Just don't shoot me.'

'I have no reason to. You have an agreement with the Minister and could be useful in the future. Just don't let any personal feelings get in the way and you will stay alive.'

Marko nodded. There was no point prolonging the conversation. Dejan was hardcore. He had broken Goran's wrist because it was deemed necessary. He would kill Marko or not depending if it was required. Doubts crept into Marko's mind, but it was too late to turn back. He drove down to Dorćol, Dejan behind him.

Inspector Jovanović snorted a line of coke before departing his houseboat. Walking towards his car, he no longer cared that he'd spent the night alone. He'd tried it on with a couple of stunners from Silicon Street, but they all knew who he was and what he was after. It would be one night, not a long-term catch.

Jova had thought fuck it, he would do coke on his own. He was aware his habit had spiralled out of control, but he couldn't stop it. Deep in debt, he'd ended up selling smack for Dragan to pay what he owed for the coke.

Not really remembering how he'd driven there, Jova pulled up outside the Chief's residence in Senjak. He looked with bitterness at the huge house. The Chief had risen to the top with Jova's help. What had Jova got out of it?

The Chief stepped out from his gated entrance where he'd been smoking. He flicked his cigarette away and walked with purpose towards Jovanović's BMW. The Inspector had never learnt to be subtle. Ivan hoped Despotović would prove a good replacement and not change his mind.

In case of all eventualities, Ivan had been to the firing range the night before, making sure he still had his aim. The handgun he carried was one he'd secretly taken when they raided the Zemun clan's Šilerova Street base.

Jovanović would be the first to go. If Despotović was really on side, then it would be the three of them versus Dejan and the odds were in their favour. If Despotović had secretly sided with the Interior Minister, it would be two against two. But Ivan felt confident with Dragan on his team. He was impatient to settle the matter.

Ivan hadn't told Vesna about the dawn meeting, not wanting to worry her. He'd told her that everything had been sorted with Despotović and his mistress. So he needed to show that was correct.

The Chief of Police got in the passenger side of Inspector Jovanović's BMW. Jovanović got the car moving and spoke rapidly:

'Morning Chief. So what's the story? Why have we got to meet Dragan so early? What's so important? And are you sure Despot is good for this?'

The Chief of Police glanced sideways at Jovanović. He was coked up yet again. It would be the last time Ivan had to be concerned. He'd already explained things to Jovanović, but he went through it point by point again:

'Yes, I'm sure Despotović will be a good addition to the team. The alternative is that his family will be killed. He has motive to do well.'

'If you say so. He still owes me though.'

'That's one of the reasons for the meeting. He will give you back what he took and a truce will be called.'

'But why does it have to be at dawn?'

'To show him how the delivery works. And Dragan has a new idea about the delivery he wants to show us.'

'He didn't tell me about that.'

'He told me.'

Jova recognised that he had been put in his place. He sniffed and made his way to the depot.

Dragan drove through Dorćol with the windows open to get some fresh air. He quickly closed them. The smell of sewage permeated the air. At the side of the street, a stray dog was sniffing the air.

Inside his Audi, Dragan smelt of sex. An hour earlier, he'd given Biljana a final fuck.

Despotović had tried to make out that she had no choice but to do what Dejan requested, but everyone had a choice. He wasn't going to harm her, but once Dejan was killed, Biljana would be out on her silicon tits. That would be her punishment.

Dejan wasn't going to be easy to kill. As a former Red Beret, he was no doubt a better shot than Dragan. So Dragan had also brought his hunting knife with him.

Marko was the first to reach the meeting point at the old docks. Dejan had taken up a position behind a storage container with his sniper's rifle. It was a long shot to where Marko was standing, but he still felt exposed. That was all part of the risk he was taking.

Jovanović drove along the riverside with the Chief of Police in the passenger seat, parking up near Marko's Ford. The Chief got out first, assuming control as always as he nodded at Marko. Jova followed, sniffing as he wiped his nose.

Dragan cruised in and parked his Audi between Marko's Ford and Jova's BMW. He swung out of the car and grinned:

'The holy trinity of Belgrade's police force.'

Jovanović reacted first:

'Cut the crap Dragan. What have you got to show us? And Despot, where the fuck are my hundred dolls?'

The Chief of Police shook his head. Jovanović had spoken out of turn for the last time. Taking out his handgun, Ivan shot Jovanović in the head.

The gunshot died and silence reigned in the deserted docks.

Dragan was impressed. Ivan clearly wasn't there to mess about.

Marko stared down at Jova's dead body, blood pooling around his head. He hadn't expected Ivan to be so quick. What had Marko expected? He'd set up the showdown and now it was in motion. One down, two to go.

The Chief of Police looked over at Marko:

'That's the first matter dealt with. What about the second?'

Marko nodded at the nearest haulage container. Ivan and Dragan both understood and went into stealth mode. Ivan gestured for Dragan to take one side and Marko the other.

Behind the container, Dejan was on red alert. Someone being shot had not been on the agenda.

If plans had changed, he needed to improvise. He sprung out, dropped to a crouch and took aim with his Heckler and Koch rifle.

The Chief of Police, the Inspector and Dragan were all in sight but at a fair distance and ducking behind their cars. Dejan shot out the windows of the BMW before moving back behind the container.

Ivan, Marko and Dragan were all crouched behind different cars, having seen Dejan open fire. With his Zastava in his hand, Marko felt the mist before he saw it. Feeling a tickle on his neck, he turned to see the dawn mist roll of the Danube. Within seconds, the mist had enveloped the cars and haulage containers.

It was now a matter of chance who would survive.

Chapter 40

Nebojša drove the Interior Minister to police headquarters half an hour before dawn. Dejan had taken the Minister's Audi, so Nebojša was acting as chauffeur in his old Yugo. The Minister quite enjoyed the downgrade, feeling invigorated to be part of an investigation.

Nebojša was more apprehensive. He could feel the adrenaline building in the knowledge that they were on the precipice of a major case. But it could go wrong at any stage. For a start, there was no guarantee that they would persuade Viktor to help them.

After earlier enquiries, Nebojša had found out that Viktor was in work that night and a phone call to headquarters confirmed the lead inspector of the anti-narcotics unit was inside the building.

Nebojša and the Minister found Viktor sitting around with two his drugs squad guys, swapping banter as they filed reports. Night often brought more crime than day, but midweek was quieter than weekends and the unit weren't doing any major surveillance.

Viktor looked up at the strange pairing of rookie inspector and Interior Minister. With the Chief's recent suspicions, the Minister was the last person Viktor expected to turn up at headquarters. The Minister tried to take charge of the situation straight away:

'We need to make an urgent arrest concerning a major drugs kingpin. The Chief of Police is unavailable, so I require you and two of your men.'

Viktor raised his eyebrows at his two men. Leaning back in his chair, he said:

'Yea? So who is this kingpin?'

The Interior Minister brandished the search warrant and stated:

'Vesna Panić.'

Viktor looked at the warrant and frowned. The warrant had been signed by the head judge that afternoon. This was real and fast. But why hadn't Viktor known anything about this? Why was the Minister delivering the warrant? And where was the Chief of Police?

Only the day before, the Chief had told Viktor to keep an eye on the Minister, who was suspected of having ties with the Germans, who in turn had made some deal with the Albanians.

Even Despot had come to him with a theory that the Minister was part of a plot to take over the heroin route.

As Viktor had told Despot, the heroin route had been carved up since the Yugoslav and Kosovo wars. They often made busts, but hadn't found out who the main financier was. Viktor had received international help in breaking up the coke cartel. He didn't have the same backing to look into the heroin route. The Chief did what he could, but on the other hand as Belgrade had become less crime-ridden, the Chief was happy to keep the route contained. Viktor got out his phone and said:

'I need the Chief's okay on this.'

Viktor got the Chief's voicemail. He left a message for Ivan to call him back and faced the Minister, who said:

'Can we talk in private?'

Viktor gave his two drugs squad guys a roll of the eyes and gestured for the Minister to enter a small office. Seeing Nebojša follow the Minister, Viktor asked:

'Are you his dogsbody or something?'

'No, I brought the case to him.'

Things were getting more and more curious. Viktor took a

seat at his desk and opened his arms:

'Okay. What's the secret?'

Nebojša inserted the USB into a pc on Viktor's desk and played the recording.

Viktor listened. When the recording finished, he sat in silence. Could the recording be a fake?

It sounded authentic. The Chief of Police and Vesna Panić discussing the heroin route as if they owned it.

Had the Chief duped him all these years? It was difficult to contemplate. With Viktor's assistance, Ivan had broken up the Zemun Clan. With Ivan's support, Viktor had broken up the coke cartel. Together, they had been a formidable police force.

With heroin, Ivan had always kept in the loop. Was that why some busts had gone down and some hadn't? Was the Chief the inside man? More than that, was the Chief of Police in cahoots with the heroin kingpin? Ivan had always been protective of Vesna Panić, but Viktor had assumed that was for political reasons. Until actual evidence had been found, Viktor couldn't desert the Chief of Police:

'Okay, so you've got a recording, which could be interpreted in different ways. How do we know it's not fake or that the Chief wasn't setting up a sting? And what concrete proof is there?'

Nebojša spoke:

'I've been working with Despotović on the case. Right now, he's trailing the Chief and Jovanović because a deal is going down. He obtained the recording. Despotović guaranteed that if we make a dawn raid on Vesna Panić's place, we will find some of the heroin still there.'

Viktor looked Nebojša up and down. Who the fuck was this rookie? And what the fuck was Despot up to? Viktor asked:

'Despot is behind this?'

Nebojša confirmed:

'He put it together. I've been helping him.'

Viktor scratched his beard. Despot was a dark horse, but

now Viktor understood why Despot had been asking questions. Despot had mentioned Panić Ajvar. Viktor racked his brains. As he recalled, Panić Ajvar had come up once in connection with heroin. Tipped off that a truck might be smuggling smack, Viktor and his guys had searched the truck. But someone must have been tipped off about the tip off because nothing was found.

Viktor wasn't surprised to hear about Jovanović. His old friend couldn't be protected forever.

Everyone knew he was snorting. Jovanović had claimed it was part of his undercover persona so he could infiltrate Belgrade's drug dealers, but Viktor would have known about any operation. And that was what niggled. Viktor secretly hoped the Chief and Jovanović were involved in a sting operation. Yet how wouldn't he have known about it?

Viktor didn't have to accept what the rookie said and for sure didn't trust the Minister. But with the Chief of Police absent, Viktor could hardly refuse to do a drugs search when a warrant had been signed by the Head Judge. If they did find heroin at Vesna Panić's place, that still didn't necessarily mean the Chief was part of it. Viktor would see what Despot had been up to.

Facing the Minister, he said:

'Okay, let's hit Vesna Panić's place.'

The mist seemed to infiltrate Marko's mind. His vision of Serbian Partizans being gunned down by German Huns came back to haunt him. He didn't believe in ghosts, but right then he felt the presence of the dead.

Marko took it to mean that he should get away from the water's edge. He didn't want to end up as a corpse floating on the Danube. It was kill or be killed. So he took a breath and moved out from behind his Ford.

He couldn't see Ivan or Dragan. Marko guessed they were also on the move. He had to hope Dragan got to Dejan Tomić while he tried for the Chief. None of them could see each other, so it would be luck as to who survived.

Feeling his way along the ground, Marko came to Jova's body. He bent down and removed the dead Inspector's police handgun. Holstering his own Zastava, Marko now had someone else's weapon. He could get away with murder.

For Dragan, the mist brought him memories of Partizan matches, in particular when Wolfsburg had come to play in the Europa league several years earlier. As usual, the Partizan fans had thrown flares onto the pitch, making visibility poor.

The German players and fans weren't used to it. Partizan had taken an early lead and Dragan had made a daring raid with two of his men into the away section. Getting into a knife fight, Dragan left a Wolfsburg fan with a fatal stab wound before climbing over the fence and making his way back to the Gravediggers.

Dragan needed to seize the initiative in the mist. Dejan Tomić had a sniper's rifle so would put himself in a firing position for when the mist cleared. Dragan had to anticipate that.

With one hand stretched out, Dragan took long steps straight ahead. He couldn't see a thing, but he knew that the near end of the haulage container was ten metres in front of him. The trick was to not look around, otherwise he'd get disorientated. After ten strides, Dragan's hand touched the metal container. Now he just had to climb up.

The mist reminded Dejan of his time as a sniper in Sarajevo during the Yugoslav War. In retaliation for the Bosnians kicking out Serbs, a siege of the city had been ordered.

From their position in the hills surrounding Sarajevo, the Serb snipers killed as many Muslims as possible. Some of the men did it out of revenge. Dejan was just doing his job. He didn't keep count of how many Muslims he killed, but he only missed twice.

Sarajevo became a ghost city, the citizens staying in their homes for fear of being shot. The fog was the Bosnians' only saviour. When it descended, the city's inhabitants came out on the streets. The Serb snipers could hear the Bosnians but couldn't see them. It was pointless shooting blind, so they waited for the fog to vanish.

Dejan needed to be in a good shooting position once the mist lifted. He felt the metal of the haulage container for holds and started to climb.

Ivan had an urge to smoke, but lighting up would give away his position. He knew cigarettes would one day cause his death, but everyone was going to die sometime. He was used to looking through his smoke-filled office, but the mist had really made everything invisible.

It made him think of the dust that clouded the air after they'd bulldozed the Zemun clan headquarters on Šilerova Street. That bust had made his name – the bust made possible because of the deal he made with Dragan.

When Ivan thought about it, the key points in his life were marked by destroyed buildings.

He had helped lead the assault on Mostar, flattening the city with tanks and mortar launches.

That had helped him rise through the army ranks. Later, NATO's bombing of the army headquarters had hardened his stance against the West and brought a career change as he moved over to the police.

Vesna had come back into his life once his position as Chief of Police was cemented. They were both back in Kosovo for her parents' funeral after they had been killed by the Albanians.

Their house in the village had been razed to the ground. Vesna had vowed revenge and Ivan had promised to keep the heroin route safe from Albanian hands. They had earned the right to control it. The Minister and his lackey Dejan Tomić weren't going to mess it up.

Dejan had been a good patriot, but it was time for him to die. Ivan edged around Jovanović's BMW and felt his way forward through the mist. He had given instructions before the mist came for Dragan to take one side of the container and Despotović the other. He assumed they would stick to orders. Despotović was more likely to back out than Dragan, so Ivan would take that side of the container, if he could make his way to it. The sound of shoes on metal halted Ivan. Someone was clambering up the container. And either there was an echo or two people were climbing simultaneously.

Dragan and Dejan both reached the top of the haulage container at the same time. As they got to their feet, the scraping of shoes on metal echoed through the mist. Both men froze. Neither could see the other, but they both knew someone else was at the other end of the container.

Dragan brandished his hunter's knife. Dejan took a sniper's aim.

Dragan crouched and charged. Either he would fall off, be shot or stick his knife in Dejan.

Well, you only live once, he thought as a shot rang out.

Marko stood still and listened. A shot had been fired and someone running on metal rang across the dock. A grunt and thud. Someone's life had ended. Marko had no way of knowing who, but he needed to do his part.

He sniffed in the mist. The unmistakable smell of Marlboro cigarettes clung to someone nearby. Speaking would reveal his position, but it was a chance he had to take. Raising Jova's Zastava, Marko spoke in a hushed voice:

'Chief?'

'Despotović?'

Marko fired at the voice, heard a gasp. He aimed lower and shot again. The mist was quickly thinning. Marko made out the prone figure on the ground. The Chief of Police was dead. As the mist lifted, Marko saw another figure spread on the ground at the base of the haulage container. He couldn't tell if it was Dejan or Dragan. With the mist now evaporated, Marko was out in the open. He heard footsteps and whipped around with the Zastava raised.

Dragan was striding towards him. Marko had a split second to shoot, but they'd agreed a deal. Marko lowered his gun and Dragan embraced him in a bear-hug. Pumped up, Dragan shouted:

'Man, we did it. Gravediggers!'

Chapter 42

Viktor arrived at Vesna Panić's mansion in one car, his two drug squad guys in another while Nebojša once more chauffeured the Interior Minister in his Yugo.

At the gate, the Minister pressed the intercom button. Vesna's security guard answered:

'What?'

Željko tried to impose his authority:

'This is the Interior Minister. Open up. We have a warrant to search the premises.'

'I don't care if you're Nikola Tesla back from the dead. It's four in the morning.'

Viktor shook his head at the Minister's inflated ego. Stepping to the intercom, Viktor said:

'You'll be joining Nikola Tesla if you don't open up.'

'Who's this?'

'Viktor Antić, anti-narcotics. You want my guys to force their way in or you going to open the gate?'

From inside the mansion's entrance, the security guard looked at the intercom screen. There were at least four men there. The anti-narcotics officer had displayed his ID, which meant that the search warrant was genuine too. Vesna had just started her dawn meditation, so it wasn't a good time to disturb her, but he had no choice. He marched down the hallway to the glass room.

Vesna was sitting cross-legged and naked, her back to the door. The guard banged on the glass.

In her meditative state, Vesna was disturbed. Her vision was permeated with mist. She couldn't see anything, just hear what sounded like a gun. But then her consciousness realised someone was banging on the door. She opened her eyes and turned to glare at her security guard, who had stepped inside her spiritual retreat. Vesna snapped:

'What is it?'

'The anti-narcotics unit and the Interior Minister are outside. They've got a search warrant. You want me to let them in?'

Vesna should have known that her vision was sending her a warning. But why hadn't Ivan warned her? Something had gone wrong, but she had nothing to hide. She waved a dismissive hand:

'Let them in.'

While the guard buzzed open the electronic gate, Vesna wrapped a gown around herself. Ivan had told her the Interior Minister was dealt with, that he'd got Inspector Despotović on side and against the Minister. Vesna knew the Inspector was a danger.

Vesna stepped out of her spiritual retreat as the Minister and four men strode towards her.

Inspector Despotović wasn't amongst them.

The men stopped in front of Vesna, who stood proud and erect, her breasts barely contained inside her gown. Before he could be distracted, the Minister held up the warrant:

'We have a warrant to search the premises.'

Vesna gave the Minister a dismissive look:

'Is this a government matter?'

'It's a matter of national importance. I'm here to support the work of the anti-narcotics unit.'

Viktor wished the Minister would shut up, but for now he was staying quiet and keeping an eye out.

Vesna wanted to ask if the Chief of Police knew the anti-narcotics unit were in her home, but instead she made a welcome gesture and said:

'Be my guests.'

Viktor signalled for his two men to start the search while he kept an eye on Vesna. For her age, she was well worth keeping an eye on. He asked:

'Is there somewhere we can all sit?'

Vesna led the way to her lounge, followed by her security guard, Viktor and the Interior Minister.

Nebojša used the opportunity to hold back. While the others entered the lounge, Nebojša stepped into the kitchen.

The packet of heroin was burning a hole in his pocket. He looked around for somewhere to put it, but the kitchen was all design and no clutter. Certainly no jars of Panić Ajvar hanging around. His eyes alighted on a big tin of Nescafe.

As Nebojša unscrewed the lid, he heard the voice of Viktor from down the hall:

'Where's Nebojša got to?'

Nebojša stuffed the packet of smack inside the coffee tin as footsteps got closer. He screwed the lid back on and reached for the fridge door as Viktor stepped into the kitchen with the Minister, Vesna and her guard.

Viktor eyed Nebojša. He trusted his two men. They would find something or they wouldn't.

He was less trusting of the rookie:

'You going solo?'

'Despotović said to try the fridge.'

'Did he really? Did you find anything?'

'Just cheese, milk and orange juice.'

Viktor watched with distrust as the rookie shut the fridge door. It was highly unlikely that heroin would be found on the premises. A small-time dealer would have it with them. But if Vesna was really a major financier, she wouldn't keep the product in her own home.

The raid didn't make sense. It took years to bring down the coke cartel. Endless surveillance and working on informers, tracing the money and gathering evidence. You didn't suddenly search someone without cause. You could do a stop and search on the street, but not on a premises.

Viktor thought about how Ivan had requested a stop and search on Despot. The Chief had said it was to check Despot was clean before entrusting him with a job. That job was checking on the Minister. Nothing made any sense. Viktor's guys entered the kitchen and gave a shake of their heads. Viktor shrugged at the Minister:

'Doesn't look like there is anything.'

The Minister had to believe Inspector Despotović hadn't fucked him over. He said:

'Are you sure everywhere has been checked?'

'You want to do our job for us?'

'I'm not doubting your expertise, just wondering where it might be hidden.'

Vesna stared at the Minister with contempt. The man was clearly an idiot. Did he think she would keep anything in her own home? With her gown half-open, she said:

'If you tell me what you're looking for, maybe I can help you.'

Viktor wanted to laugh. Either Vesna Panić was a great actress or the Minister had fucked up.

The Minister took a firm stance. Vesna's aggression reminded him of his wife. Combined with her amazing breasts, it was hard not to be turned on. He went on the attack:

'We have a recording in which you clearly reveal yourself as being in charge of the heroin route. We know you have heroin in your possession. So why don't you tell us where it is to save us all time.'

Vesna burst into laughter. The Minister's first sentence had worried her. How had he got hold of the recording? Ivan had promised that had been taken care of. But she quickly calculated that a recording wouldn't be enough in court. A good lawyer would get the case dismissed.

And heroin never came near her house, so that wasn't something to worry about. Not letting her concerns show, Vesna said:

'While you are guests in my home, can I make you men a

drink?'

Viktor suppressed a smile. The woman had balls. The Minister didn't know how to respond.

Nebojša said:

'I wouldn't mind a coffee.'

'A coffee for the young inspector coming up.'

Vesna sashayed over to the kitchen counter, her breasts ready to pop out of her gown. All the men's eyes were on her as she opened the coffee tin.

Vesna froze for a second as she saw the packet of heroin. Quickly putting the lid back on, she said:

'Ran out of coffee. How about some juice?'

Vesna smiled at the men, but it was too late. They'd seen her hesitation.

One of Viktor's guys stepped in and took the coffee tin. Taking the lid off, he showed the packet of smack.

At a glance, Viktor guessed it was a hundred dolls as they said on the street. With that in your possession, you'd go down for dealing. But if Vesna was the kingpin, why would she keep one packet in a coffee tin?

Vesna protested her innocence:

'It's obvious one of you put it there. You won't get away with this.'

Viktor had thought something similar. He glanced at Nebojša, but the rookie was feigning innocence. Viktor was sure the rookie had planted the smack. He didn't know what game was being played, but until he knew the rules, he had to go along with it. He gestured to one of his men:

'Cuff her.'

Vesna wanted to fight, but her pride stopped her. As one of the men put her hands in cuffs, she said:

'My lawyer will end all your careers. How do you think you will frame me for this?'

Viktor shrugged:

'Easy.'

Putting on plastic gloves, Viktor removed the packet of heroin. With Vesna's hands cuffed behind her back, Viktor forced her hands around the packet. Now they had her fingerprints.

Evidence was quickly building.

For now, Viktor would go along with the Minister. But he still wanted to hear from the Chief.

Not to mention Despot.

Chapter 43

The Interior Minister watched as Vesna Panić was driven away by the two anti-narcotics officers. The arrest had gone to plan. Now he just needed to hear from Dejan and Inspector Despotović.

In his mind, the Minister started planning his speech for the cameras. This was going to be major news. The heroin kingpins had been arrested and the route cleared. Željko had not only been at the head of the operation but actually taken part in the arrests.

He felt like phoning his wife and Boris Hoffman to boast. The Germans would have to back him now. He would be on the path to becoming Prime Minister and Željko would be First Lady.

As Vesna was driven away, Marko turned into the street. The two cars passed each other and Vesna seemed to look right at Marko. He couldn't tell if she was staring at him or through him.

Either way, it sent a brief shiver up his spine. Parking by the gate to Vesna's mansion, Marko dismissed the feeling. He'd just taken part in real violence. Vesna's spiritual hate wouldn't kill him.

Relief flooded through Marko. Nebojša had sent a text that Vesna had been arrested. Now he'd seen it with his own eyes. Everything had gone to plan. Marko and Dragan had left the bodies of Dejan, Jovanović and the Chief of Police to be discovered. They'd thrown their weapons into the Danube and driven away. The murders wouldn't be connected to them. Now Marko just needed to tie up a few loose ends.

The Interior Minister, Viktor and Nebojša were waiting for Marko by the gate. Each had unspoken questions they wanted to ask.

The Minister wanted to know where Dejan Tomić was. It was a good sign that Inspector Despotović had arrived, but the Minister needed to know about his right-hand man.

Viktor wanted to know where the Chief of Police was. If Despot had been trailing the Chief, what had gone down?

Nebojša was relieved that Despotović was alive, but wondered what that meant. What had happened to the Chief?

Marko said:

'I see you've arrested Vesna Panić.'

The Minister spoke:

'Yes, we found evidence on her premises. It has been great work all around. Inspector Vranac was instrumental in the arrest and the anti-narcotics unit proved invaluable. Do you have any additional news for me?'

'Yes, I've got news for you, but I just need to speak with Viktor first.'

Marko turned his back on the Minister, patted Nebojša on the shoulder and nodded at Viktor.

The two inspectors stepped away from the gate so that they could confer. Viktor had let Marko take the initiative, but now he got straight to the point:

'What the fuck have you been up to Despot?'

'It's a long story. Did you hear the recording?'

'Yea, I heard it.'

'And you found Vesna with heroin in her possession?'

'The packet the rookie planted, yea.'

'Vesna and Ivan were the kingpins Vik.'

'Where is the Chief?'

'He's dead.'

'What?'

'That's what I heard. Apparently there's been a shoot-out down in Dorćol docks. It might be a good idea to check the scene.'

Viktor looked at Despot in a new light. He wasn't sure he liked what he saw:

'You know that even if the Chief was corrupt, no-one on the force is going to be happy about this.'

'I know.'

'You'll be left out in the cold.'

'I'm just the messenger. Nebojša's in charge.'

'The rookie ready to make enemies where he works?'

'Says he is.'

'And I guess you've got the Minister behind you?'

'Doubt it. Not after what I'm about to tell him.'

Marko left Viktor to call in the murders in Dorćol docks and walked back to the Interior Minister, who was waiting impatiently. In a hushed voice, the Minister asked:

'Where's Dejan?'

'He's dead.'

'What?'

'Dragan killed him.'

'Dragan's alive?'

'And well. Afraid you'll have to fight him for the route.'

The Minister couldn't contain his anger, raising his voice:

'What are you playing at Despotović?'

Marko took a step closer to the Minister, got into his face as he said:

'Your man is dead. You don't pose a threat to me anymore. If anything ever happens to my son, I will kill you.'

The Minister stumbled back and spluttered:

'Your career will be over.'

Marko shrugged as he turned away. He suspected his career wasn't over, just that he would never be promoted. That was fine by him. Getting in his car, Marko nodded at Nebojša, who nodded back – an unspoken agreement between them. Marko turned on the engine. He was going home to his family.

The Minister, Viktor and Nebojša watched Marko leave. Nebojša understood that he'd been left the case. He would get the plaudits, but also face hostility as he gained promotion.

Viktor had to hand it to Marko. He'd managed to get Vesna Panić arrested and the Chief of Police killed. Not only had he made his job on the force untenable, he'd clearly fucked with the Minister too.

The Minister thought about the threat he'd just made and knew it was his own career which was about to implode. He turned to Inspector Vranac, needing a lift home.

Chapter 44

As Nebojša drove the Minister from Vesna's place, the Minsiter asked:

'Did you know what Inspector Depotović was up to?'

'Only what he told us both.'

The Minister looked at the young inspector. He seemed genuine, but he'd also answered like a politician. The Minister knew right then that Inspector Vranac's career was on an upward trajectory, unlike his own.

They lapsed into silence and didn't speak for the rest of the journey to the Minister's home on Francuska Street. The Minister had a lot to think about. He would have to say that Dejan had gone rogue, taken the Audi and got involved in some drugs deal. He would spin it so that he looked innocent.

What he couldn't rectify was Dragan having taken control of the heroin route. Hoffman and the Germans weren't going to back him anymore. And he wasn't going to make Prime Minister any time soon. He might resurrect his political career, but it would take years.

The Yugo pulled up outside the Minister's residence, but he didn't want to get out. Never mind the Germans, the press or his own political party, the Interior Minister couldn't face the disdain of his wife.

Chapter 45

Branka was at the oven when she heard the front door open. Only Marko had keys, but for all she knew he'd been killed and someone else had taken the keys. Marko hadn't told her everything, but enough to make her fearful. She held her breath.

Marko appeared in the kitchen doorway. He strode over to his wife and embraced her. With his head buried in her hair, he said:

'See, I said I'd be back for breakfast.'

Branka smiled in relief. Her husband was alive and her family were safe. But what were the consequences? She wanted to ask: 'What have you done?' But she kept silent.

Marko sniffed and gestured to the oven:

'Smells good. Should I get Goran?'

Branka nodded. She needed a few seconds to herself. While Marko went to get Goran, Branka tried to come to terms with her thoughts.

What had Marko done to survive? Had her husband become a murderer? It was too much to take in. She needed the normality of everyday and turned to take her strudel out of the oven.

Marko ushered Goran into the kitchen. His son had come reluctantly and without saying a word. Goran sat at the table with his head bowed and his arm in plaster. Marko knew it would take time for Goran to heal. Mentally as well as physically. But Marko would be there for his son.

Looking at his wife, Marko didn't know if their relationship could be repaired. He had made his family safe, but only after putting them in danger. To survive, he had killed. Branka might not forgive that. Not to mention his affair with Milica.

With neither Branka nor Goran speaking, there wasn't the usual breakfast banter, but Marko was happy. His family were safe. He smiled as Branka placed the poppy seed strudel on the table and cut it into slices.

Epilogue

Abdul-manan scored the poppy pod with his three-bladed *nushta*, a tool he was adept at using.

If you cut too deep, the milky fluid would ooze out too quickly and drip to the earth. If the cut was too shallow, the opium latex wouldn't drip quickly enough and harden inside the pod.

His father had shown him how to make the right cut, allowing the 'poppy tears' to seep out and harden on the outside of the pod.

Abdul-manan worked backwards through the field, making sure the sleeves of his *shalwar kameez* didn't rub against the poppies he had scored. To his left, Abdul-manan's two younger brothers were working backwards through their rows. His father, mother and sister worked to his right.

If he pictured the scene from a distance, it would have looked beautiful. A family at work in a field of red, white and lavender poppies. But the work was hard and had to be done before mid-morning. He was already sweating under his *pashtun* cap and it would soon be too hot to continue.

The whole field had to be finished so that the opium could harden in the day's sun. The next morning, they would scrape it off into containers that hung from their necks.

With the field finally complete, Abdul-manan stretched his back. At fourteen he was almost as tall as his father and had to bend to do the poppy scoring.

Back at the farmhouse, his mother made the yogurt and

mint drink they all loved. Abdul-manan hoped he could play on the Xbox his father had recently bought for the children, but instead he was summoned to watch how heroin was made, so that he could soon help out.

Abdul-manan watched as his father mixed a batch of hardened opium with hot water and a calcium solution. He saw how it was siphoned, had chemicals added to it, was filtered, dried in the sun and finally crumbled into white powder. The whole process took up most of the day.

His father told him that it was a deadly drug that should never be consumed. Abdul-manan didn't understand:

'If it is deadly, why are we making it?'

His father answered:

'Because people in the Western world crave it.'

'Will they be killed by using it?'

'Sometimes.'

'But isn't it wrong for us to sell it to them?'

'It is Allah's wish. Why else would he plant these poppy seeds next to us? Perhaps it is meant for non-Muslims to die.'

Abdul-manan was confused, but he didn't ask any more questions. He trusted his father and believed in Allah, but not everything made sense. A few years ago, the family had been poor.

As his father had told him, the ruling Taliban had outlawed opium poppy cultivation. Since the American invasion, they had been free to harvest more every year and become rich. Were the Taliban bad and the Americans good? Yet the Taliban were Muslim and the Americans not.

One night, a convoy of 4x4s had arrived at the farm. Abdul-manan had listened as a man gave orders to his father about how much heroin should be produced. The man was not Taliban or American. His father had been silent, accepting the orders he was given.

Abdul-manan was too tired to think about it anymore. With his father's permission, he was allowed to join his brothers and sisters who were on the floor inside, staring in

264

awe at the wide-screen TV.

In the last year, his father had bought a new multi-terrain vehicle, put up an electric fence around the farm and paid a security guard to man the entrance. Abdul-manan wasn't sure he didn't prefer it when they were poorer. Then they'd been free to run around where they wanted.

But he liked the Xbox, which had been delivered by the fat Turkish lorry driver who came to pick up the heroin. On the Minecraft game, his sister had just finished building a farmhouse that looked very similar to their own, as did the valley it was situated in. She handed the controller to Abdul-manan so he could have a go. He thought it was better to be more imaginative and started creating a glass building that towered into the sky. He wanted to soar above the valley, not be contained by it.

Čem drove through the entrance to the farm, eyed by the armed security guard. It was bizarre really. Fields of beautiful flowers fenced off and guarded. Of course, he knew why, but it was kind of funny when you looked at it.

Stepping down from the lorry, Čem nodded at the farmer. He didn't know his name and they never shook hands. It was fine by him. The less he knew the better.

As usual, he was guided into the farmhouse, where the farmer's wife served him lamb and rice. Through the open doorway, he saw the children sitting entranced in front of the TV and Xbox he had delivered last time.

Čem wanted to laugh at the oddness of it. A stone farmhouse, a hundred years old and in the middle of nowhere. Fitted with the latest technology.

The farmer had definitely been making money in the last few years. But then so did Čem with his long-haul transportation. It was the risk that almost killed him. Every time, he said he would stop.

The farmer's wife poured Čem some coffee boiled in a pot. It wasn't as good as his own wife's Turkish coffee, but it was strong. When he'd finished, the farmer beckoned him outside.

Wooden crates containing boxes of poppy seeds were loaded into his lorry. That was a good joke. On the surface, he was transporting poppy seeds to be used in cakes and bread.

Somewhere hidden, he was delivering several kilos of heroin. Was this Afghan humour?

Čem wanted to laugh, but wasn't sure the farmer would respond. He heaved himself back into his truck and trundled out of the farm.

He was soon at the Iranian border, the most risky part of the journey. If he got stopped in Iran and heroin was found, he'd be executed before he could say 'Allah have mercy'. Not that he knew Farsi and they wouldn't understand his Turkish.

The mountain crossing went without a hitch. Maybe the Iranian police were fed up of being killed by better armed drug cartels. He'd heard about the running battles, not that he was connected in any way. He was just a driver delivering poppy seeds.

It took twenty-four hours to drive through the north of Iran, including a brief sleep outside Tehran. Čem didn't like stopping in a country where he could be beheaded, but had to rest. His sleep was fitful, so he drank coffee from the flask his wife had given him and carried on.

When he reached Turkey, Čem farted in relief. Yes, he could still be chucked in prison, but at least he wouldn't be executed. He spoke out loud:

'No, just bum-raped for twenty years.'

Čem thought about it:

'So maybe it would be better to be killed.'

He concluded it was best to relax:

'You're in your own country. If anything happens, you'll talk your way out of it.'

He realised he was talking to himself and shut up. It often happened on long-hauls. He was happy to take a break in the Iğdir warehouse depot.

While Čem ate and rested, the crates of poppy seeds were taken out of the lorry. Through the café window, Čem saw that the boxes of poppy seeds were removed and the crates filled with lemons, half of the crates fork-lifted back into the lorry.

So the heroin was hidden in the crates thought Čem, instantly wishing he hadn't thought. If the police stopped him, he had to appear to have no knowledge of heroin. It was the same if he was ever stopped by cartel guys. His job was to be an ignorant driver. Ignorant, but alive.

Lemons to Macedonia. It almost sounded like a song. He sang it all the way through Turkey, imagining he was on stage with a group of scantily-clad backing singers, the women fawning over him as they sang the chorus. He stopped for a few hours' sleep outside Istanbul, then skirted northern Greece, a country that was well and truly fucked. Served them right for joining the EU. No pride, not like the Turks.

Several hours later, Čem parked up at the factory just inside the Macedonian border. He wanted to smile in relief that the risk-taking leg of his journey was finally over, but first he had to wait while the crates were unloaded and checked by the Macedonians. To make him more nervous, a lorry with Serbian registration plates was also parked up, two huge guys watching proceedings from the side.

Satisfied that the crates were intact, one of the Macedonians handed over a fat envelope. Čem nodded his thanks, got in his lorry and drove the fuck away. Laughing in nervous relief, he vowed not to take on another heroin transportation.

The two Serbs were part of Dragan's crew, sent to watch as the Macedonians cut up the heroin before they transported the repackaged goods to Belgrade.

Serbs and Macedonians had always worked well together, so they didn't expect any problems. It had been agreed that the heroin would be powdered down to eighty per cent purity. This meant more money all around.

Saša and Radovan watched on as the Macedonians knocked off the corners of the wooden crates. The Serbian anti-narcotics squad had previously had a tip-off about heroin being hidden in this way, so from Macedonia onwards it would be hidden differently.

The cut heroin was repacked in sealed plastic bags and carefully inserted into jars of *ajvar*.

The operation took over an hour, but was smoothly done. Most of the jars were labelled with a Macedonian brand name, but one set of jars had Serbian labels.

With the lorry loaded, Saša and Radovan drove north to the Serbian border. They were both armed in case the Albanians tried anything, but there wasn't a *šiptar* in sight. Dragan had told them the Albanians wouldn't be a problem.

If the border control guys caused any trouble, they would be bribed. Failing that, they'd have a gun pointed at their heads and their families would be threatened. The guy on duty wasn't bothered about checking:

'What you got?'

'*Ajvar.*'

'From Macedonia? What's wrong with our own?'

'Not for us, for the Germans.'

'They're welcome to inferior shit.'

The guy opened the barrier and waved them through. Dragan's men drove through the night and arrived in Belgrade by dawn.

Dragan was waiting by the haulage container in the Dorćol depot. The dead bodies of Dejan, Inspector Jovanović and the Chief of Police had long since been removed. A bit of police tape was stuck in the weeds, but the police wouldn't be coming back so soon. Dragan no longer had inside information, but with the police sorting out their own corruption, he was free to be the kingpin of the heroin route.

Only one crate of jars was staying in Belgrade, so they unloaded them by hand. The rest was going to Germany.

Germans had more money to spend on drugs than Serbs so that's where the market was.

Serbia was a transit country, not a distribution centre. Dragan laughed to himself. Only a few days into the new role and he was already using the terminology.

The lorry from Germany arrived. Dragan and his men stood alert. They wouldn't be caught unaware like Milan. Dragan didn't like the Germans. His grandfather had been a Partizan and was killed by the Huns in the Second World War.

Dragan had got revenge when Partizan had played against Wolfsburg, stabbing a fan to death.

He'd got the scar above his eye in that fight. He didn't know if he'd avenged his grandfather, but at least he'd got rid of one German. The world should have smashed the Germans to bits when they had the chance. The Germans never changed. They didn't have Hitler anymore, but they still wanted to control Europe. They did it with economics these days.

Just look how they were fucking Greece over.

Dragan didn't shake hands with the German lorry drivers, but he didn't kill them either. They needed to be alive to transport the heroin to Munich. And there, Dragan hoped as many Germans would die of an overdose as possible.

The Germans trucked into Munich without a hitch. A German lorry entering Croatia didn't raise any suspicions. And once in the EU, there were no serious border stops.

In Munich, the heroin was taken out of the *ajvar*, unpacked and further cut. The street dealers did their own cutting. Everyone trying to make more money at each stage.

By the time Kamel had his bag of smack, the heroin was only 70% pure. He didn't care as long as he got his hit, unaware that his body was usually used to ten per cent less purity. He'd got it from a businessman instead of his normal dealer, paying with a blow job rather than cash.

Kamel sat on the mattress in the grotty bed-sit, injected the needle into his pockmarked arm and felt the heroin flow through his bloodstream.

As he sank onto his back, Kamel's eyes took in the faded reproduction of van Gogh's *Sunflowers*. His mum had hung it there years ago.

Kamel saw his mum in a field of sunflowers, the yellow petals bright as the sun. The plants were as tall as his mum, who smiled down at Kamel.

He couldn't ever remember his mum taking him through a field of flowers, so it was a false memory, but he didn't care. Better than the real ones.

They'd emigrated from Turkey when he was a baby, leaving behind an abusive husband. But without work, Kamel's mum had turned to prostitution. It was how he learnt to suck men's dicks. And inject heroin.

The endorphins surged through the nerve reactor sites in his brain's pleasure centre. Kamel felt himself sinking deeper into the earth, the sunflowers towering over him on their long stalks.

He beamed a smile up at his mum as his body jolted.

THE END

270

Acknowledgments

I had the idea of writing a Balkan Noir thriller for a long time, inspired by living in Belgrade in the late nineties (I was kicked out as NATO prepared to bomb the city). In 2015, I was awarded a Literature Wales bursary to carry out research for the novel. Publisher and author Aleksandar Šurbatović set up a meeting with a Belgrade police inspector who told me about the Balkan heroin route, combatting drug smuggling and corruption. 'Hvala mnogo' to Aleksandar and the police inspector who wished to remain unnamed. Thank you from my heart to Nela Tomić who translated during interviews, proofread for linguistic accuracy and provided insights into the Serbian underworld. Many thanks to the author John Yorvik and poet Carole Satyamurti for their invaluable feedback. And a huge thank you to the super-cool, hot-punk Fahrenheit Press for making me part of the gang. More Balkan Noir is on the way…

About the author

Cal Smyth has lived in Serbia, Japan, Italy and the UK. He has met wanted criminals, interviewed police inspectors and escaped NATO bombing. He's had three novels published and his new Balkan Noir series is being published by Fahrenheit Press. He teaches creative writing, has two ex-wives and lives with his son.

More books from Fahrenheit Press

If you enjoyed The Balkan Route you might also like these other Fahrenheit titles

Boondoggle By Mark Rapacz

Jukebox By Saira Viola

Hidden Depths by Ally Rose

In The Still by Jacqueline Chadwick